Hearts in Training

Annie J. Kribs

This book is a work of fiction. Names, characters, places and incidents are works of the author's imagination and are used fictitiously. Similarity to actual people, places and events are entirely coincidental.

All right reserved, including the right to reproduce this book or any portions in any form whatsoever. For information, email anniekribs@gmail.com.

Copyright © 2020 by Annie J. Kribs

ISBN: 8695802603
ISBN-13: 979-8695802603

Dedication & Reader Note

#metoo

A note for those affected by the *#metoo* movement:

This is a workplace romance. The intent of the author is to present a sweet romantic story between two equally engaged individuals. No harm is meant by any scenes that take place in the workplace.

I share my empathy with all those impacted by unwanted advances who are now living with the memories.

Chapter 1

*R*eed rushed through a cup of coffee before heading to the floors below to the executive offices of Decatur Industries. As the recently appointed CEO of his family's international shipping business, he liked to get to the office early to get a jump on things before the chaos of the day took over.

He waved his keycard in front of the lock to his office door and wondered what his mystery woman would be wearing today. He nearly smiled to himself as he pictured her blonde hair swept up in a neat twist complemented by her sedate but classy work attire. If he wasn't the boss-No! He had to be honest with himself. If he wasn't so damned shy, he would know her name by now. As far as he could tell she hadn't been with the company long, but she'd certainly caught his attention.

He logged into his computer and considered looking through the company directory again. His previous searches hadn't produced a staff photo. Maybe she was a contractor? He smiled. Even better. If she was only here on a temporary assignment, maybe she wasn't off-limits after all.

None of that changed the fact he'd have to work up the nerve to speak to her first, and that was a lot to ask of himself. His interest in the woman bordered on an obsession. It had become something of a ritual to seek her out each day. Some days were so full of meetings and critical decisions that the anticipation of seeing her bright smile was often the beacon that pulled him through.

But, right now he was wasting time. He checked his calendar and then opened his email and focused his attention on Decatur Industries.

Two hours later, Reed resisted the urge to leave the Board of Directors meeting. In his imagination, he slammed the enormous, heavy door with a reverberation heard on all thirty floors of the lower Manhattan skyrise. When he'd agreed to take the reins after his father's retirement a year ago there hadn't been a single word said, not a single hint that the board planned a long transition in which they would exploit his age and looks to modernize both the company's image and its productivity. He clenched his jaw in disgust. His father, a man he loved and respected, had presided at the head of the table and delivered the announcement with a damned twinkle in his eye. Reed knew that twinkle. In his younger years, it had signified something was about to happen *for his own good*. Except he couldn't see how making him the centerfold of such a project could benefit him personally. Reed Decatur might be the next CEO of Decatur Industries, but he still answered to his father and the Board of Directors, and they were not to be deterred.

"The first phase of our leadership transition was to contract a Transition and Training Coordinator. She's spent the last two months assimilating herself into our culture," his father announced at the meeting. Reed looked around the table and wondered if he was the only one there who hadn't known this person had already been with the company for that long.

"For more than seven weeks she's walked among us incognito. Working her way from the ground up as she's learned our corporate culture, structure, and goals. Getting to know us from the inside out. And she's here now to give us her impressions."

Reed leaned forward and steepled his fingers in front of him as he watched Human Resources director, Bill Burns, stand to usher in their guest. Reed prided himself in being involved at every level. How had he known nothing about this?

Fred Decatur, Chairman of the Board and Reed's recently retired father, rose to his feet as a stunning blonde in a perfectly cut business suit entered the boardroom. Reed stood with the rest of the board until their guest reached her seat just to Fred's left. "Gentlemen, let me introduce Caroline Trumbull."

Disgust for the Board's trickery gave way to disbelief and knocked the breath out of Reed as he recognized his mystery woman. With a level of discomfort at nearly one hundred, he pulled his emotions behind an indifferent mask while she smoothly took control of the meeting. He was forced to listen to her assessment of the corporation he'd only recently taken the reins of. A corporation he was tasked with revitalizing. Presumably now under her guidance. Why had the Board appointed him if they believed he wasn't ready? He swallowed hard and suppressed the idea the Board thought he was a child in need of a babysitter. No one could do the job better than he could, except perhaps his father.

The fact that her observations were dead-on, or even that she seemed to share the same view of the company's strengths and weaknesses as him, did nothing to soften the irrational feeling she'd betrayed him. Going out of his way to spot her in the common areas or riding an extra floor in the elevator just because she was in it had become his habit of late, only now to find she'd been planted by his Board, his father. She had to have sensed his interest. Had she known *his* identity all along? Had it been a joke with her friends over drinks after work? His gut burned and he resisted the urge to fold an arm over it. That would look like a defensive position. Only to himself would he admit he was embarrassed to learn he'd been flirting with someone hired to tell him what the company was doing wrong. Perhaps the burning feeling was disappointment he'd have to stop his imagined game of cat-and-mouse with her. It was conceivable that one day he'd have worked up the nerve to ask her out on an actual date. Now, he let that dream crash and smolder as he came back to the present and listened to her impressions.

"I'd like to put him front and center as the image of the company. A young philanthropist, responsible and upward." She slanted a look at him as if challenging this for the truth. "But also, interesting and attractive. That will address the positive publicity objective."

She was going to use him as an example to support her agenda. The *Board's* agenda.

"In partnership with your CEO, I'd like to create a training division to improve productivity within various departments and attract workers with new skills."

Reed's gaze slid around the table noting that every head was bobbing in eager agreement as she cast her spell on them. He hated that he agreed with her goal for the training division.

"Exactly how will exploiting my age and looks translate into company gain?"

He felt his face getting hot as the men around the table looked his way. It was impossible not to sound combative. What did his looks have to do with his ability to do his job anyway?

The burning in his gut spread through his veins as anger replaced embarrassment again. The one saving grace to the situation was there would be an opportunity for the Board to vote. He still had a voice in the situation. He telegraphed his disdain to the blonde bombshell as she wound down her presentation. She glanced his way and faltered. It was immature of him and he fully knew it, but he sat back and gave her a satisfied gleam. It lasted only a split second, but he'd cracked her seamless veneer. Score one for Reed.

Thirty minutes later and resolutely overruled, Reed yanked his lavender tie loose and planted his hands on the credenza in his office staring out across the East River at the Brooklyn skyline. Yesterday he would have secretly thought it was cute that his mystery woman's gray suit matched his own so perfectly. Today he had to wonder whether she contrived her wardrobe selection for her success. Disappointment ate at him. He took a swig of liquid antacid that he kept in his desk and forced his gaze back to the calendar open on his computer screen. Two meetings this afternoon. He'd originally planned to use the free time to review several proposals that had come across his desk. Now he wasn't sure he could be fair to the prospective business partners. He closed his laptop and called his sister. She always knew how to distract him.

CAROLINE THREW a smile at Reed's executive secretary, Jamie, when she bypassed the woman to reach Reed's office. From now until the conclusion of her contract she had unrestricted access to the CEO. For that reason, she didn't wait to be announced, but out of respect for his work, she opened the heavy wooden doors silently. Her heels made no sound on the thick carpeting as she neared his desk. She slowed and took in the view that greeted her. Two entire walls of the office were glass from floor to ceiling. The corner and one wall were devoid of furniture giving the illusion of being able to step right off the edge into the expanse of the city below.

Her gaze moved from the skyline to the stiff shoulders of the man before her. Either he was still angry, or this was his normal personality. His back was to her, his hands planted on the low cabinet before him. Even from the back, he was an imposing figure. Even without seeing his expression, she felt the anger radiating from him. She could have been intimidated. She chose not to be. She was equal to this task. Besides, failure simply wasn't an option for her right now.

She knew most people saw the younger Mr. Decatur as stoic and unfriendly. Caroline thought he was fascinating and sexy but she doubted many other people saw him *that* way. His quiet appeal would help her with the project the Board had given her. Reed was good-looking, sure, but how could she get people to see him as relaxed, confident, and capable as well? He didn't appear that way to the general public, and that was the image the directors wanted to create.

"What can I do for you?" He didn't bother to turn around when he spoke.

"I have the impression you were caught off guard by your role in this project, Mr. Decatur."

He turned to face her, his indifferent mask back in place. "Not at all."

She raised her eyebrows at him, amused. His tie was haphazardly tugged loose. He looked down, made an exasperated noise, and fixed his tie.

"So, what's next on your agenda? World domination?"

She accepted his sarcasm and tried to keep the conversation light. "Well, I generally start small, you know, one company at a time. But I think you mean, where do you and I go from here?"

He looked into her eyes. "Yes, that's what I mean."

She held his gaze. "There are a couple of options. You can choose which works best for you."

"That's kind of you."

She gave a single nod. "I can lurk in the background and shadow you while I formulate the best method to go public with you."

It was barely a split second, but she was sure she saw him flinch when she mentioned going public.

"Or?"

"I can fully immerse myself in your work life."

"Gee, those are some great choices," he muttered. She gave him a commiserating smile. He dropped his head. "Which choice gets this whole project over faster?"

"Immersion." She let him hear her sympathy.

He seemed to examine her for a moment and his expression softened. "Immersion? That seems excessive for a simple decision on how to exploit me."

She shrugged. "It is the fastest way for me to see how you operate. The research and interview route can take months. I've been here two months already. It's also less personal, *less effective,* and therefore more expensive. I prefer quick and to the point. Like ripping off a Band-aid."

"That's certainly effective," Reed agreed. "And every bit as painful as I imagine this will be."

She wanted to laugh. She could add humor to his list of attributes. "I'm very good at my job, Mr.

Decatur. I promise not to make this any more painful than it needs to be."

"Are you placating me?"

"You appear to need it."

She saw his smile just before he turned his back on her. He spoke to the window. "What does immersion involve? Let's iron this out right now while you have me trapped here."

She didn't bother to hide her pleased smile. "For the next month or so I will work your schedule. I'll attend meetings with you, listen, and watch how you interact with your peers, learn what makes you tick."

"Do you plan to stalk my personal life too?"

She cocked her head and studied him with a curious smile. "Do you have one?"

Reed leaned back against the credenza with his hands in his pockets and studied her. "I'll let you decide. I keep long hours. Are you sure you can keep up?"

If he only knew the kind of hours she kept. "I'm tougher than I look."

This time he did laugh. "I hope so."

Giving him a bright smile to show she wasn't offended that he was laughing at her, she hitched her leather tote higher on her shoulder. "Immersion it is then. I'd like to get started right away. Tomorrow, if that works for you."

"Jamie will be happy to put you on my schedule."

Caroline acknowledged that with another nod. "She can schedule me into meetings with you, of course. But you and I both know you do so much more in a day than what is covered in a few impersonal meetings. I'll need to know what that is as well." She deliberately kept her voice calm, cheerful even. He wouldn't be able to dismiss her so easily. She had a job to do.

Regardless of her tone, he impaled her with a look that managed to convey both his displeasure and incredulity. "You intend to follow me around all day?"

"I believe I just explained that. The more you share with me the more I have to work with. And the more I have, the quicker and more successful our project will be."

"The more I share with you?" She watched his gaze travel down her body, and she hoped he couldn't see the effect that had on her.

"It's not personal, Mr. Decatur." Unless he wanted it to be. Then, she was all in.

"Tomorrow will be soon enough to work out your role here." He looked down at his monitor and then fixed his gaze on her again. "Unless your idea of getting to know me involves watching me read contracts for the rest of the day?"

"Not until tomorrow," she added, injecting a little levity again.

He sat down, dismissing her.

"Thank you, Mr. Decatur." She looked at the time on her phone. She'd barely been there ten minutes. "I'll see you tomorrow."

"I'll be in at six A.M." He looked at her steadily, but she knew her expression didn't falter.

"I'll see you at six then."

Caroline waited until the door closed behind her before releasing her pent-up breath. To her right, Reed's assistant, Jamie, nodded her head. "He has that effect on everyone. I've forwarded you his schedule."

Caroline laughed, but she doubted Jamie understood the exact effect he had on her. She hugged her bag a little closer, straightened her spine, and gave Jamie a little wave. "See you tomorrow, Jamie. And thanks."

She checked her messages as she rode the elevator down to the fourth floor. Two voicemails, both from bill collectors. The cable company and a grocery delivery company. She deleted the messages and sighed. How did these places even get her number? She knew, of course. Her mother had given it out as a contact number. What she wouldn't give to change her number, she thought. But it just wasn't possible. Her family needed her.

Inside the office she'd been given for the duration of the project, Caroline made a few notes from the Board meeting. Her office was nowhere near the size or caliber of Reed's office, but it was spacious, and the windows faced East where she would have direct sunlight in the morning, her most creative time of the day. It had been thoughtful of the company to give her a place to call her own for a while.

She plopped into her chair, kicked off her shoes and swiveled to face the windows with her laptop balancing on her knees. She scanned Reed's calendar. "He has no life!" How could she revitalize a company led by a robot?

Knowing she wouldn't find an answer to that tonight, she let her mind wander back to her mom's situation. Her mother and Tony loved each other, in their own mutually needy way. Caroline could understand that. Her father had been a good man, a big man in every way, and his death had left big shoes to fill. Her mother wasn't brave enough to stand on her own. But Tony? She knew her mother couldn't see it, but Tony was every bit as needy as she was – and even more irresponsible with their money.

While she logged off the network and packed up her things to head home, Caroline considered the benefits of kidnapping her mother and hiding her somewhere to see if Tony would move on, like a parasite finding its next host. She had to be fair. Even though he and her mother had never married Tony treated her like a stepdaughter and her mother like a queen. Her mother could have done worse. But she could have done better.

She decided to forgo the expense of a cab and walked the ten blocks from the Decatur Building to her Battery Park apartment. It was November and the temperatures hovered in the low forties, but at least the buildings would block most of the wind. Tomorrow she would remember her tennis shoes and a real winter coat.

She scolded herself again on her choice of shoes

as she noted the out of order sign on the elevator doors in her apartment building. With a sigh, she took the stairs to the third floor. Maybe after this project her company would promote her, and she'd be able to afford a place in a better building.

She unlocked the door and tossed her keys in the little metal dish on the table in her entry. Before dropping her bag on the floor next to the table she dug out the mail, a few catalogs, more bills for her mother and Tony. At this rate, not only couldn't she move to a better place, she would have to take on a second job, and find jobs for both Tony and her mother to dig them out of all this debt. She resisted the urge to moan that this wasn't fair. Life wasn't fair. She'd learned that lesson as a teenager when her father died so suddenly. Her father had taught her to believe that life was whatever you made from what was dealt to you, and she was determined to give her mother the same good life that her father had provided for them. Even if that meant supporting her and Tony during their struggles.

She tossed the mail aside and selected a microwave dinner from the meager selection in her freezer. While it heated, she changed into a stretchy T-shirt and leggings and found a romantic Christmas movie on T.V. Perhaps a dose of happy-ever-after would take her mind off the things in her life that she couldn't change.

Chapter 2

Reed was in his office at a quarter to six and already feeling irritated with himself. He was nervous. He hadn't even been nervous when his father announced he was retiring and offered him the presidency. He frowned and went to start a pot of coffee in the little machine in an alcove of his office. There wasn't any point in getting started with his work when Caroline would be coming in any minute to *immerse* herself in his life.

Of all the office fantasies he'd indulged involving his mystery woman, this was not one of them. A tryst in his office, taking her up to his penthouse, those images he'd entertained. But having her follow him around watching him work, judging his every move? Nope. Never that.

She was lovely, and now he knew she was entertaining as well. But to spend all day at the office with her while he acclimated to his new role? He was already too distracted by her presence. What would he be like after a few weeks with her? An incompetent idiot, probably. This was pressure he wasn't prepared for.

He was frowning over the very real possibility that he would make a complete fool of himself when she opened the door to his office and stepped inside.

"Good morning." Her voice was soft and slightly rusty.

"Morning." Reed studied her for a moment and then took a few steps closer. Her face was flushed, and she looked tired. He'd only ever seen her looking bright eyed and confident, almost irritatingly so. But this morning some of that brilliance had dulled. Despite his teasing the previous day about keeping up with his schedule, he'd seen her around the building often enough to know that she kept long hours, too.

"You look tired." He commented after scrutinizing her up close. "Too early?"

She scrunched her brows together. "No."

He cocked his head, curious that she was so withdrawn this morning, especially after teasing him so blatantly the day before. "Wake up on the wrong side of the bed then?"

She huffed. "I didn't wake up in a bed at all."

"That sounds interesting."

She gave him a chagrined expression. "Unfortunately, not in the way you think. I woke up in my loveseat. To an infomercial."

He offered her a small smile. "You might want to come up with a better story than that. That one's kind of lame."

She laughed, her expression clearing. "So noted." Helping herself to a cup of coffee, she turned and propped a hip against the counter. "What's on our plate for today?"

Reed seated himself behind his computer and brought up his schedule. "Back to back meetings from seven-thirty until four." He scrolled down. "Dinner with one of our vendors at seven."

Caroline stared past him at the Brooklyn skyline outside his office windows. "Okay."

He sat back and made eye contact with her. "Miss Trumbull, you don't have to stick it out all day. It's going to be a long, boring day. Feel free to take off when you need to."

"Boring, huh?" She straightened away from the counter and moved closer to his desk. He liked the way she walked. So tall and graceful.

"Do you dance?"

She paused. "Excuse me?"

He almost laughed. Geez, had he said that aloud? "Sorry. I meant to ask if you've ever been a dancer?"

She blinked at him, clearly not sure how to read that. "Uh, yes. I danced until my second year of college. Ballet and lyrical. Not, you know, the other kind."

"What other kind?"

She pinned him with a warning look. "The naked kind."

Until she'd said spoken the words, he hadn't considered any other kind. Now he couldn't get that image out of his head.

He laughed. "Maybe the day won't be so boring after all."

She lifted one side of her mouth in a forgiving smile. "Wouldn't matter either way. You selected the speed round so like it or not, I'll be hanging by your side for a while."

He nodded in acknowledgment and turned to pull a page from the printer behind his desk. In addition to being under a microscope, spending time in her presence and hearing her sexy voice all day, he'd have to be more careful not to cross the line between banter and sexual harassment. "Here is an itinerary for the off-site meetings on my schedule this week." She took it and glanced at it when he turned back to his computer. "You'll be able to plan ahead and adjust your wardrobe," he looked her up and down, "or whatever, for the schedule."

She looked away from the paper and directly into his eyes with her eyebrows raised. "Is there something wrong with my wardrobe, Mr. Decatur?"

"Of course not."

She held out the page as if asking him to explain his remark.

"We have a full day of meetings which will likely run late. Then we'll have a dinner meeting. You'll want to change into something more formal for dinner. If we're running all day, you might want to rethink your shoes." She was wearing gray heels, the kind with a little wedge cut out giving a tantalizing peek at her painted toenails.

"I'll be fine. I'm used to being on my feet all

day." She raised one side of her mouth again. "Are you trying to scare me away?"

Reed tried to keep the exasperation from his voice. "I'm trying to give you the information you need to make good decisions. To know what to expect so that you can be comfortable."

She tipped her chin up, looking thoughtful. "My comfort is important to you? Even though I'm here to do something you clearly disagree with?"

Reed's stomach churned. She was reading into his motives already. Less than an hour into her project she was already taking notes, spinning ideas. He ground his teeth. "I'm human."

This time her smile reached all the way to her liquid blue eyes. "Yes. And I'm here to make sure everyone else knows that as well."

For the rest of the day, Reed focused on meetings, decisions, and emails. He was surprised to realize that once he got to work Caroline's presence hadn't distracted him from getting things accomplished after all. He was always aware of her, it was impossible not to be, but she was more like a welcome support than the irritating presence he had anticipated. Though she wasn't a direct stakeholder in any of the meetings they attended, she was surprisingly good at understanding multiple points of view, and more than once she served as mediator when tempers started running hot. As Reed had little patience for finger-pointing, Caroline's patience and diplomacy were a helpful addition.

It had been a long day and Reed had intended to dismiss Caroline before the dinner meeting with their lead packaging vendor but after several hours in her company, he decided he wasn't ready to part with her yet. When their four o'clock meeting convened at five-thirty, he hurried upstairs to his penthouse apartment to change into a more formal suit. Most of his executives were in favor of a more casual appearance, but Reed agreed with his father that dressing well was a sign of respect for their business partners.

Belatedly wondering how to introduce Caroline to his dinner guests, he punched the elevator button for the lobby where they had agreed to meet. The elevator made several stops on its descent. Reed paid no attention to any of them until the doors opened on the fourth floor. His heartbeat tripped over the sight of Caroline dressed up for dinner. She'd chosen a sedate navy blue dress. There was nothing inappropriate about the way she looked, yet Reed couldn't stop himself from visually undressing her.

Thankful that the elevator already held three other people, he moved further back and kept the others between them as she entered. The brief interested look she gave him made him wonder if he hadn't done enough to conceal his own interest.

Caroline exited first when they arrived on the ground floor and walked slowly toward the fountain, probably waiting for him to approach. He paused a few minutes to let more people clear out of the lobby before reaching her side.

She didn't wait for him to speak. "I'll take a taxi once you've left for the restaurant. I didn't want to arrive ahead of you."

Reed frowned at her. "I have a car waiting for us."

She tipped her head the way he now knew meant she was considering something, as if every decision was a chess move. "If that's what you want. Sometimes those small actions are misconstrued. I don't want to start any rumors."

Reed pressed his lips together and spoke. "It's both polite, and the way I would treat any of my executives if they were joining me. Male or female."

"Perfect. Then, thank you."

He looked down into her eyes, liking the way she seemed genuinely pleased at his offer.

The ride from Wall Street to the Midtown restaurant took several minutes in the evening traffic. Rather than sitting in uncomfortable silence, Caroline shared her thoughts on the meetings they'd attended that day.

"I suspect Adam's department is having trouble with Jeff's department because Adam and Jeff have different goals. I already have some ideas for getting those teams to work together more smoothly." She offered a few suggestions that they debated for several blocks before arriving at the restaurant.

"Shoot." Reed placed a hand on her forearm as she reached for the door. "I forgot to ask earlier. How would you like me to introduce you to my vendors?"

She gave him a knowing look. "You might want to fudge my title a little so that it doesn't give people the impression that you're a leader under construction."

Even though she was dead-on, Reed laughed. A leader under construction? "I was thinking more along the lines that it might seem strange that I'm bringing a development coordinator to a meeting with my vendors."

She nodded. "Do these men often visit your office?"

"No."

"Then just introduce me as your date." She flushed. "I'm not suggesting anything. But they would be less likely to ask questions, and hopefully spend more time focusing on your agenda."

It didn't really matter to Reed one way or another, but he liked the idea of introducing Caroline as his date. He liked it a little too much.

As far as business meetings went, the evening was a success, though Reed hadn't been particularly worried about that. His company's relationship with the packaging supplier was solid and mutually beneficial so this had been more of a formality than anything. As far as dates went, he'd never been more impressed with a woman. Caroline was poised and said all the right things. His pleasure lessened a fraction when he remembered that she was merely a contractor and tonight she had been playing a role for him.

The dinner ran long, mostly due to the easy and entertaining conversation, but Reed felt guilty for keeping Caroline out so late. He was used to the long hours, but he wasn't sure that a sixteen-hour day was quite what she'd signed on for. As soon as his guests departed, he turned to offer her a ride home.

"It's gotten pretty cold out tonight. Where's your coat?"

Caroline shook her head. "The coat I wore today didn't match the dress, so I left it at the office."

That was a serious sacrifice to fashion, but it played into his plans perfectly. "That's alright. I was planning to take you home anyway."

She wrapped her arms around her middle and looked at him, her uplifted chin accentuating her stubborn response. "I'll grab a taxi. There's no need for you to take me all the way back downtown."

"I live downtown. It's not exactly out of my way. Where do you live?"

"Oh. Ah, no. I insist on getting a taxi." She gave him a teasing smile, though even in the dark he could see that she was uncomfortable. "It's only our first date." She held out a hand as if she was going to place it on his chest. "I'm kidding. But it really is late, and you must be as tired as I am. Please, don't put yourself out. I'll grab a taxi and be home in a few minutes."

Reed's sense of chivalry warred with his realization that she was right, and responsible for her own decisions. He clenched his jaw and tried not to stare at her. "You're right. I am exhausted and we have another long day tomorrow. Why don't you come in at nine tomorrow?"

She cocked her head. "What time are you coming in?"

Reed shrugged. "Seven, probably."

She nodded. "I'll see you at seven. Goodnight, Mr. Decatur."

Reed watched her step up to the curb where a taxi immediately angled out of traffic for her. One quick wave and she was gone.

IT WAS TEN-fifteen by the time the taxi pulled up in front of Caroline's building. Reed had forced her hand by insisting on taking her home, and there was no way she wanted him to see where she lived so she'd broken her self-imposed no-frivolous-spending rule and took a taxi home from the restaurant instead. She couldn't fault him too much; Reed had been right about one thing. It *had* been a long day and she was dead on her feet. Without his insistence on seeing her home she might have walked the distance from mid-town to Battery Park, and that would have been a terrible idea.

Tomorrow she'd wear sneakers to work. She'd also bring a couple cocktail dresses to keep in her office. She had to give him credit, Reed was certainly organized, and he'd known from the outset exactly what she'd need to keep pace with his hectic life.

Once safely inside her apartment, Caroline stared out the window, the buildings and streetlights blurring into the background of her thoughts as she reviewed her day. Seven hours of meetings and Reed had walked into each one of them confident, prepared, and ready to make a decision. She marveled at the extent of his knowledge and the deference his employees already showed toward him.

He was young, just over thirty, and had been CEO for less than a year and already his peers followed his lead. Of course, it was just as likely that his quiet, unsmiling demeanor put people on edge.

Caroline took a quick shower, dressed in her favorite flannel pajamas, and flopped onto her bed. Next to her, her phone signaled a voice message. "Carrie, honey? This is your mother. Please call me when you have a chance. It's really important."

Caroline deleted the message, clicked her phone off and tossed it onto the worn bedspread beside her. Everything was important to her mother.

Unfortunately, it was nearing the fifteenth of the month which meant her mother, or more accurately, Tony, had run out of money. Caroline sighed and flipped through a few more channels. What did it say about her lonely existence that her best prospect for company was calling her mother back?

She gritted her teeth and muted the television. With the usual combination of guilt and dread, she dialed the number and waited. Like clockwork, Tony answered her mother's phone.

"Hi Tony. Can I speak to Mom?" She listened to Tony's rustling as he jostled himself to shout.

"Heather, ya got Carrie on the phone."

"Caroline," she muttered under her breath.

There was a pause and then, "Carrie? Is that you?"

"Yes, Mom. What's wrong?"

Her mother made a clucking sound. "Why do

you always assume something is wrong when I call?"

"Maybe because you only call when something is wrong?"

"Well, maybe this time I just wanted to congratulate you on your big contract. I'm so proud of you, Carrie. So proud."

The burst of joy Caroline felt at her mother's praise was short-lived. In the background she could hear Tony's reminder, "Find out how much she's getting paid." With an angry thrust, Caroline kicked a throw pillow off the end of her bed.

Her mother crooned, "Ooh, I'll bet you got a nice bonus for this, huh?"

"I get a negotiated rate for each project. You should know this by now."

"Oh well. I don't know anything about how all that works."

And yet, Caroline thought, she knew how to spend someone else's money just fine. "It's not a new contract, Ma. I've been there nearly two months now."

"I guess I knew that. But it just seemed important to tell you how proud we are."

"You mentioned that. What do you need?"

Her mother seemed to hesitate. "A few hundred, I think. A thousand at most."

Caroline frowned at her television. No more taxi rides for a while. She sighed. "I'll make a deposit for you tomorrow."

"When is the last time I told you that you're the best and most beautiful daughter a mother could ever have?"

The last time you asked for money. "Goodnight, Ma."

Chapter 3

Caroline's carefully chosen navy suit gave her the perfect disguise. Today two other executives had worn the same dark color. She would be able to blend into the group more effectively. For all that she'd been there in the Decatur building for a couple of months already, she'd spent very little time on the top floors. It was quieter up here, more focused. She wondered how the men and women could work in such an uninspiring environment.

Caroline checked the calendar on her phone for the location of the conference room. She was early, which was exactly the way she liked it. She preferred to acclimate herself to her surroundings and choose a strategic seat. In the case of today's meeting her perfect position would be nearest the door, unobtrusive, and hopefully, unnoticed. She knew Reed would be there, of course. From now until she finished observing the executive team, she was going to be his shadow. Despite yesterday's teasing, she felt bad for him. She'd figured out pretty quickly that he was a strong introvert, and her constant presence invaded his privacy. She only hoped that by now he'd realize she didn't expect him to entertain her. Remembering his handsome, angry face as they discussed her plans for his company sent a tingle from her chest to the tips of her fingers. She stowed her phone and hugged her laptop closer as she entered the conference room.

Low voices halted her in the doorway. She got a glimpse of a beautiful red-haired woman leaning into Reed intimately. They looked up when she entered. Caroline was caught in Reed's angry expression. She sucked in a breath and reversed her step, backing out of their view. Embarrassed, she leaned back against the wall outside the door and released her breath slowly. Damn! Walking in on Reed was not the way to start off the day on a positive note. She ignored her twisting gut and reminded herself that whether she had a crush on him or not, Reed had a life of his own.

Caroline waited outside the door until another executive entered the room before going in again. He seemed to have collected himself. He'd chosen a seat, not at the head of the table as was his right, but on the side facing a long bank of windows. Deliberate? She'd bet on it.

She chose a seat adjacent and across the table from him, near the door as she'd planned. From this vantage she'd be able to see everyone without putting herself in the limelight. The redhead had seated herself at the head of the table. She appeared to be pouting and from the random clenching of Reed's jaw, he was irritated as well. Had they seen her enter? She opened her laptop and brought up a note-taking program, more to keep herself from looking at either of them than from an actual need to take notes. Her role in the meeting was only to watch and evaluate. She didn't normally make notes until afterward.

Before the meeting got underway, one of the executives, a graying mid-fifties aged man beamed a smile at Caroline before turning to Reed.

"Who's the new face?"

Reed slanted a glance toward her. "This is Caroline Trumbull. She's a professional team builder that the Board hired to work with us. She's going to be my right-hand man for a few months while she works on setting up a new training division for us, among other things."

There were several polite greetings, but the redhead, she noticed, had not reacted so favorably. Caroline exchanged smiles and nods around the table while the meeting was brought to order. Caroline tried not to be obvious as she watched Reed work. In truth, she could be content to watch him all day. He was organized and methodical, and so intense that she could nearly feel his focus. She let her mind wander as a presentation was delivered, imagining what it would be like to have Reed's focus on her. She felt herself flush and shifted in her seat. His gaze transferred from the screen to her. She quickly lowered her eyes to her computer and made a few brief notes. Since the meeting had only just started and she had yet to identify anything worth noting, she tapped out a to-do list.

Sneaking a quick peek at his face gave her the idea that he knew she wasn't focused on the meeting. Was the man a mind-reader, too? The meeting dragged on in a blur of reports and decisions that meant very little to Caroline, though she had learned a few things about their new CEO.

First, he knew his market. Caroline was impressed at the breadth and depth of his knowledge about the shipping industry. He didn't need to ask for a single detail in order to make a decision. Second, his staff was quick and organized. Except for the woman she'd seen him with, the other executives asked for, listened to, and accepted his suggestions without the need for a lot of discussion. For a man in his early thirties and relatively new at the helm, his opinions were treated with a great deal of respect.

At the conclusion of the meeting, Caroline fell back to allow others to precede her so that she could follow Reed back to his office. The redhead pushed past them, clutching her laptop to her chest. Reed's jaw clenched one more time, she noticed, before he turned back to Caroline, his expression clearing.

He walked by her side without speaking. In the space of two heartbeats the silence became awkward. "I feel like I should be walking behind you?"

Reed cocked an eyebrow at her in question.

"You know, if I'm your shadow?"

The tiniest glimmer of a smile appeared in his eyes.

"I'm sorry for walking in on you earlier."

"You didn't." His clipped response suggested it was a sore subject.

She nodded, which seemed to make him feel the need to explain himself. "I don't condone that kind of activity in the office."

Caroline stopped in her tracks and looked up at him. "She came on to you?"

Reed looked up and down the wide, carpeted hallway before returning his gaze to hers. "Does that surprise you?"

"Ah, no." She could feel her face burning. "No, sorry. I just-I didn't expect that at this level, you know?"

"Flirting from my executives?"

"Yes." Could she have sounded more obtuse? Reed seemed to soften as he looked at her.

"I didn't hire Elizabeth, Miss Trumbull. And I haven't really worked much with her. She indicated her interest, I informed her of my expectations for my employees and now she knows."

Caroline smiled and started walking again. "That was very gentlemanly of you, Mr. Decatur."

"Thank you." Reed held the elevator door for her. There were others in the elevator with them, so Caroline held her questions until they'd exited and were safely away from the curious glances.

"So, what's next on the agenda, Boss-Man?"

Reed had entered his office ahead of her and turned now with an almost playful expression. "I'm not your boss."

Unable to resist the verbal sparring, especially since it seemed to cheer him up, Caroline moved closer and smiled at him. "Does that mean all the usual rules don't apply?"

Both of Reed's eyebrows rose before his interested gaze swept down her body. "Which rules are you planning on breaking?"

Too late she realized it sounded like she was flirting with him, exactly what he'd just spoken to Elizabeth about. Caroline blushed and Reed smiled wider making her feel naked under his gaze. Apparently, he didn't have the same qualms about flirting with contractors. Relieved by his response, she took an involuntary step forward and moved around him to perch a hip against the corner of his desk. "Once I decide, you'll be the first to know."

He appeared to consider that with one side of his mouth tipped up. "I'd rather be surprised."

Caroline swiveled to watch as he moved around his desk to look at his calendar. "Huh."

He frowned at his screen and then raised his eyes to her. "Huh-what?"

Caroline shook her head and straightened away from the desk. "I wouldn't have pegged you for a guy that likes surprises."

His frown disappeared. Clearly, he enjoyed teasing her. "I don't like surprises. Usually. But you're entertaining as hell. So, if you're planning on breaking the rules, seriously, surprise me."

With that enigmatic response he gathered a file and notepad and left his office, leaving Caroline staring after him, wondering whether she'd just received a compliment or an insult. A moment later, Reed poked his head back around the door. "Are you coming?"

"YOU REALLY do work a grueling schedule." Caroline told Reed around a stifled yawn. They were returning from the third back-to-back meeting that afternoon. Reed stopped short and turned to focus on her face. "I'm used to it. You don't have to attend every meeting. This has got to be pretty boring for you."

Caroline shrugged one shoulder. "To be honest, I don't bother to follow along all the time. My job is to see how you interact with your employees. At some point I'll even see you in action in public."

"Well, you're a trooper for sure."

Caroline gave a small laugh. "I think, by definition, you're the trouper. Seriously. You must have the patience of a saint."

His shoulders straightened. "I have a lot more respect for my dad." He started to turn away and turned back. "And like I said, you're entertaining to have around. So far, having a shadow is not that bad."

"Wow. Thanks."

Caroline's phone dinged a text. She pulled it out of her pocket and glanced at it. *Damn!* Tony was coming to see her, may even be there waiting for her already. Her hand shook a little as she stuffed her phone back in her pocket.

She stewed on the reason for Tony's visit as they traveled the hall from the reserved conference room to the bank of offices for junior executives and herself. If Reed noticed her sudden distraction, he didn't comment.

Reed had never visited her office. In fact, she wasn't sure he was even aware they were near it and suddenly she was glad of that. A quick glance toward the glass interior wall of her office showed her Tony was indeed waiting on her. She stopped and angled her body so Reed's back was to her office and tried to appear casual. "I'm going to stop off here and make some notes. You know, let you off the hook for a few hours."

He tipped his head and half-turned toward her office. Her face was heating, she could feel it. He needed to go now, before Tony decided to come out and introduce himself. Heaven only knew what he would say. Just the thought made her want to melt through the floor.

Clearly in no hurry to leave, Reed's eyes focused on her face, making her blush intensify. "Are you okay?" He looked around. She knew when he spotted the back of Tony's balding head. She prayed Tony would just stay put until Reed had left.

"I'm fine. I just had some thoughts I wanted to capture while they're fresh."

"Who's that?"

"No one," she answered too quickly. *Dammit.* "Sorry, I mean, I don't know yet." She tried to give him a confident smile, but from the look in his eyes she knew she failed.

He pressed his lips together and slanted a suspicious look toward her office before looking back at her with something like disappointment.

"Have a good evening, Miss Trumbull."

Caroline nodded but she wanted to slam something. It was as if the minimum ground she'd gained with Reed the past few days was gone, just that fast. She stomped down her anger and breezed into her office. Tony stood when she entered. At least he had manners.

"What are you doing here?"

"Can't a man visit the young woman he thinks of as a daughter?"

Caroline stared at him. Sure. Except he never did. "You can't just show up where I work!"

He held his hands out to the sides. "They let me in and they even told me where to find you."

Caroline's insides froze. If Tony was confident enough to come and find her at work for money, when would he stop? "What do you need, Tony?"

He sighed. "A couple thousand. That should do it."

Caroline closed her eyes to shield her murderous thoughts. A couple thousand! Tony threw numbers like that around as if they were tens and twenties.

"I gave you a thousand dollars last month. What happened to that?"

Tony hitched his chin back, looking defensive. "We paid for stuff with it. The bills come every month, you know."

"So do paychecks," Caroline muttered. "I don't have that kind of money on me, Tony. Go on home and I'll visit you guys later."

He hitched his thumbs in the pockets of his jeans and looked around. "This is a nice office. You must be doing really well here."

"I'm a contractor. I don't work for Decatur; I work for Johnson & Jenkins. This office is just a loaner I use while I'm here. In another month I'll move on to my next contract." Except that she hadn't lined one up yet.

"Don't matter. This is nice and it suits you. Maybe you should stay."

Caroline huffed. "Really, Tony. I'll come over tonight and we can all talk." She walked around her desk and opened her laptop. "I have a few things I really need to take care of right now."

Tony nodded. "I get it. You're busy." He slouched to the door and turned back with a smile. "We really are proud of you, you know."

Caroline nodded and sat while she watched Tony make his way to the elevators. Great. Now she felt angry, frustrated, *and* guilty. Needy or not, they were her family, and they cared about her.

Chapter 4

*I*t only took a week for Caroline to decide that Reed's schedule was going to kill her. His work life was grueling. And if he had a personal life, she'd seen no evidence of it. Since the day Reed saw Tony sitting in her office, he'd been distant. There hadn't been any playful conversations, no shared looks.

Today in particular, had been a hellish day and all Caroline could think of was a glass of wine and a binge session with her favorite show when she got home. Reed had done his best to ignore her all day. Although it hurt, she was getting used to his indifference toward her. During those first few days she'd been sure he felt the same shocking chemistry between them that she had, but after a week of being in his presence without exchanging more than a few necessary words, she'd decided the attraction was one-sided after all. It was probably for the best because workplace relationships were tricky, and she knew how he felt about them. Besides, after watching him work she was starting to understand that she was not in his league.

The worst part about working with the leadership team was the way the female executives treated her. Caroline was well-aware of their competitive nature. Understanding personalities and helping companies use them to their greatest advantage was her trade. She also knew that the senior Mr. Decatur hired only the best for his company, but for all the time that Caroline spent in the executive wing, the other women made it clear she didn't belong there. She knew, even if the executives didn't, that so much of their disdain for her really stemmed from their resistance to change and the fact that she was the one promoting it. Fighting with them just to prove she was right would have been contrary to her goals for the company, so every day she manned up and pretended their petty insults weren't wearing on her. Things would improve, as they always did, but she usually didn't stick around long enough to build relationships with anyone once a contract was finished.

Caroline's role gave her virtually unrestricted access to everywhere Reed went, which put her in meetings, lunches, and business dinners where she was the recipient of the women's snide remarks and suggestive comments, and undoubtedly gave business partners and other employees the impression she was Reed's plaything rather than a highly sought-after corporate trainer. Often Caroline went home feeling cheap instead of accomplished.

Tonight, had been no exception. Reed's five o'clock meeting had lasted until seven-thirty, so it was well after eight by the time she left the building for the night. Their Director of International Shipping, Diane the Dictator, as Caroline secretly referred to her, had made a comment to her assistant Julie implying Caroline would earn overtime pay at Reed's apartment later. Neither Reed nor Caroline reacted to the barely veiled whisper, though Caroline knew Reed had heard it. Instead of rebuffing the employee, Reed turned his inscrutable eyes to Caroline. As if the innuendos weren't bad enough, his lack of reaction could have lent enough credence to start rumors. Now, it was nearly nine o'clock and well below freezing outside. Time to get off the Manhattan streets.

Caroline spotted her mother waiting at her apartment door even before she'd climbed the final flight of steps. A rotten day, the elevator broken again, and now her mother. How much could a woman take? She let out a slow breath and pasted a smile on her face.

"Mom!" She pulled her mother in close for a hug. "I wasn't expecting you."

"Oh, I'm sorry, dear. I didn't realize you would work so late." Heather paused, "Oh! Or did you meet someone? Were you on a date?"

"No, Mom. I worked late." Caroline unlocked the door and let her mother precede her into the apartment. Who had time to date?

"Your place is fixed up so cute. I always feel so peaceful here."

Probably because you know I'll take care of you when you're here. But Caroline kept her thoughts to herself. She set her satchel on the little entry table and hung her coat in the closet prolonging the time before she would have to face her mother.

Heather had made herself comfortable on the loveseat and was fidgeting with her phone until

Caroline perched on the chair adjacent to her.

"All right. Lay it on me, Ma."

For a split-second, her mother looked irritated and then quickly changed her expression to one of humility. Caroline rolled her neck to loosen the muscles in her back. She'd been sitting far too long today.

"Well, you know how far we are from you now, Tony and me. We're up in Harlem and you're all the way down here in Battery Park. Alone. And I–we worry."

Caroline shot out of her seat. "No!"

"Think about it, dear. It's practical. We don't take up much space, and this way you wouldn't be alone."

"No, no, no. No." Caroline turned away from her mother, half afraid she would strangle her if she didn't put some space between them. "I like to be alone."

"No one likes to be alone," her mother snapped, and then appeared to think better of it.

Caroline paced back to the chair and sat. "What's wrong with your apartment, Ma?"

Her mother burst into loud tears and it was several minutes before she could collect herself enough to speak. "We're being evicted."

"Again?"

Heather's sobbing grew louder.

"I'm sorry." The response came more out of

habit than any actual regret. It wasn't the first time her mother had been kicked out of an apartment and neither of them liked to be reminded of it. "I gave you two month's rent just last week." And it had definitely cut into her budget. "Didn't you give it to the landlord?"

Heather waved a hand. "Most of it. But I guess we owed more than two months."

There was so much wrong with that Caroline didn't know where to start, but she knew that blowing her top would get her nowhere with her dramatic mother.

"Ma, last month I gave you two month's rent, too. The money I gave you last week should have put you ahead. What happened to the rest of it?"

"Oh, well. I let Tony borrow it sometimes."

Caroline could feel the pulse tripping in her neck. "Do I even want to ask what he does with it?"

Her mother brightened. "It's nothing bad. Sometimes he likes to buy a few rounds at the Blue Feather."

Caroline was aghast. "For a thousand dollars a month?" She was working long, crazy hours for her mother's boyfriend to drink it away?

Heather sat back, looking defensive. "It's how he gets all his leads."

Leads that seldom got him anywhere and certainly didn't pay the bills. No, they had Caroline to do that.

Going on as if expecting her daughter to be

excited about the idea, she brightened again. "Just think of it, Carrie. I could cook and keep the place picked up for you. That would help you, right?"

Caroline shuttered her expression. "And Tony?"

Another hand wave. "You know. He'll be hitting the pavement looking for the right job."

Caroline resisted the urge to roll her eyes. "After this many years *any* job would be the right job, Ma."

"That's not fair! You know Tony is used to a certain lifestyle and the kinds of jobs he's been offered are beneath him."

In the eight years that Caroline's mother had been with Tony DeLuca, she'd never known him to have a job. Leads, he had plenty of. But follow-through always seemed to come up short. They'd been over all of these points too many times to count.

"What skills does he have? What kind of job is he looking for?" She must have asked this question a hundred times in the past eight years.

"A good job."

Caroline closed her eyes, then looked at her mother and tried again. "What constitutes a good job to Tony? What does he want to do at his good job?" Sometimes talking to Heather was like reasoning with a toddler.

"Something like what you do. An office job. He could wear suits. Don't you think Tony would look great in a suit?"

Caroline rushed to get her mother back on track.

"Absolutely. So, an office job? Can he use a computer? I guess I've never really asked before."

"No, but it's not hard, right? I mean I see commercials all the time saying these programs are so simple a child could use them. Besides, all the richest executives do everything on their phones these days. And Tony's a whiz with a cell phone."

Caroline kept her opinion of Tony's aptitude to herself and tried again to get a logical response out of her mother. "What experience does he have? Trade? Advertising? Insurance? Sales? What did he do, Ma?" It was times like these when Caroline missed her father most. Her dad knew how to read Heather. Somehow, he'd made her naivete seem endearing rather than silly and needy. Or maybe it was because he took such good care of them both that Caroline never paid attention to her mother's personality flaws. Richard had loved her mother, loved them both so completely that even after nearly sixteen years, Caroline still felt the hole his passing had made in their lives.

"You mean, before he met me? He was a mechanic down at the taxi garage."

Caroline let out a whoosh of breath. "He's a mechanic?"

"He *was* a mechanic," Heather amended. "Now he wants to work in an office."

"Ma, you can't just go from fixing cars to working in an office, just like that."

"You did."

Caroline frowned at her. "I did what?"

"You went from waiting tables to working for billionaires."

That was certainly rewriting the past. "I waited tables to put myself through college. I got a Master's degree, Ma. I gained experience to work in an office." She paused and then added, "And I don't work for billionaires. I work for an agency that handles change management and training. My current contract is to set up a training department and transition a new CEO. He's probably not even a millionaire yet. He's young. Like my age."

Of course, Heather would seize on that. "Ooh! Is he single? Good looking? Straight?"

"For heaven's sake, Ma! He's a job." Unable to resist, Caroline flashed a quick smile. "I drive him crazy."

Heather blinked at her. "Dressed like that? The man must be a prude."

Caroline glanced down at her work attire and frowned. She dressed in an intentionally sedate style to blend into the background of every setting. Her job was to put her clients at ease and that often required her to be inconspicuous. "No, I mean he hates that I'm his shadow. I feel bad for him really. He's such an introvert and he's been thrust not only into a new job as the head of this enormous company, but the Board also wants him to be recognizable as part of their brand. This is all making him miserable and it's not making my job any easier either."

Talking about Reed Decatur succeeded in distracting her mother from her case of moving in with Caroline.

"What does he do for fun?"

"Fun?"

"Yeah fun, silly goose. Everybody needs to play, one way or another. Sometimes it's just not obvious to everyone else."

Caroline dropped back in her chair and stared at the wall just beyond Heather's head. As far as she could tell, Reed didn't have fun.

"Oh, I know that look," Heather mumbled to the room. "I'll get out of your hair while you puzzle through whatever it is you're thinking."

Caroline heard the wood floors creak and the door snap shut but she was still focused inward, considering a new angle from which to show Reed. How did he play? Did he enjoy a sport? She could almost picture him sweaty from a game of basketball. Did he attend plays? She tried and failed to imagine him at a rock concert. Without any real intention of doing so, Caroline began to stalk the perimeter of her small apartment.

Reed was a good man. She'd seen enough of him now to be sure of that. Perhaps he participated in charities. She knew one of his sisters was a museum curator. Perhaps he donated to the arts. Caroline got ready for bed, fixated on images of Reed in various leisurely pursuits and finally gave up when those images began to include herself.

The next morning, Caroline dressed again in something classy yet understated, a short black and white sleeveless dress with black heels that she knew would kill her feet by lunchtime. Not one to complain, she tugged the messenger bag containing her wallet and laptop over her shoulder and hurried the ten blocks to the office. Today she would greet Reed with her ideas, ideas that could get her job done and out of his hair quickly. Win-win.

HER SCHEDULE today was lighter than usual, so she used the time to send out a few resumés for her next assignment and then planned to use the down time to put together some training materials for one of the departments she'd finished evaluating. She only had one meeting with Reed which meant she'd be able to use the afternoon to focus.

Two minutes into the meeting, Caroline snatched her phone off the tabletop and transferred it to her lap. She snuck a look at the name on the display and set it face down on her thigh. She should have left it in her office. Sneaking a peek around the room she noticed Reed watching her. She met his gaze for a split-second and then turned her attention back to the notes she was taking. This group functioned well so she didn't think they would need much team building. She typed a few ideas for activities that would work well for them, and then tipped her laptop away from the group and spent the rest of the meeting searching online for affordable places to rent for her mom and Tony. Apartments in Manhattan were everywhere, and so were the people looking for them. When the meeting wrapped up and people around her were getting ready to leave, she gave a quiet growl and snapped her laptop shut.

Beside her, one of the younger managers gave her a commiserating smile. "Looking for a new place?"

He must have seen her screen. Damn. "Something like that."

Softly, he continued. "My sister is a Realtor. I can give you her info if you need help."

Brightly, pretending she wasn't frustrated by the whole situation, she responded. "Thank you. That would be very kind. Send me her info and I'll get in touch with her when I'm ready."

He nodded and turned to address another colleague. Caroline swiveled her chair away from the table and pulled her phone out. Sixteen messages from her mother. Two from Tony. She scrolled through them. The usual rambling mish-mash of silly, hopeful, desperate, dramatic, and guilt-laced messages. The two from Tony were succinct. *Let me know when I can pick up a key to your place.*

"When hell freezes over, that's when," she muttered.

"Problem?"

Caroline froze. She turned around with what she hoped was a polite smile. Randy Atkinson was standing with Reed beside her chair. "Not at all." She cocked her head and addressed Randy. "Good meeting. Your group works really well together."

Reed nodded. "I agree. I seldom get anything but positive results from them."

"Excellent." Randy beamed. Caroline scooped

up her laptop and stood. Randy moved aside to give her room, but Reed took his time backing up a few steps. She almost thought he was going to help her out of the chair. She directed her comments to Randy again. "I made a few notes, but I'm guessing you won't need much from me."

"It's good to hear that something is going right." Reed answered even though she wasn't speaking to him.

Caroline's stomach flipped unpleasantly. He had no idea how true that was. If only she could find an area of her life where something was going right. She threw them a distracted smile as Randy stopped Reed for another topic and made a beeline for the elevators. It was time to change her focus to damage control.

Chapter 5

*R*eed watched Caroline leave as he listened to Randy's update. Something was different about her today. He appraised her while she waited for the elevator. She was dressed just as tastefully as always, her hair perfect. It wasn't anything physical. It was more like she'd lost her...glow.

He could feel the tension increase in his shoulders. Just thinking that something had happened to upset her made his blood burn. Caroline's happy-go-lucky attitude was one of her most precious assets. He looked around the hall assessing his lingering staff for a possible cause, but no, it hadn't been anyone here. She'd been distracted by her phone so it must have been something outside of work. He reviewed what he knew about her personal life, but he knew it was precious little. She'd hinted once that she lived nearby, though whether that was in Battery Park, or in one of the surrounding neighborhoods, he didn't know. He was so intent on Caroline's mysterious life he almost missed his cue when Randy stopped speaking.

He nodded at his executive, a mid-fifties gentleman with sandy blond hair that hid a touch of gray. "I'll entertain the idea, Randy. Can you email me a recommendation? And I'll need the numbers to back it up."

He hurried down the hall and then slowed when he realized Caroline was still waiting for an elevator. She met his gaze and quickly looked away. Interesting. Was she avoiding him?

He stayed at the back of the group crowded near the doors so that he wouldn't spook her but kept an eye on her as she got into the elevator. Someone tried to engage her in conversation. She smiled at him, but Reed could see it in her eyes for those thirty seconds before the door closed between them. She was upset.

He pulled out his cell phone and dialed Jamie. "Can you let Ed know I'll be a little late? If he doesn't want to wait, go ahead and reschedule."

Jamie was used to his last-minute schedule changes. "Sure."

Reed took the next elevator down to the fourth floor. He wanted to rush to Caroline's office, but he knew actions like that would start rumors, so he forced a casual pace and offered friendly nods to the employees he passed. Caroline's door was open just a crack as if she'd swung it shut too weakly for it to catch. Perfect, Reed thought. He wouldn't have to knock.

The door opened silently at his push and he found her standing at the windows with her back to him, arms hanging loosely at her sides.

"Everything okay?" Reed asked in a low voice. It was inappropriate to close her office door, but he wanted to respect her privacy, too.

She swung around giving him a glimpse of her unguarded expression before she pasted an insincere smile on her face.

"Of course." She raised her eyebrows at him. "Did you need something?"

She'd offered him the perfect segue. "I, or rather, we, have another meeting."

She bobbed her head. "I'm sorry. I have to cut out early this afternoon, so I won't be joining you this time." She looked at her watch. "You're probably late though."

Reed narrowed his eyes at her dismissal. "He'll wait. Or he won't. Doesn't matter." He folded his arms across his chest. "Everything is fine, but you're cutting out early? Playing hooky today?"

Caroline blinked at him. "I'm not paid by the hour, Reed."

"It's unusual for you, that's all."

She hitched a shoulder and appeared irritated. "You chased me down here to find out why I was leaving early?"

"I didn't chase you anywhere. And I didn't know you were leaving early until a minute ago."

She pressed her lips together and leaned forward to scoop a few things from her desk into her satchel. "Let me rephrase that. You are willingly late for a meeting so that you could come to my office and ask me if I'm okay?"

Reed nearly smiled. "Yes."

She shook her head as if she thought he was nuts. "I'm fine. But I really need to go. Whoever you're meeting is probably getting impatient."

Reed stood back and held the door open for her. "Ed will reschedule if he waits too long."

"You could have told me it was Ed," she grumbled.

Evidently, she also knew that Ed was as easy-going as they come. Since they were now in the hall where any number of people could see them, Reed kept his laughter to himself. "Are you sure there's nothing you need?"

"Besides a little downtime and a whole lot of patience? No. I'm good." He must not have looked convinced because she lowered her voice and added, "Honest. But thank you."

"I'll see you tomorrow then?"

"You bet, Boss."

Reed shook his head. Even with whatever was bothering her, she didn't fail to give him attitude.

ON A HUNCH, Reed texted his driver and took the elevator to the lobby to find a spot where he could watch the elevators. Within minutes he spotted Caroline exiting the building. Thankfully, she didn't notice him. She was preoccupied and more serious than he'd ever seen her.

He was too curious to feel guilty for spying on her. He got into his waiting car. "Mason?"

"Yeah, Reed?"

"Do you see that blond up there?"

Hearts in Training

"She's kinda hard to miss." He wiggled his eyebrows at his boss.

"Can we follow her?"

Mason looked at Reed through the rearview mirror. "She's walking. You want me to pull alongside and offer her a ride?"

Reed gave it a half-second's thought. "No." She wouldn't appreciate that, and then he'd lose the opportunity to see what she was up to. "She's having a rough day, so I just want to make sure she gets home safely."

"Lucky for you, the traffic's moving at a walking pace right now. I'll see what I can do."

"Thanks." Reed called Jamie to let her know he would be longer than anticipated. Ever efficient, she had already rescheduled his meeting with Ed. With a touch of embarrassment, he suspected she knew his absence somehow involved Caroline. If only it was for a more pleasing reason!

They tailed Caroline three blocks until she looked around and stepped to the curb where she hailed a cab.

Mason and Reed watched her slide into the back of the car. Mason looked back at Reed for instruction.

"Follow it."

Mason nodded and maneuvered into a space leaving one car between them.

They followed cab 528 north for nearly the length of Manhattan, Reed's stomach clenching as he watched the scenery deteriorate. Where on earth was she going? It wasn't safe for a woman in this neighborhood. It wasn't safe for *anyone* in this neighborhood.

At last, the cab pulled to a stop in front of a run-down building in the south of Harlem. Mason pulled over far enough back that they could watch her without being recognized. Reed frowned when Caroline pulled a key out of her pocket and let herself into the building. Trash littered the sidewalk, and near the door was a careless pile of someone's belongings. Someone had recently been evicted.

Reed leaned forward to get a better look through the windshield. Indecision tore at him. Caroline's personal life was none of his business, and yet part of him wanted to follow her through that door and pull her back out. She couldn't live there; she'd said herself that she lived downtown. And yet, what would a successful woman with a good salary be doing in Harlem?

"Sorry Reed, but we probably shouldn't sit out here very long. We're already getting attention."

"You're right. Dammit." He gave one last long look at the building, wishing Caroline would step out the door. "Let's head back."

Mason pulled away from the curb slowly and looked back at Reed. "Sure you don't wanna grab her out of there first?"

Reed groaned. "I can't. And for the record, we were never here."

Mason nodded. "Gotcha."

The whole trip took just a little over an hour, hardly longer than a business lunch, and yet when Reed got back to his office, it seemed like his world had shifted from sunny and bright to cloudy and gray. Jamie was waiting for him outside his office door with a frown.

"I'm sorry, Reed." She tilted her head toward the closed door. "Elizabeth is waiting in your office. She would like to speak with you privately. She looked angry."

Reed exhaled. Cloudy with a chance of storms. He trusted Jamie's judgment and respected her greatly. He hated what he had to ask her to do. "I have no idea what she's angry about, but I need to be sure the door stays open." Jamie immediately nodded. Clearly, she understood his need to protect himself from a sexual harassment accusation. "Can you please sit within view of the door? Maybe even interrupt me if an opportunity pops up?"

Jamie gave him a kind smile. She was nearly the same age as his mother, and he'd known her practically since childhood. It was times like these when he really appreciated that intimacy. "I've got you covered, Reed." She patted his shoulder. "Go on. Get it over with."

Reed nodded and stared at the floor for a moment. "I really hate this part of the job."

Jamie shot him a smile that reminded him of Caroline when she was being cheeky. "Maybe it would help if you got married. You know, keep the wolves at bay."

Reed blinked at her, a little shocked. And then

laughed softly. "Let's make that your next project."

"Already on it," she quipped.

Reed removed the smile from his face and entered his office with all the authority of a man who'd earned his title. The attractive red-haired executive was standing behind his desk looking out over the East River.

"What can I do for you, Elizabeth?"

She turned and perched on the credenza behind his desk. He tried not to react to her audacity. She was in his space. No one went behind his desk. Except Caroline.

"With an open-ended question like that, a few things come to mind." She looked at him, over him. Then she seemed to notice the open door and straightened away from his desk, coming around to take a seat in one of the chairs intended for guests.

Reed gave her a stern nod and took his own seat. "I understand you have an issue you need to discuss. How can I help?" He checked the time on his watch. Did he have any meetings this afternoon? Something to serve as a bookend to this uncomfortable discussion? He looked to the door. He could see Jamie sitting at a small end table, just outside. She could see him clearly, though probably she wouldn't be able to hear the conversation.

"I just wanted to apologize for my actions before the meeting the other day. It was inappropriate to come on to you in such a public way." She looked at her fingernails. "I wanted to be sure we're okay."

He tried to imagine what his father would say in a time like this. It was likely that his father had never been in a situation like this. He folded his fingers together and gave her a serious look.

"While it's not against our company policy to engage in activities of a," he hesitated, not sure of a good word without reading the company policy to her, "dating nature when you're not a direct report, it still isn't a good idea to act on them at work. Particularly in a place where anyone can walk in on you."

"I understand. I really do." She shifted toward him and lowered her voice. "I just feel like there's something between us, Reed. In fact, I've considered taking a different position with the company so that I no longer work under you." She searched his face. "What do you think?"

She'd put him on the spot. He hated to deliberately hurt someone's feelings but in this case, it couldn't be helped.

"I'm not sure what it is you think is between us, but I value the work you do. You're terrific at your job, Elizabeth, and that is where I think you should stay."

"Are you already seeing someone?"

Reed squinted at her, wondering how to avoid being blunt. Maybe he needed to spell it out for her more specifically. "I don't bring my personal life into the office." He glanced toward the door, hoping Jamie would see him and take the hint but she was focused on her computer.

"You see, that's not what people are saying. There's all sorts of conjecture about you now that that Caroline Trumbull's always hanging around."

Reed felt that like a shock to his heart. People were reading into his non-existent relationship with Caroline? The first flames of anger entered his bloodstream. It would be one thing if there *had* been a romance between them, but the fact that his staff was making up rumors about something he was working so hard to abstain from really burned him. He leaned back and didn't bother to mask his irritation. "I'm not sure what rumors you're referring to, but Caroline is a contractor, hired by the Board to implement a training program as well as to evaluate the health of each of our departments. Her job is literally to evaluate my leadership team."

Elizabeth gave him a dirty look. "Well, she certainly spends a great deal of time evaluating you!"

"There is nothing personal going on between Miss Trumbull and myself. She's spent time here evaluating several departments and not once have I heard that her behavior was anything less than professional. Now it's time for the executive team to be evaluated. As the head of the executives, that means she reports to me on her findings." He looked up when Jamie gave a tentative knock on the doorframe. "I'll be interested to see what Miss Trumbull has to say about the overall health of this department. I have another meeting now. Thank you for sharing your concerns, Elizabeth."

Elizabeth brushed past Jamie on her way out of the office. Jamie stood in the door for a moment longer, then gave Reed a thumbs up. He nodded his thanks and opened his computer to check his schedule. He seriously needed a distraction.

THE NEXT morning Caroline went straight to her office to collect her notes before heading up to Reed's office for her daily briefing. It was later than her usual seven A.M. start time, and as a result, Jamie was already at her desk when Caroline arrived.

"Morning Jamie," Caroline called as she sailed past.

"Morning – hey!"

Caroline paused just outside the door to Reed's office and turned back.

"He's in a mood this morning. You might want to give him some patience."

"What's wrong? Has something happened?"

Jamie shook her head. "Not that I know of. I just wanted to give you a heads up before you get it bitten off."

Caroline gave her a smile and a nod. "Thanks." She'd seen Reed angry a time or two, that first day it had even been directed at her so she knew she could take it. She took a breath and pushed the heavy wooden doors open. As usual, she didn't speak until she was certain he wasn't on the phone. She approached his desk quietly and seated herself in one of the chairs that waited across from him.

Slowly, he turned around and pulled a file from the corner of his desk. He didn't spare her a glance.

Feeling it was safe to speak, Caroline leaned forward. "I had some ideas for your public image that I wanted to run by you."

"I have a busy day today."

"I know." She smiled. His schedule was her schedule.

"So maybe we should talk about this tomorrow."

"Ah-? I'm going to be with you all day. I'm certain we can find a few minutes to chat. I really need to get started on the plan to blend you with the brand."

He finally raised his head to focus his gray eyes on her. In them, she saw anger, regret. Her stomach clenched. "What's wrong?"

"Nothing is wrong. It's just going to be a crazy day and I need to prioritize what I'll be able to get done. If you don't mind, I'd rather wait until tomorrow to discuss this with you."

Caroline's heart dropped to somewhere around her belly button. Something really was wrong. Speaking as a friend, instead of a contractor hired to help him, she leaned forward and lowered her voice. "Reed, how can I help?"

He sighed, but his expression remained hard. Closed. "You can't. Your job is assisting with my company's transition. That isn't needed today. I just need to focus, and I can't do that with you hanging around."

Her stomach gave another lurch that she tried

to ignore. She'd thought they had a good camaraderie, the tender beginning of a friendship, even this past week when he'd been distant. But maybe she'd misread those signs as well. "That was, um, direct." She stood and arranged the chair back the way she'd found it. "I'll get out of your hair and have Jamie set something up for us."

She let herself out of the office, gave Jamie a wave and headed down to her office. Jamie had been right. He was in a mood. But unlike Jamie, she didn't want to give him time. She wanted to make it all better for him. If only she knew how.

By noon Caroline considered leaving early to go home and clear out her spare room for her mother and Tony when an instant message from Jamie popped up on her screen. Caroline had had no luck in convincing their landlord to let them stay long enough for her to find them a new place. Mentally backing away from that horrible memory and all that it meant for her immediate future, she read Jamie's message instead.

There's a benefit tonight at the Met. It just occurred to me that you wouldn't have received an invitation.

You're correct. Do you need me there? Caroline responded.

You should come. It'll be a good opportunity to see Reed in a public setting. I'll make sure you're on the list. 8 P.M. Formal. Jamie told her.

I'll be there. Thanks.

Caroline looked at the time. If she left now, she'd still have time to clear out the room and get ready for a party at the Met. She added the details Jamie emailed her to her cell phone and logged off her computer. She thought about Reed again. What was bothering him? After weeks of being near him almost constantly, it hurt to receive the cold shoulder. It was especially strange since he'd gone out of his way to check on her the other day in her office. Even if nothing more than as a concerned colleague, she knew he cared.

Knowing that she would see him later, even if she couldn't solve his troubles, made her feel a little happier. If he was only a job, why was she so invested? She got into the elevator and shook her head at herself. She'd moved way past crush stage.

Chapter 6

ℜeed watched Caroline from his spot along the wall. He'd had no idea she would be at the benefit ball and the sight of her lifted his spirits just enough to make the tedious evening bearable. He would be happy to stand in place and observe her all evening.

She wore a long light rose colored gown with her hair gathered into some curly concoction, sexier than the way she wore it to work. Not for the first time he wondered how long her hair really was. He could picture it down, brushing the middle of her bare back and he clenched a fist imagining his fingers against her skin, feeling that hair spill over his hands. She spoke animatedly with a group of mid-level executives showing none of the exhaustion he knew she must be feeling. His heart constricted for a moment, allowing a hint of jealousy that she no longer showed him that same level of enthusiasm, even though he'd brought that punishment against himself. The instant he'd caught wind of the office gossip he'd made the decision to drop a lid on their light-hearted banter in order to spare them both further embarrassment. He'd practically sent her away. He was surprised to realize how much he regretted that now. He'd done what needed to be done, the first step in putting some distance between them, but the fact remained that he missed her bubbling personality, the impertinent way she teased him, but mostly the easy friendship.

He spotted his date, Melanie, coming toward him carrying two glasses of champagne. Hadn't he told her he didn't care for champagne? In his periphery, he saw that Caroline was also watching Melanie. It only lasted a split second but clearly there on Caroline's face was an expression of disapproval. *Huh.* His gaze tracked over Melanie and flicked back to Caroline. Outwardly, Melanie was perfect. She was no more to him than an old friend and his favorite go-with date because neither of them wanted a relationship, but Caroline wouldn't have known that. Could the great and impervious Caroline Trumbull be jealous? It was such an appealing thought that Reed nearly smiled.

Melanie reached his side and offered him one of the glasses. With a nod of thanks, he took the glass but did not drink it. Over the next half hour several people stopped to congratulate Reed on winning various contracts, and he was thankful when Melanie had finished her glass. He traded his full glass for her empty one without anyone being the wiser. Or so he'd thought.

A few minutes later Caroline appeared before him. With a dismissive smile for Melanie, she moved to Reed's other side and handed him a new glass with raised eyebrows. "You can't walk around with an empty glass," she teased.

Reed accepted the flute of bubbly amber liquid, concealing the confusion he felt in her offer. Clearly, she expected him to drink it. He brought the glass to his lips but inhaled before taking a sip. Beer? With a hint of a smile, he took a sip. "Thanks."

Caroline excused herself with a slight nod and moved on to another group. The fact that she'd noticed and brought him his preferred drink concealed as champagne, was both clever and thoughtful. He was honest enough with himself to admit that seeing her tonight in this setting, especially after his self-imposed distance only made him want her even more. While Melanie was gorgeous and came from a great family, she lacked the depth of character that truly made a woman appeal to him. On the other hand, he knew next to nothing about Caroline's personal life and yet he already respected her greatly.

Reed paid more attention to Caroline as the evening wore on, sometimes surprised it was even possible. He watched as she circulated from group to group, seeming to find something in common with each of them. He noticed that she left each group wanting more of her. He could relate.

Every so often she glanced his way. Each time he wondered briefly if she was talking about him and then just as quickly realized that no one else turned to look his way. Even though it wasn't her role with the company, she seemed to be playing hostess, and was doing very well at it. No, she was keeping track of him. With a wry laugh, he remembered she wanted to see how he interacted in public.

Being an introvert, Reed hated the part of his job that required entertaining the company's guests. Caroline, on the other hand, was more than capable of picking up his slack. He cut his attention to Melanie. She was also chatting with a small group, but unlike Caroline, her intent was clearly more selfish. The men in the group fawned over her as she smiled and preened.

For the first time, Reed gave thought to what it would be like to be married as Jamie had jokingly suggested. An image of Caroline on his arm immediately filled his mind.

When she glanced his way again, he subtly raised his glass, to which she responded by blushing. Cute. Knowing it was a bad idea, Reed kept her in his sights and made his way to her side. The group she was speaking with had just moved on leaving her alone. Even better.

"Thanks for the beer. How'd you know?"

Caroline gave him a look that suggested he was obtuse. "It's the only alcoholic drink you order."

"Noticed that, did you?"

"Don't get a big head over it", she teased. "It's my job to notice things about you." She hitched one side of her mouth up in a half smile. "Does that make you feel special?"

He grunted. "Intimidated."

She rolled her eyes and turned more fully to face him. "Oh right. I don't intimidate you, Big-Shot CEO."

He leaned down toward her, intentionally getting in her personal space. "That's Mr. CEO to you."

"I'll try to remember that." She looked around as

if sizing up the crowd. "There's an opportunity here."

"Opportunity for what?"

"To put you out there."

"Out where?"

Caroline laughed. "Don't look so worried. I told you earlier that it was time to start working on your image. Part of my job is to bring your company's image into the twenty-first century, and I firmly believe changes like that should start from the top." She looked around again. "You should dance. Where's your date?"

Reed looked around with Caroline, and spotted Melanie leaning on the arm of a man Reed knew to be a lawyer. With his eyebrows raised, he looked to Caroline for another suggestion. Did she think he should interrupt Melanie's obviously personal intentions? Caroline shrugged and glanced around the room, presumably to find someone else suitable for her task.

Reed sighed. He was forced to be blunt. "Would you like to dance?"

She seemed surprised by the question. "Me?"

He gestured between them. "You're standing here, and you made the suggestion. You told me you were a dancer. Seems like an obvious conclusion to me."

"Ah." Caroline tipped her head back to meet his eyes. Even with heels, he towered over her. "No, it's not like that. I'm not trying to be coy with you."

"No, as I recall you ordered me to dance. You're here alone?" He touched her elbow and ushered her onto the dance floor.

"Of course. I'm working."

Reed looked around as he gathered her in his arms to lead her in a slow dance. "Why? No one else is."

She gave him an obstinate expression. "It's my job to watch you interact with your peers. Besides, I wouldn't want to offend your date."

Reed kept his eyes locked on Caroline. "Does she look concerned to you?"

Caroline slanted a glance at the woman. "Not really, no."

Reed shrugged. "We have an arrangement. Jealousy isn't part of it."

Caroline groaned. "Don't say any more. I don't think I want to know about your arrangements."

He cocked his head. "I thought you needed to know everything. Full immersion, remember?"

"You're confusing that with full disclosure. No, I don't want full disclosure from you."

"Mm. That's too bad. You might be interested."

Caroline pressed her lips together and shook her head. Her eyes laughing, expression indulgent.

"So dancing is going to make my company relevant in this new age?" He asked when she was silent for a while.

"It'll draw attention to you. Puts you in the spotlight."

"Awesome." His sarcasm came across loud and clear. Under his breath he started singing along to the tune of the classic love song.

Caroline squeezed his bicep where her hand rested on his arm. "Maybe don't sing. You don't want that kind of attention."

Above her head, Reed grinned down at her.

The music changed to a faster tempo forcing them to step apart. A quiet chirp sounded from Caroline's wrist.

"Oh!" She looked at the little gold watch on her wrist. "I've got to go."

"What's the rush, Cinderella?" Reed asked with a laugh.

She gave him an embarrassed smile. "I don't want to be on the streets too late."

Reed couldn't believe he heard her right. "You're planning to walk home, at this hour? Dressed like that?"

Caroline looked down at herself and when she looked back up her expression was resolute. "I'll be fine. I'm tougher than I look, remember?"

Reed took Caroline's elbow and ushered her to the mezzanine where they would have a little more privacy. "You don't always have to be the tough guy, Caroline. Not tonight anyway. I'll have my driver take you home."

She was already shaking her head. "It's really not nec-" He pressed a finger to her lips.

"No, it's not necessary. But I can't stand the thought of a beautiful woman walking the dark streets of lower Manhattan alone." He pulled her into the circle of his arms and put his forehead to hers. "Humor me. Let me take you home."

Caroline laughed, but she sounded nervous. "Don't be silly. You can't leave yet."

"Did you just call me silly?" He knew she was right. It would be inappropriate to leave before most of his guests, and they certainly shouldn't be seen leaving together.

"Well it would be silly," she whispered.

When she tipped her face up, presumably to argue with him, he silenced her by pressing his lips to hers. He hadn't planned to kiss her, had in fact been resolute in distancing himself from her just that morning, so it came as much a surprise to him as it likely did to her. Wanting to wrap his arms around her and fit her tight against him, Reed decisively set her away from him. Even as he removed his hands from her waist, he couldn't take his eyes from her flushed face.

"I'm sorry," she whispered.

He shook his head. Words were impossible against the strength of the feelings flooding him.

"I'll get my coat." She didn't wait for his response.

Reed pulled his phone from his pocket and

texted Mason to bring the car around to the front of the building. He waited until Caroline had returned with her coat and then helped her into the waiting limo, giving Mason instructions to take her home. He gave her one last look and closed the door, cutting off anything more they might have said.

Chapter 7

Caroline gave her address to Reed's driver and sat back with as much calm as she could fake under the circumstances. She wanted to grin, maybe even squeal and kick her feet, but since she had no idea how well Reed and his driver knew each other, she kept a lid on her giddiness.

He'd kissed her! Oh, it had been hardly more than pressing their lips together, but in those few seconds she'd felt his barely leashed restraint. She closed her eyes hoping she looked calm on the outside while in her mind she went over the events of the night. She'd made many contacts, several of whom showed interest in her professionally. There were also a few men who'd shown interest in her at a personal level, but as with any time Reed was in the room, she'd been unable to reciprocate. What other man could possibly compare?

No matter where she'd stood in the enormous ballroom, she was aware of him. She tried not to be obvious as she watched how he interacted with his peers. He mingled and chatted, and from people's expressions, he'd said all the right things. But Caroline could see that he was not enjoying himself. A black-tie evening was clearly not his thing.

He'd perked up some when she brought him a beer and Caroline wanted to believe that it was, in part, because he was happy to see her even with a gorgeous date by his side. Dancing with him hadn't been a great idea, considering they were in such a public venue, but resisting him was impossible. For a few precious minutes, she'd touched him. He'd held her in his arms. Those arms! Who would have guessed he hid such muscular shoulders under sedate business suits? She curled her fingers, still feeling his heat and strength on her fingers.

She opened her eyes when she felt the car slow and pull to the curb. Reality took the shape of a dirty brick building fronted by a bent iron railing. Home.

Caroline thanked the driver and offered to pay him, though she wasn't surprised when he refused. The driver waited until she'd entered her building before pulling away and she wondered if Reed had asked that of him as well, or whether he was just making sure she was safe. Regardless, she appreciated the gesture.

Caroline floated through the ritual of getting ready for bed, all the time picturing Reed's handsome face as he sang to her.

IT HAD TAKEN Caroline hours to fall asleep last night. Between the excitement of the evening and the knowledge that her mother and Tony would soon be moving in with her, she was out of sorts and not at the top of her game when she arrived at the office the next morning. She logged onto the network and was immediately greeted by an instant message from Jamie. Reed wanted to see her the moment she got in.

Caroline smiled, tucked her cell phone into her pocket, and snatched up her laptop. She spent the short elevator ride schooling her expression into one that she hoped wouldn't give away the pleasure she was feeling at the prospect of seeing him. All things considered; he would be the bright spot in her day.

Caroline entered his office and headed straight for the corner of his desk where she liked to perch when they went over the daily schedule. "You wanted a word?"

Reed looked up from his computer and seemed to regroup for a minute. "This company is often like a small town."

Caroline raised one side of her mouth in an almost-smile. "Offices often are."

Reed flattened his lips together and looked away. "I'm trying to say that we need to stop flirting. I should have discussed this with you yesterday. People are getting the wrong idea and word spreads fast around here. Especially when it involves me. It's probably not a good idea to continue meeting alone."

She huffed a quick laugh though there was nothing funny about the situation or his words. "Okay. No flirting. Got it." She could feel her face turning red, humiliation settling into her chest, choking her. She wanted to be brave and ask him exactly how his kiss last night figured into things, but she feared that her emotions were too close to the surface to be able to hear his explanation without making a fool of herself. There was no telling whether she would get angry or cry. Time to make a quick exit. "Anything else, Mr. Decatur?" The slip back to formality was petty, but she couldn't help herself. She wanted to him to know she got the message.

"Staff meeting at ten."

"I'm not staff."

"Then we won't wait for you."

He still hadn't looked up from his screen. His voice was clipped, and for once, she couldn't sense his mood. Was he angry with her? With himself?

Feeling chastised, but also concerned, she ignored her burning face and cocked her head at him. "Is everything okay?"

She took an involuntary step back when he impaled her with his gaze. There was so much there to decipher. Anger, yes. But also heat and...regret?

"Of course." His tone held a hint of warning.

"Then I'll head back to my office now." She reversed a few more steps and concentrated on holding her voice steady. "Ah, have a good day."

Damn, damn, damn. Caroline buried her face in her phone to avoid making eye contact with Jamie as she exited Reed's office and cursed herself all the way down to her own office. She had no idea what had changed between them overnight, but she knew a dismissal when she received one. On the surface, she knew Reed was right. It was unprofessional to act so familiarly with the new CEO, and it could damage his reputation if he appeared to be showing her anything more than polite interest at work. She dropped into her chair and plopped her chin in her hands. She wanted to cry. Only, crying at work wasn't a good choice, so she lectured herself instead.

She was a professional and she'd been hired to help the company adjust to changes the Board wanted to see. She was not here to flirt with the sexy new head of the company. It didn't matter if the chemistry between them could be cut with a knife. It only mattered that she did the best job possible for Decatur Industries. Her stomach clenched a little, though, as she considered how very perfect Reed was for her. She'd never met a man who could challenge her intellectually while being funny, sexy, and humble at the time.

Of course, she couldn't begin to guess how he felt about her. Sometimes it seemed that he was interested in her as a woman, and at other times, like today, he appeared to have no trouble keeping her at arms-length. Clearly, she'd overstepped a boundary with him last night. Except that last night he'd kissed *her*. Then she remembered that he'd gone to the event with a date. She swallowed the growing lump in her throat and turned to face the New York skyline. Reed had acted as though the woman was no more than a convenient date, but maybe his date saw things differently. Had she seen them dancing last night? Caroline wasn't sure. It would have been so much better if she could talk to him about this. But he'd made it clear he wanted nothing from her.

Reed had never withheld his interest in her before, so it was possible that he was feeling his words and actions as strongly as she was. Still, knowing that didn't ease Caroline's hurt. Instead, the idea of him hurting only intensified the ache inside her. Taking a step back from her was his choice, his reputation was on the line. She had to respect that.

To distract herself, she opened her laptop and forced herself to focus on the job at hand. Only, when she logged into Decatur Industries' social media sites, the pictures that greeted her made her sick to her stomach.

Each of the sites boasted the same picture, of Reed and Caroline locked in an embrace in the middle of the dance floor. Reed was smiling down at her while she laughed up at him. Some headlines hinted at his playboy status. Others declared he was off the market. *This* must have been what prompted Reed's abrupt change of heart. Caroline's heart beat painfully. She'd caused this. She'd provided an outlet for speculation. The wrong kind of publicity. She dropped her head in her hands and closed her eyes. What next?

Fighting down shame and embarrassment, and wishing again Reed would just talk to her about this, Caroline spent the rest of the day in meetings where the attendees didn't make eye contact, or only offered awkward greetings in passing. One dance with the boss and she was a pariah.

Back in her office at the end of the day, she shut down her computer and considered the impact of the media response on the success of her project. To the public, she was a stranger, just a random woman in a picture. She had hoped to take advantage of his good looks and single status to increase their brand recognition, but with the way he was looking at her in the picture she could see how the headlines were chosen. Would this attention help or hurt the company's image? In his industry it likely wouldn't hurt, but she knew how much he hated to be in the limelight. All teasing aside, it was never her intention to paint Reed as a playboy, or even anything less than the amazing man he was. She could only assume Reed was angry over the press. Did he think she'd used him? She swallowed back the lump threatening to choke her.

Would he take his issues to her superiors? She'd never received any feedback that was less than stellar on a project. It would kill her to hear complaints, especially from a man she respected so much. She couldn't imagine Reed going to Johnson & Jenkins without speaking to her first. No, he would address this head on. She frowned. So why wasn't he? If he was truly upset or disappointed in her maybe she should get in front of it and offer to relinquish her contract to an associate.

Her chest ached, as much from holding herself rigid all day as from the deep regret that whatever fledgling relationship they'd had was over. She waited for the elevator, willing it to be empty when it opened. From the corner of her eye she saw she saw Keith from Accounting coming to stand with her. She gave him what she hoped was a distracted smile. He seemed to take it as an invitation to talk.

"Hi Caroline." His smile and the way he dragged out her name hinted at more than casual interest.

Her stomach knotted. *Not tonight, please not tonight.* Knowing that Reed was upset with her and going home to learn what kind of chaos would ensue at her apartment, Caroline's facade was ready to crack, and she wasn't sure she'd be able to hold it together much longer. She certainly wasn't up for being hit on.

"Hi Keith. Long day for you, too?"

Keith moved a step closer to her side to make room for someone else. She forced her stomach to relax. Surely, he wouldn't hit on her in front of witnesses.

"It's just gotten better." He winked at her.

She resisted an eyeroll and managed a nod. At least he hadn't mentioned the pictures. It gave her hope. Maybe there were still people in the company that hadn't seen them.

"Hey. You want to grab a drink with me tonight?" Keith was standing so close now that she could feel his sleeve brushing hers.

She took a small step to her left to put some room between them and bumped into someone. She mumbled an apology. She was feeling anxious and boxed in and desperately wished for those doors to open before she did the unthinkable and cried in public. "I'm flattered, Keith. But I already have plans." With a tub of ice cream and her pillow. Unless Tony had found the ice cream. Could she take the stairs instead without making it obvious that she was fleeing? "I'm totally slammed tonight."

Keith nodded, whether from agreement or acceptance, she couldn't tell. "Yeah, I get it. Another night, then."

The elevator doors finally slid open and she stepped in and all the way to the back. She could feel tears gathering in her eyes and tipped her face back to try to keep them from falling. Damn! She glanced up to see who was going to witness her humiliation and her heart slammed into her chest. Dark gray eyes impaled hers as Reed entered behind Keith and took a place against the back railing. Beside her.

"Keith." Reed acknowledged him with a nod as he passed.

For a second Keith looked surprised, and then quickly regained his composure. "Mr. Decatur."

Reed's jaw twitched. "Just Reed. Mr. Decatur is my father. Every time someone says that I feel like a kid being caught doing something naughty."

Caroline couldn't prevent a smile. *Nice save, Reed.* At least he'd been paying attention to some of what she was trying to instill in his leadership team. If they wanted to appear

down-to-earth and approachable, they had to put their employees at ease.

Keith adjusted his computer bag and turned his attention to the downward progression of the lights on the door panel. Reed half-turned to face her, pride glowing in his eyes. She couldn't help but give a nod of approval before tipping her face down to hide the tears that still threatened her.

A few deep breaths got her back under control as they reached the ground floor. Then Keith inadvertently ruined the moment by handing her a card. "Here's my number. Let me know if you change your mind." He gave her one last admiring look and then headed for the parking garage.

Caroline heard Reed's angry growl beside her as she followed Keith out of the elevator letting distance accumulate between them.

She chanced a look at Reed's face, but she couldn't read his expression. She hitched the strap of her laptop bag across her body for better protection and gave him a polite nod.

Reed dipped his head, still giving her no hint of his mood. "Have a good night, Caroline."

Caroline walked a few steps toward the exterior door before Reed stopped her again, somehow not more than a step behind her. "Wait. Do you need a ride home?"

The last thing she wanted was for Reed to see where she lived, especially now that it would be occupied by her family. "It's not far. Thanks though."

"It's freezing outside." Reed pressed his lips together. "You live in Battery Park?"

She was careful not to confirm or deny his question. Instead, she tipped her head up to look at him. "It worked out that this contract gives me a shorter commute." With a small smile she raised a hand in farewell and pushed out the doors before he could stop her again.

The wind had a deceptive bite tonight, and Caroline was thankful that she'd packed a hat and gloves that morning. She walked the usual three blocks that she gave herself for appearances before digging out and donning the fluffy apparel. She shivered and rubbed her hands together to warm them in the gloves. She had many blocks to separate herself from her job and find some patience to deal with her mother and Tony. She considered calling ahead to let them know she was on her way and then decided against it. She would deal with them soon enough. Though bitterly cold and windy, at least the streets were quiet. Hardly anyone else was foolish, or desperate, enough to brave the weather tonight.

When she reached her building thirty minutes later, her eyes were burning, and her nose was running. Perfect. When she cried later, she could blame her red eyes and runny nose on the wind. She steeled herself and unlocked the outer door. She took two steps to the elevator. Out of order. Again. She pressed her lips together and shook her head. *Don't cry. Don't cry.* Thirty-three more steps and she'd be able to sit down, put her feet up. And enjoy her first night with roommates. A single tear let loose of her eyelashes and she swiped it away with her fist. Now was not the time.

Before she cleared the final landing, Tony poked his head outside the door. He beamed and hollered back into the apartment. "Carrie's home!"

That's when Caroline had another depressing thought. Her neighbors were going to hate her.

Chapter 8

*D*eciding that honesty was the best policy, Caroline called her employer the next morning and explained about the photos creating speculation with her and Decatur's CEO. She offered to hand over the account to another member of their team, but her boss turned that down. Caroline knew she worked for a great company, and that they had a lot of faith in her as an employee, but that didn't bring her much relief right now. Reed had been impacted by her lack of self-control. Caroline went in to work, but she didn't feel any of her usual enthusiasm for it.

She switched focus on the project from branding to training and spent the next two weeks working with the Human Resources department setting up their new training division. She worked with the director, Bill Burns, to hire energetic and dynamic trainers, and to set up class offerings and training opportunities specific to their industry. The work was fulfilling. This was always her favorite part of any project, but she still missed Reed. As much as she wanted to see him, she avoided the areas of the building he frequented, and still having access to his meeting schedule, avoided meetings with him as well.

For the most part, his executives were back to being civil to her. Some of them even stopped into her office now and again to invite her to lunch or just to chat about ideas for improvement on their teams. That was nice, but she was still lonely.

Life with roommates was also wearing on her. She couldn't deny that sometimes it was nice to come home to find dinner waiting for her, or to play card games with Tony on a Friday night. But her parents' unpredictable hours and complete disregard for her budget were interfering with her productivity. She was losing her energy and her edge. She could feel it.

Caroline plunked her head on the desk beside her keyboard and rested there for a few minutes. The urge to cry always simmered close to the surface these days so she took a steadying breath and let a few tears escape. Sneaking a peek at the time, she turned her back to the door and did her best to fix her makeup. She had a status update to deliver to the Board, including Reed, in a half hour. It was almost showtime.

Jamie was already in the conference room when Caroline arrived ten minutes early to hook her computer to the wide screen on the wall. Jamie's warm greeting nearly brought her tears flooding back. She gave Caroline an appraising look and pulled her into a hug.

"We miss you upstairs. It's been forever since you've been up to visit us, and I can tell you that some of us are really feeling your absence," Jamie told her as she checked the coffee bar to be sure it was fully stocked.

Caroline sucked in a breath and faked a smile she didn't feel. "You'll see in a minute the project is nearly complete. The only part left is to introduce

Reed to the world."

"Heaven help the world," Reed announced as he stalked through the doorway and headed straight for the coffee machine.

Embarrassed at being caught talking about him, Caroline hovered in front of her computer and brought up the presentation. She was ready, and not at all nervous about her status report. Her grand plan to get through the meeting without looking at Reed, though, would take Herculean effort.

Thankfully, the rest of the Board trickled in and took their respective seats. Several of the gentlemen, including Reed's father, Fred, engaged her in friendly conversation which helped distract her from his presence.

Caroline's update was diligently met with detailed questions, and ultimately, the Board's acceptance of the project's progress. "Overall, the project is ninety percent complete and on track to finish slightly ahead of schedule." She paused to send a smile around the room, even managing to flash it over Reed without looking at him. "While it's completely normal to be resistant or at least suspicious of change, most of your employees have embraced it. They've really been a dream to work with." She added a nod to drive home the point. "Honestly, your leadership is strong and competent. I have no doubts that once the training division is running, and new meeting techniques are being utilized, this company will be ready to soar into the next fifty years." She wrapped up with a reminder that Jamie would be scheduling another meeting once she'd completed the project.

Caroline shook hands with a few of the Board members and then closed her presentation and unplugged her laptop while the rest exited the conference room. Caroline planted her hands on the desk in front of her and let her head hang for a few seconds to stretch the tension out of her neck and shoulders.

"What's wrong?"

Caroline quickly debated pretending she hadn't heard him. Except knowing Reed, he would probably follow her around until she answered him. She sighed. *Plan B. Time to play dumb.* She straightened and turned around. "I don't know what you mean."

He cocked his head with a look of disbelief. He wasn't going to let this go. She hitched her chin and held her proverbial ground.

He visibly hesitated when she made eye contact and then glanced around to be sure they were alone. Interesting, since not that long ago he'd made it clear that being alone with her was the last thing he wanted.

"You've been crying. I want to know why."

She frowned at him, though what she wanted to do was fall into his arms and let him explain why he was so intent on keeping his distance, maybe even ask him for guidance with her parents. Strangely, she knew he would help if she asked, cancelled relationship or not. That's just who he was. But that thought gave her an idea.

"We need to schedule a brief meeting to talk

about my ideas for associating you with the company brand. I have a plan that would be, I think, pretty painless for you." *There. Change of subject.*

Reed stared at her as if catching up. "What does that have to do with why you were crying?"

Caroline pretended confusion. "Nothing. What makes you think I was crying?" Apparently, he wouldn't be diverted.

Reed looked at her like it should have been obvious. Maybe she needed to check her makeup.

Reed lowered his voice. "Call it intuition. I don't know. Your eyes are red, and you've been faking a smile since I walked in here." He narrowed his eyes and folded his arms across his chest. "Last time I just assumed you were upset over my decision to pause things between us, but it's been more than a week so either you're still heartbroken or there's something else going on."

"Pause?" Caroline whispered, wondering at his choice of words. He went on without clarifying. "You've been avoiding me for nine days. Granted, I don't know you as well as I'd like, but you don't strike me as the kind of woman to pout that long."

Caroline had the sudden image of a cartoon with its jaw on the floor.

"Am I wrong?" Reed unfolded his arms and slid his hands into his pockets. "Is it me?"

Caroline mentally picked herself up from the floor. Despite his concerned tone, she laughed softly. "Not today, no." She shook off the intimacy she felt directed toward her and hitched her chin.

"Sometimes women just cry."

"Not you though." He leaned back against the coffee bar and perched his hands on the counter behind him. The action made his shoulders bunch. She wanted so badly to step forward and put her hands on his biceps. She remembered what those shoulders felt like. She craved his strength.

"I've seen you take on the hardest audiences and leave them wanting more. You might bend, but you don't break, sweetheart."

The endearment wrapped around her like an embrace and brought the tears right back to the surface. Damn him. She cleared her throat and shrugged as if to laugh it off. "I'm just having a rough day. It's nothing a glass of wine and a good night's sleep can't fix." Unfortunately, neither of those were readily available right now.

"Why don't you go home? Take a little down time for yourself."

She shook her head. "I'm good. Thanks, though."

Caroline picked up her computer and edged toward the door. "I should head back to my office. We've been alone in here too long, and I know you're busy." She stepped into the deserted hall and looked over her shoulder. "I'll have Jamie set up a couple of meetings to talk over my ideas for you. Can you please let her know who else should participate?"

His brows knit together. "Does anyone else need to participate?"

Kind of hoping he wouldn't ask, she sighed and

turned around, and lowered her voice. "A chaperone, then. So that we're not *alone*."

Reed clenched his jaw. For just a second, she was fascinated by the strength in his face, even if it was the result of his frustration with her.

"I think I'd rather be alone for whatever it is you have planned."

Geez. He hadn't bothered to lower his voice or check his temper. The hall was still blessedly empty, but she thought of how his words could be misconstrued if someone had heard them, exactly what he'd said he wanted to avoid.

She shrugged. "It's your call. There isn't much time left on this project anyway, and once I'm done the women will realized I wasn't competition after all."

"Excuse me?"

"Never mind," she snapped.

Reed frowned at her. It didn't matter if he understood what she was referring to or not, she shouldn't have spoken the thought aloud. She needed to get away from him to regroup. And she needed to do her job.

Reed looked at his watch. "We start tomorrow. And you'll tell me why you were crying."

Caroline stared after him. He was an arrogant jerk.

And she was in love with him.

REED WAS too keyed up to sit and wondered if it could be attributed to the coffee or to Caroline's impending arrival. Honestly, she had the same effect on him as a double espresso. Probably a combination of the two would be deadly.

He considered pacing his office to work off some anxiety. People did it in books all the time. He pictured himself walking back and forth with no determined direction and shook his head. Thankfully, before he could come up with an alternative solution, he heard Caroline enter.

"Morning." She stepped up to his desk and set her laptop down before turning to look at him. "What are you doing?" For once, he couldn't make out her mood.

He realized he'd been standing still in the middle of his office. He shrugged. "I was thinking about pacing."

She seemed to take a moment to assimilate that. "Why?" She dragged out the word as if she were talking to someone who could blow up at any moment.

"I was considering giving it a try." He laughed at himself, relieved just to have her back in his presence. She probably thought he was crazy.

She watched him; her expression concerned. "Are you okay?"

He shook off the question and wondered if he'd ever be okay when he was around her. It seemed she always kept him on edge. "Let's talk about your plan." Reed pointed to a chair and took his own seat across from her.

Caroline seemed to regroup for a minute before opening her computer to consult her notes. "I think the fastest way to get this part done is to systematically publicize photos of some of your philanthropic work."

Reed wanted to groan, or maybe hide. "Have I done any philanthropic work?" He wasn't an idiot. He knew what the word meant. But he honestly never considered anything he did to be philanthropy. Maybe he'd misunderstood her. "What kind of photos are you looking for?" He tried to avoid being in photos, so it was unlikely there were very many of them.

"Pictures of you doing volunteer work." She leaned forward. "Pictures of you serving food at a shelter, donating items to help the homeless. Things like that." She paused. "I'd prefer photos of you in action rather than you all dressed up and giving money though. Action is real." She fiddled with her keyboard, not meeting his eyes. Was she uncomfortable? "Should I get with Jamie for all that?"

Reed stared at her from across the desk. "I doubt pictures like that exist."

Caroline looked disappointed. "I know you do a ton of charity work."

He acknowledged that with a nod. "But I don't do it for recognition." He smiled, not bothering to conceal his embarrassment. "And I'm not a fan of having my picture taken."

She seemed to deflate before his eyes. "Well, shoot."

Reed chuckled. "Pun intended?"

She rolled her eyes at him but didn't laugh. "Not intended. But now I will have to arrange to get shots of you somehow." She tapped her fingernails on her keyboard again. It was something she did when she was thinking, another thing Reed found endearing about her.

"Or I could come up with another plan." She pursed her lips and looked at him, but he could tell she wasn't really seeing him. Maybe he should offer her the chance to pace. "Okay. Well, I'll have to think about this some more. I thought for sure Jamie would have a press package of you or something."

"Couldn't we just recreate some activities for photos?"

"It wouldn't be authentic. You have a different expression when you're helping people for real."

Reed was taken aback. "I do? Or everyone does?"

Caroline waved a hand. "You do. I don't know everyone."

"Huh." Reed thought about that. When had she seen him serve anyone? But that gave him an idea. "Then let's go do some real activities."

She blinked at him. "That would take a while. And it would take a lot of your time."

He sat back and stabbed her with his best CEO expression. "In a hurry to be rid of me?"

Hearts in Training

"I think it's the other way around, actually."

It took him a minute to work that out. "I'm in a hurry to be rid of you?"

Caroline didn't meet his eyes. "Of course. This whole project must be keeping you from getting a lot done. Dealing with the rumors and drama, that can't be fun. And now there's pictures of you in the news with all sorts of interesting conjecture about your personal life."

He didn't need to give that a second's thought. "Working with you in this capacity is my job. You're not keeping me from anything I need to do. And I thought the pictures of *us* looked great." Reed considered her for a minute. "Is that why you were upset yesterday? Because you think I want to get rid of you?"

Caroline scrunched up her face in an expression of denial that was almost plausible. "No." She sat back looking annoyed. "I'm a woman, Reed."

"Believe me, I've noticed. So?"

"So, when too much builds up, some of us cry to blow off steam. You know how some guys hit to release some pressure? Well, some women cry."

Trying to lighten the mood, he added, "There are other ways to blow off steam."

"Yeah? Like what?"

He pretended to think about that. "Hmm. You could take a brisk walk."

"It's ten degrees outside," she protested, but there was a glint of cheerfulness in her eyes now.

"You got any warmer ideas?"

"I've heard sex works pretty well."

She laughed but gave him a little head shake. "Well, I wouldn't know about that."

Not allowing himself to dwell on that, he changed tact. "Ok. So, what has you steamed?"

Caroline looked down at her computer, shutting him out from seeing whatever was going on in her head. Predictably, she shook her head again. "Family stuff," she hesitated, and then added, "it won't interfere with the project."

Reed sat back, unaccountably disappointed. He knew her performance wouldn't suffer. She'd proved herself to be a hard worker, conscientious and talented. But he wanted to help with whatever was troubling her. He hated that their relationship had taken such a step back that he couldn't be there for her the way he wanted, needed to be. Here was yet another reason to get this project over fast. He wanted her in a way that was entirely unprofessional, and he was struggling to find ways to keep his reasons for caution forefront in his mind.

Caroline looked up and tears spilled from her eyes and tracked down her face. "Sorry." She gave a watery laugh. "I guess I'm not done blowing off steam yet."

Reed moved around his desk to sit in the chair beside her. She pulled a tissue from somewhere and attempted to stem the flow without smudging her makeup. It was magic to him how women could do that.

Knowing it was contrary to everything he was trying to do, not to mention might very well spook her, Reed pulled her out of her seat and onto his lap. "How about we try it my way now?"

Caroline stilled for just a second and then leaned into him and tucked her head under his chin. She felt so good in his arms that at that moment he didn't care whether it was inappropriate to be holding her in his office where anyone could walk in and see them. Right now, she was with a trusted friend, and she needed him.

"What did you have in mind?" She mumbled against his shoulder.

Reed leaned back to share a smile with her. "A good old-fashioned distraction."

"Sounds good to me."

Tenderly, he leaned in and pressed his lips to hers. She was soft and sweet, and he knew as soon as his tongue touched hers that they were both in too far to step back again. After a few heated minutes exploring her mouth, he remembered that his office door was unlocked. Though it was unusual for someone to walk in without knocking first, he knew it could happen. Without breaking the kiss, he lifted her into his arms and carried her to the other side of his desk where he could reach the button for the automatic door lock. He set her gently on the desk and hit the lock, all without parting from her intoxicating mouth.

Caroline shifted on the desk so that he could step between her knees, his hands automatically sliding up her thighs to her ass to pull her tight against him before returning to her shoulders and down, finding the top button of her blouse and working his way down. Willing himself to go slow, he moved from her mouth to place feather light kisses down the side of her neck, to her shoulder and then lower still until he reached the swell of her breasts. Leaning back to take her in, he breathed, "Beautiful."

Caroline's response was to tug him closer, using her arms around his neck and her legs around his lower back to anchor him to her.

"I've never done this before," she whispered.

Reed's hands stilled on her breasts; his cock pressed against her. Something about the wonder in her tone cooled his blood. To be sure, he asked, "Never had sex on a desk?" His lips, now against her neck, could feel the increase of her pulse. He wanted so badly to plunge into her with the same insistence. But first, he needed to understand her comment.

"Any of it."

With huge effort, Reed took a step back, gently closing her top across her amazing cleavage. Regret and disbelief fought against his need for her. He adjusted himself and moved to sit beside her on the desk. Their arms connected shoulder to elbow, neither seemed willing to sever the connection completely.

Embarrassment and something defensive hovered in her explanation. "I've been, you know, pawed. Once or twice even some decent foreplay." She hesitated. Reed gritted his teeth. He didn't want to hear the details of her past exploits, but he needed to know where she was going with this.

"Define *pawed*."

She blushed. "I've had guys hold me and touch me. But it wasn't what I'd consider romantic."

He nodded for her to continue. "Go on."

"Do I really have to spell it out?"

Reed wasn't about to let it go now. He didn't want any misunderstandings. "Yeah, I really think you do."

"What I mean is, I've never had sex."

Even suspecting that confession was forthcoming, Reed blinked at her. She looked up from smoothing her skirt down over her long legs to study his face. He kept his expression neutral, though inside he was shocked. He raised a hand to caress the side of her face, hardly believing they were having this conversation. "You're still a virgin? At twenty-seven?"

She dipped her head and Reed regretted his incredulous tone.

Perhaps seeking to lighten the mood, Caroline gave a short laugh and gestured down her body. "Honest to goodness. Nothing has been inserted anywhere."

Reed's heart stopped for a beat and then ran into overdrive. Amazingly, she flushed an even deeper shade of pink. But she met his gaze, honestly and openly.

"No one ever felt right, Reed. It just never seemed worth it."

"Until now?" he guessed.

"Until you," she whispered.

A little freaked out by hearing it confirmed, Reed stood and moved to the window. With one hand he smoothed his hair and then tucked in his shirt. Despite the evidence that she was all in, they wouldn't be going any further today. Making love with her on his desk had been one of his favorite fantasies but there was no way he would disrespect her by letting her first sexual experience be on a cold hard desk facing a city full of windows.

In the reflection he could see Caroline still perched on his desk, making no move to straighten her own appearance. He couldn't make out her expression, but her posture was worried, maybe rejected.

Hating this moment for its confusion, Reed turned to face her and confirmed the wariness in her eyes. His instinct was to put on his game face, the same face he used while negotiating a business deal or protecting his innermost thoughts, but Caroline deserved his emotional honesty. She was worth the discomfort this brought him.

He let her see the confusion, regret, tenderness, whatever his heart was feeling as he approached her. Placing a gentle kiss on her lips, he buttoned her top and then circled the desk to retrieve her shoes. One at a time, he put her shoes on her, while she watched him soundlessly. He smoothed her hair and rested his forehead against hers.

"Are you turning me down?"

Her voice trembled, and he was impressed that she was bold enough to ask despite the extreme awkwardness.

"We got carried away today. With you, it seems I'm always being carried away."

"Is that good or bad?"

He closed his eyes and breathed for a moment. "That's good. You're good." He straightened and let his hands fall to her hips, anchoring her so that she couldn't move away, or move closer. "But what you have is rare and special. And probably shouldn't be given away to some horny guy. On a desk."

Caroline's face flushed again, but he could see the first sparks of anger there. She straightened her shoulders and slid off the desk to square off with him. God help him, Reed nearly smiled.

"Isn't this *gift* mine to offer as I choose?"

"Of course."

"What if I choose this?" She swept a hand toward the desk.

Reed slid his hands in his pockets to prevent himself from reaching for her. "But I can do better."

She reacted as if he'd slapped her. "Thanks for that." Angry sarcasm hung between them.

"No. God no. I don't mean I can do better than you. I mean I can do better than a quick fumble on my desk between meetings. I don't want to just have you. I want to blow your mind."

Her shoulders dropped and her anger

evaporated. "Oh." She stared at him as if considering that. "Oh."

Reed stepped forward to pull her into his arms. Caroline bit her lip and looked up at him and then her eyes swept his desk. "Can I get a raincheck on the desk, though?"

Reed grinned. "Hell, yeah. This is one of my favorite fantasies of you."

She cocked her head. "You have fantasies about me?"

"At least a thousand." And he added to that list every day.

"Wow."

Reed let his hands fall to her ass. "Don't worry. If you're game, we can work up to it. Just not today." His heart softened along with his voice. "Not the first time."

The calendar on his computer chimed a notification. "I've got a meeting in fifteen minutes."

Caroline stepped out of his embrace and straightened herself again. "Mind if I skip out on this meeting?"

Reed gave her a wry smile. "I think that would be an excellent idea. I now have an image of your sexy underwear branded on my brain, and if you're in the room I'm fairly certain I won't be able to concentrate."

She raised an eyebrow, all traces of her earlier embarrassment replaced with a flirtatious look. "Good to know." She swooped past him to pick up her laptop and paused by the door. "Enjoy your meeting."

WHILE HAVING CAROLINE out of sight did help him concentrate on his meeting, he couldn't keep her from his thoughts completely. She'd chosen him to be the first man she slept with. The fact that she'd never had sex gave him pause. The noble thing to do would be to gently turn her down, but in his mind, he'd already made a list of the reasons he wouldn't. First and foremost, he *couldn't* resist her. What he felt for Caroline was nearly tangible, and he fully knew some of his staff was already aware of his infatuation with her. Secondly, and probably most importantly, it really was her decision, and she'd chosen him.

That brought Reed around to the possible repercussions of making their relationship an intimate one. After sleeping together would she imagine herself in love with him? Would she stake a claim on him that he wasn't ready for? Reed immediately dismissed that thought. His heart had staked a claim on her the first time he saw her across the lobby. Months ago.

No, the real issue was what it could do to their professional relationship. They weren't employer and employee, so technically it wasn't against company policy to see each other. But it could be viewed as unprofessional. Caroline was representing her firm. Could her career be damaged by crossing that line? He couldn't do that to her. And yet, he wasn't prepared to say no to her either. He dropped his fist on the conference room table in frustration, startling the people around him. "Sorry," he muttered, returning to the present conversation. "Continue."

What if things didn't work out between them and she was still working for his company? Could she be moved to another contract? Bring on someone else to handle the branding part while letting her continue with the training division? He stopped just short of shaking his head, this time remembering that he had an audience. He was rearranging her future just so that he could have sex with her guilt-free. Or was there more involved than just his conscience? Was the risk worth the possible disruption to their jobs? Oh yes. She was worth it.

What they really needed was a place they could get away to just be themselves where no one would recognize them. Reed suspected Caroline had no trouble being herself in every situation. She seemed perfectly comfortable in her skin. But Reed knew he was different outside of his work responsibilities and suddenly that was a side of himself he wanted to share with her. He considered going somewhere tropical for a long weekend, or to the West coast maybe, but somehow those settings didn't seem right. They all felt contrived to him. Fake.

An hour later, his sister Savannah, handed him the perfect solution.

His phone signaled a text. He smiled at Savannah's selfie, her tongue sticking out at him. She was clearly happy, and he was happy for her. Unfair circumstances had taken her to Wolf Creek, New

Hampshire where she'd found not only a new calling she was passionate about, but also the love of her life, Daniel Harrison. The two were engaged and presumably planning their wedding, though Reed never asked.

Feeling remiss in his brotherly duties, Reed called Savannah back immediately. She answered on the first ring.

"Hey, Skids. What's going on in Wolf Creek?" Reed heard his sister huff over the phone and smiled. She hated the nickname he'd given her as a child.

"As a matter of fact, there's a wedding going on around here. We'd sure love for you to come and be a part of it."

Reed's smile turned to a grin as he continued to rib his sister. "I don't have to wear lumberjack plaid or anything, do I?"

"And work boots!" she quipped. "We follow the latest style trends around here too, you know. It's just not as important to you city-folk. Mostly we care about function."

Reed snorted. Savannah might be a born-and-bred New Yorker, but she had never paid much attention to fashion. She left that to their sister, Angela. In a lot of ways, Wolf Creek was a good fit for Savannah.

"A nice suit will be fine. We're planning a small wedding and it won't be super formal."

"Great."

"I'll email you the dates and stuff. It would be

nice if you could come for a visit before that though. You know, take some time to shake off your title."

At that, Reed laughed. "Am I that bad?"

"Lately? Yep. You're stuffier every time I talk to you. Which is less and less, by the way."

He could always count on her for the absolute truth.

"You're at work right now, aren't you?"

Knowing her better than nearly anyone, he couldn't let her slide on her unspoken censure. "You've got no room to talk, Skids. You've been known to work twenty-four-seven yourself."

"Not anymore. Daniel has me on this work-eat-play-sleep cycle."

Reed laughed at her antics. "Yeah, it's called a life."

"It's kind of nice," she added more seriously. She paused, and then, "You should get one."

"I was thinking the same thing just this afternoon." He rubbed his jaw and turned to face the skyline.

Seeming to sense his mood, Savannah injected concern into her voice. "How's the publicity stuff working out? Dad says you have a shadow. How bad is she?"

Reed expelled a breath. His father must have shared more than Savannah was letting on for her to know that his shadow was a woman. "She's not bad. Not at all. She's outgoing and smart."

"Interesting." Savannah drew the word out.

"What's interesting about that?"

"She's outgoing, and you didn't say that like it was a trait of the devil. Plus, you don't mind that she's following you around all the time with the expressed goal of making you recognizable." She laughed. "Am I detecting a crush?"

He didn't bother to deny it, since Savannah's interest played into his plan. He never could lie to his sister anyway. "She's beautiful in an understated way. And she has a great sense of humor. She thinks she's blending into the background, but the fact is she distracts me. A lot."

"Hmm. Distracts you in a good way?"

"Is it ever a good thing to be distracted at work?"

Savannah made a noise. "For you? Yes. I've never met someone more in need of a distraction."

Reed turned his back on the skyline and perched on the credenza. "It's stupid, but before I knew who she was – her role here, I mean – I did have a bit of a crush on her. I'd even considered asking her out."

Savannah let out a whistle and he knew why. He rarely dated. "I guess that's out of the question now, huh?"

He sighed. "It's definitely complicated." He was silent for a moment and then groaned. He had to get this said. "I was thinking of bringing Caroline up for a weekend sometime. We need to get some photos of charity work and I know Wolf Creek can always use the help."

"Why don't you come up and see Daniel and I this weekend? Take Friday off and spend a long weekend. You can stay with us, or in the cottage. Your choice."

"The cottage would be great."

"It only has the one bed, but hey, we won't ask questions."

Reed could practically hear the wink in her voice. But, it was the perfect solution. The cottage would give them privacy, and although there was only one bedroom, there was also a pull-out couch if it came to that. "Sounds great. I'll clear my calendar and check with Caroline. Thanks, Skids."

In response, Savannah sighed and hung up on him. Reed grinned.

He sent his instructions to Jamie. The muffled whoosh of the door told him without looking that Caroline had entered. He didn't even need to look up, he could *feel* her standing there.

"What's up?" He sat back and worked to keep his eyes on her face. Now that he'd gotten a glimpse of the body hiding beneath her clothes, he was having a hard time putting it out of his mind.

"I was giving thought to other angles we can use to humanize you to your employees. What do you do for fun?"

"I work. For fun."

She cracked a smile at his sarcasm. "I'm sure you do. But it would go a long way toward making you more relatable if I could show people a lighter side of you."

He held his hands out to the sides. "What you see is what you get."

Caroline frowned. "Then they're not really seeing you."

He let that go for now. "You think I need to be humanized? Like a dog that needs to be housebroken?"

She looked amused. "More like Superman that needs to be brought down to Earth."

"Humanized, huh?" He looked at her for a minute, once again considering the ramifications of his invitation. Damn the repercussions, he decided. His family, even past girlfriends accused him of being too set in his ways. "I thought of a way we can kill two birds with one stone. What are your plans this weekend?"

Caroline stepped up to his desk. "I don't really have any, I guess. What are the two birds?"

"Come to New Hampshire with me this weekend."

"What's in New Hampshire?"

"My sister. Charitable activities." He lowered his voice. "A snowbound cottage with a stone fireplace."

Her face flushed. "That sounds relaxing."

"Well, some time will be spent with my younger sister. She's not relaxing. Are you interested?"

She nodded and then appeared to consider something. "Who else is going?"

He studied her face, watching for any signs of hesitation. "Just you and me."

She cleared her throat and nodded again. "Okay, sure. Just let me know the flight information and I'll be there."

Feeling more and more confident in his plan, Reed leaned back in his chair and laced his fingers behind his head. "We're driving."

"Isn't that...several hours?"

"About four, yes. Problem?"

"Ah, no. That's fine. Road trip, yay!" Her happy glow was back.

He chuckled. "Road trip." He turned back to his screen before he jumped the gun and pulled her around the desk and into his lap. Again. "Leave me your address and I'll pick you up."

"I can meet you. Here?"

"You'll have luggage, right? It'll be easier for you if I just pick you up in front of your building."

She straightened her spine and retreated a few steps. "It's really not necessary, Reed. I can meet you."

He cocked his head. There it was again. She avoided disclosing where she lived. Granted, they didn't know each other well yet, but he resented that she was willing to have sex with him, but she didn't trust him enough to share her living arrangements. Unless- "Is there something wrong with my showing up at your apartment?"

She tipped her head down and he saw her shoulders drop a little before looking up at him again. "I don't live in the best area."

"Harlem?"

"Not quite."

Reed contemplated her. He'd grown up with many advantages, and for that reason he knew that people often made assumptions about him. "I'm not a snob, Caroline. I don't care much where you live, as long as you're safe and comfortable there."

She moved around to the side of his desk and pulled a sticky note from the pad near his elbow. He held still as she scribbled her address. She was so close that he could smell her skin. He wanted to lean in and bury his face in her hair, but he'd had too much temptation today. Anything further was just pushing his luck.

He glanced at the address and silently agreed that she didn't live in a great area. "I'll pick you up at five on Friday."

"In the evening?"

He smiled at her expression, able to breathe now that she'd moved away again. "In the morning. It'll put us in Wolf Creek around nine. That'll give us three full days. You can sleep in the car if you want."

"Can I wear pajamas?"

She'd probably intended her comment as a joke but once she'd put it out there, Reed couldn't get the image out of his mind.

"I guess that depends on what you sleep in."

She shook her head a little, clearly understanding what he must have been imagining. "Yoga pants and a t-shirt?"

"Yeah? Me too."

"Really?"

He cocked an eyebrow at her. "No. Five A.M. on Friday."

She nodded and snatched her laptop off the desk. She gave him a quick wave and left, closing the door quietly behind her.

Chapter 9

Caroline was thankful she'd planned to spend the afternoon in her office answering emails because now she couldn't focus. Reed had invited her to spend the weekend with him in New Hampshire. Just the two of them. Was this his way of working up to having sex with her? A cottage with a stone fireplace sounded like a romantic weekend getaway. Or was it merely a convenient opportunity for her to get pictures of him doing charity work and other normal things? She propped her chin on her hand. Why hadn't she thought to ask him those questions while she was still in his office? Because all logical thought fled her brain whenever she was alone with him, that's why, especially since that morning when they'd made out in his office.

As attracted to Reed as she already was, it would be nearly impossible to keep a professional distance from him for a whole weekend, especially alone with him. And along that line, what the heck should she pack? What was appropriate for a winter weekend in the north with a man who may or may not be expecting more?

She managed to push her fixation on Reed's motives to the back of her mind for a few hours and got through her most pressing messages. Knowing he would still be in his office she decided to swallow her embarrassment and ask him. Seeing he was online via the company's instant messaging software, she sent him a quick message.

What do people wear in Wolf Creek?

Jeans

Anything else?

Wondering what to pack on my little trip.

She didn't reference Reed in case he wasn't alone.

We won't be working. Dress comfortable. You can pack as little or as much as you choose.

Caroline stared at her screen for a minute, tapping her nails on the desk next to her keyboard. Well, that wasn't much help.

Ok, TTYL, she typed, and then logged off before he could cause any other enticing thoughts to pop into her head.

THE ELEVATOR ride should have been quiet at this time of night. Much of the staff had left hours ago and those that were still in the building would be stuck in their offices. Because she'd just talked to him online, Caroline didn't expect the doors to slide open and reveal Reed standing perfectly still, looking as if he'd expected her all along. It would have looked cowardly to refuse the lift now, and yet she was inexplicably nervous to be alone with him.

His eyes seemed to brighten as he looked at her but because the rest of his face didn't change, she couldn't quite be sure.

"Reed," she acknowledged.

"Caroline." His lips twitched. Was he laughing at her? She couldn't decide. The doors slid shut, cocooning them in dim silence.

"So, are you packed yet?" Reed asked her quietly.

She turned to look up at him. His stare was direct, warm, and a little unnerving. "We only discussed this, what? Maybe ten minutes ago?"

"As organized as you are, I figured you'd have been home, packed, and back again by now."

"How do you figure?"

"You're always two steps ahead of me."

Adopting a playful tone, Caroline cocked her head and teased, "Maybe I prefer the view from the front."

Without so much as a smile, Reed stared down into her face. They were mere inches apart. "That's perfect then. I don't mind at all looking at the backside of you."

Caroline felt herself blush and then took a hasty step back when the elevator paused at the next floor. The doors opened again, and a good-looking man stepped in. He offered Reed a polite nod and greeted Caroline with a huge, friendly smile.

"Hey Caroline."

"Hi Ridley."

Normally, Caroline would have welcomed

Ridley's easy-going attitude and even returned it. He had a great sense of humor. But having Reed barely a foot behind her made her too nervous to focus on small talk. Fortunately, Ridley didn't seem to notice her tongue-tied state.

"You're cutting out of here earlier than your usual twelve-hour day. Got a hot date?"

Damn her propensity to blush! "It's been a long day."

Ridley accepted that with a nod. "It's been a long week too. Hey, I've got tickets to a comedy show this weekend. There's a group of us going but I've got an extra ticket. Interested?"

Caroline could nearly feel Reed's gaze burning into the back of her head. "Thank you, but no. I'm actually heading out of town this weekend."

"Bummer. Would have been a lot of fun to have you."

Caroline smiled. "Maybe next time."

The next floor added two more people, squishing Caroline further back and close enough to Reed that she could smell his cologne. Heavenly. She wanted to lean into him.

Ridley chatted easily with the other occupants giving Caroline a chance to let out a few slow breaths and will the blush out of her cheeks. By the time the elevator reached the ground floor, Caroline had herself under control. She smiled and waved goodnight to Ridley and the others. She turned to include Reed in her generic dismissal, but he stuck by her. With a sharp gaze and a voice that was far too personal, Reed stepped close enough to avoid being overheard and said, "Sleep well, Caroline."

Caroline could only nod and hope to get away before her knees failed her. What would it be like to spend the whole weekend with him?

The long and bitterly cold walk home helped to clear some of the giddiness from her mind. Back in the safety of her apartment, she worked through various ways she could present Reed as the "guy next door" for the Decatur brand as she tossed things on her bed to pack. Reed, she knew, was a true introvert. He needed quiet, peace, and solitude to recharge his energy. Calling attention to the personal habits that made him such an amazing man would be invading his privacy. How could she satisfy the Board's expectations without changing their new CEO in some measurable way?

She wasn't naïve, she knew perfectly well that it wasn't really her job to watch out for Reed's feelings. He was the president, and it was his responsibility to lead his company. Her job was to facilitate trust from his employees to make a smooth transition. In past campaigns she hadn't put as much thought into the personal impact of her target. But Reed was different, she'd known that from the first time she laid eyes on him, before she'd even known that he was her assignment. And somehow, she would figure out how to show him in a follow-him-into-the-future sort of way without changing the essence of who he was.

Caroline fell asleep early and woke feeling harried. It was Thursday. Tomorrow, before dawn,

Reed would be waiting outside her apartment to whisk her away to – what? It was the possibilities and the unknown that had her on edge.

To say the day was awkward was an understatement. If Reed had any reservations or was even looking forward to the weekend, Caroline couldn't tell. He was once again his handsome enigmatic self. Where Wednesday had started with tantalizing promise, Thursday was a complete turnaround. Caroline appeared in Reed's office first thing as was customary, to find him unusually focused on her publicity work.

Not bothering with a greeting, he led with, "My mom was able to find some older pictures of me helping out at different functions. Will that help with your campaign to humanize me?"

"Yes." She stood beside his desk, waiting for him to look at her. He was hard to read this morning. She had hoped to follow his lead in deciding how to act, but he wasn't making it easy on her. Inside she was giddy but seeing him so serious made her worry about a repeat of their earlier attempt at keeping their distance.

"I'll have her drop them off later today so that you can see what she has." He still hadn't looked at her. "Hopefully that will give you an idea of what angles you still need."

"In a hurry to finish this project?" she teased.

Reed didn't take time to think about that. His answer was instantaneous and certain. "Yes."

Hurt and a little confused, Caroline could only

nod. Reed further confused her when he finally looked at her and added softly, "But I am really looking forward to this weekend."

His sexy tone sent a zing right down to her toes. "So am I." Relief made her knees weak. She perched on his desk next to his elbow. "Will I finally get to see the real you?"

Reed narrowed his eyes, a smile lurking on his lips. "How much more of me did you want to see?"

"The side that relaxes and smiles."

"That's *this* side," he teased.

Caroline gave a small laugh and twisted to look at the schedule on his monitor. "Back to back all day, huh?"

"That's what it takes to get a day off."

No wonder he was so serious all the time. "What does it take to get a whole week?"

"What, like a real vacation?" She read the sarcasm on his face. "A miracle."

Caroline straightened and stretched her legs out in front of her. "We need to work on that."

"We, huh?" He tipped one side of his mouth up in a smile.

"Sorry."

He shrugged and pulled a file out of his drawer. "I think we make a great team."

She smiled, her heart storing away the compliment. "I might even figure you out yet."

"Take your time," Reed offered as Jamie ushered in the first meeting's attendees. Caroline excused herself to head down to Human Resources to work on the new training division.

The rest of the day passed in a blur of faces, numbers, and decisions. Caroline finally got a break at three P.M. and headed back to her office. She sat down and swiveled her chair around to face the windows. She stared out the window for several minutes when she heard the door open and glanced over her shoulder to see Jamie placing a Styrofoam container on her desk. In response to her unasked question, the woman provided, "Reed was concerned that you'd missed lunch, so he asked that I have something delivered for you."

Caroline turned fully around and raised her eyebrows. "Thank you." She cocked her head. "Just out of curiosity, what if I had eaten lunch?"

Jamie chuckled. "He was confident enough to call your bluff. He also suggested that I stand here until you'd taken a couple of bites, but I assured him that you knew how to feed yourself."

Caroline shook her head in amusement. "It's really kind of you to take care of this for him. For me."

There was a twinkle in Jamie's eyes. "It's no trouble at all. I love being involved in this-" She stopped herself. "I love seeing Reed happy."

Caroline opened the box as soon as Jamie left. Reed had sent a Caesar salad with a wedge of homemade bread from a nearby deli that delivered to the Decatur offices.

Hoping he didn't have an audience around his computer screen, Caroline sent him an instant message to thank him for the salad. He responded immediately with *You're very welcome. Call it an early night. Knowing my sister, tomorrow is going to be a long day.*

Aye, Captain, she answered with a winking emoticon. She logged off, stowed her things in her bag and floated home on a cloud of giddy pleasure at the prospect of a long weekend away with Reed.

Her mood quickly sobered when she reached her apartment door and heard the voices inside. "No, no, no," she whispered, and then swung the door open. Sure enough, there was Tony lounging on her loveseat entertaining his misfit group of friends while her mother was in the kitchen cooking.

As if she had a radar, Heather turned around and smiled at her daughter. "Hi Carrie. You're home early. We weren't expecting you for a couple more hours."

Caroline set her bag against the wall in her little entry and looked around her apartment. "What are the guys doing here?" She knew the answer, of course, but she was willing to give her mother the benefit of her doubt.

Wiping her hands on a dish towel, Heather turned around and stole a nervous glance at Tony. "I told you, Tony's always looking for leads."

"Nobody ever mentioned having parties in my apartment, Ma."

Her mother waved a hand as if to say it didn't matter. "Well, it's done. Everyone's here and the food is almost ready."

Caroline chewed on the inside of her cheek and headed for her bedroom. She could always spend the night on the couch in her office and text Reed to pick her up there instead.

In near defeat, Caroline sat on the side of her bed and stared at the rug. Would it be better to stay and talk this out with her mother and Tony? She was sick at the thought of them taking over her apartment while she was away, and yet to give up this rare opportunity to spend time alone with Reed in a totally new setting was too good to pass up. If she cancelled on him now, would he ever ask her again?

She dropped her head into her hands and groaned. Even though they'd never really spent any time together outside of work, she cared about his opinion of her. When her contract was over with Decatur Industries, she hoped to still be able to count him as a friend. Or more. The idea of not seeing him again after her job with him was done caused a painful knot behind her belly button. She couldn't stand him up now.

She stood to relieve the gathering anxiety and pulled her suitcases out of the closet. He'd invited her on an impromptu weekend away, and for once, she wasn't going to let her parents ruin her fun.

Without her usual regard for organization, Caroline dumped the clothes she'd laid out into her suitcase, comfortable clothes, and even lingerie she'd been saving for something romantic. She swept her toiletries and cosmetics off their shelves into a smaller case and carried it to her bed next to the suitcase. Before she could second guess herself, she slipped on her tennis shoes and carried her bags into the living room. She yanked her favorite fuzzy throw out from behind Tony, located her iPod on the end table, and tucked it into her jacket pocket.

Giving Tony a wave, she turned to her mother. "I'm going to be out of town on a business trip for a few days."

"Are you going with the CEO you drive crazy?"

"Yeah, Ma."

"Nice!" Her mother winked at her.

"We're going to get some shots of him volunteering and such."

Her mother clucked her tongue. "It could still be fun. Will you be safe alone with him?"

Caroline nearly choked. Define safe, she wanted to ask. "Yeah, Ma. He's a good guy. I'll be perfectly safe. I'm going to stay at the office tonight to shave some time off the commute tomorrow."

Her heart thawed just a little at the relief on her mother's face. She knew her mother had assumed she was leaving out of anger. There was some truth in that, but Caroline knew it wouldn't do any good to dwell on it. After so many years, her mother wasn't going to change. Caroline tried for a smile. "Try not to burn the place down while I'm gone, okay?"

Heather pulled her in for a hug. "Your place will be just like you left it. I promise."

"I know, Ma."

"Be careful."

"I will, Ma. See you later."

CAROLINE HAILED a taxi rather than wheel her luggage across town to the Decatur Building. Since it was late in the evening, there were few employees in the building when she wheeled her bags onto the elevator. Thankfully, no one appeared to be working on her floor, so she didn't have to explain her reappearance, or her luggage, on the way to her office.

Tossing her fuzzy blanket and iPod onto the narrow couch against the wall, she dug out her cell and texted Reed. *Change in plans. Long story. Pick me up outside the DI building instead.*

She set her phone on the little glass table beside the couch and plopped down next to her blanket. For just a few minutes, she let anger at her mom and Tony consume her. Once the initial flame burned to embers, she was left with frustration and defeat. Would they ever learn to stand on their own feet? Would Caroline ever be rid of them? By all rights, this contract with Decatur was paying her well enough to live in a much nicer place. But not if she had to continue to support her parents.

Her mother was all she had left for family and she loved her deeply, for that reason she couldn't bear to see her flounder, and yet their relationship was an emotional and financial burden. Mother-child love shouldn't be a burden. Feeling tears building behind her eyes, Caroline dropped her head back and squeezed her eyes shut. She refused to cry again. It seemed all she ever did was cry these days.

Her cell dinged a response from Reed. *I have time. Need to talk?*

Caroline stared at the message, unable to decide on the best response. Did she want to talk? *You bet.* Should she talk about it? *Probably not.* The last thing she needed before spending the weekend with the man of her dreams was to dump her problems on him.

She started to respond that she was fine and would see him in the morning when a rap on the door startled her. She knew it was Reed on the other side, but that still didn't prepare her for the sight of him. He'd probably been in the office for eleven hours and still his tie was tight, his suit unwrinkled. In comparison, she felt like a wrinkled, frumpy mess. *Unfair!*

She didn't bother to conceal her expression when she opened the door. She knew her eyes were red, and she'd already hinted that something was wrong. He could already read her better than anyone she knew so there would be no point in denying it. She just had to decide how much, or how little, to share with him.

Reed didn't speak. He just strode past her and closed the door behind him, something he never did with his female employees. With his arms folded over his chest he stared down into her face and then nodded for her to sit.

She pushed her blanket out of the way and saw his eyes sweep the room, taking in the suitcases. His tone was gentler than she expected given the intensity of his stare.

"What's going on?" He took off his jacket and tossed it across her desk before pulling a chair away from her desk to sit across from her. She watched him silently as he pulled off his tie and rolled up his sleeves. A big part of her was sort of hoping he wouldn't stop there. She could certainly use the distraction. When he leaned forward with his elbows on his knees, she tucked her hands under her thighs to keep from reaching for him.

"I didn't mean to bring you down to check on me."

He shook his head, dismissing that, and waited for her to continue.

"I got home this afternoon to find a little party going on in my apartment. It was--I thought it would be less complicated if I just stayed here tonight. It'll be so much closer in the morning anyway. Now you don't have to come so far to get me."

"Closer. But not comfortable," Reed added. He gave her another piercing stare before speaking again. "Is there a man in your life?"

Caroline let out a surprised giggle making Reed frown. "You asked me to go to Wolf Creek with you. Isn't it a bit late to wonder if I've got a boyfriend?"

Looking uncomfortable, but honest, Reed explained, "After our ah, meeting on Wednesday I didn't really care. If you had a significant other you would have turned me down, right?"

"Of course."

He nodded as if that proved his point. "But you've always been careful to keep me from knowing where you live, and now something has changed, so I had to ask."

Caroline was mortified over what he would think of her once he knew about her family and yet she owed him more than what she'd shared in her cryptic text.

"Like I said, it's a long story. My mom and her long-time boyfriend are staying with me for a while. When I got home tonight, I found out that Tony had decided to have a little party." When he looked like he was trying to read between the lines she tried a diversion. "It's a small place and I didn't want to deal with all of that tonight." That seemed to satisfy him.

"So, you're planning to sleep here?"

She shrugged. "It's not bad. And it'll be quiet."

He raised an eyebrow. "Until the cleaning crew arrives, or some ambitious employee comes in early."

Caroline sat back with a thump. "Yeah."

Reed gave her an almost-smile and stood. He returned his chair to its spot, picked up his jacket and grabbed the handle of the larger rolling case. "There's an apartment one floor above my office. You can stay there tonight. I'll come get you in the morning."

Caroline thought about it for a few seconds and decided the comfort and privacy were worth the mortification of telling him that her parents lived with her. She nodded and stood. "Thank you."

Reed waited in the doorway with her suitcase and laptop bag while she gathered up the smaller bag, blanket, and iPod. Without any further questions on his part, Reed led the way to the elevators to the penthouse apartment that occupied the floor above the executive offices.

Reed opened the door with a keycard and then handed it to her. "It should be stocked with anything you need. Help yourself. I have some things to finish up tonight, so I won't bother you again."

Caroline just had time to shoot him a grateful smile before he turned back to the elevator, leaving her standing in the foyer of the beautiful apartment. She wheeled the bags across the shiny tile floor and peeked into an office and a half bath before locating the bedroom suites with attached bathrooms.

Caroline was exhausted from the pace and emotions she'd been keeping at bay, and knowing that tomorrow would start early, she decided to forgo dinner and go straight to bed.

There were two bedrooms in the apartment, so she chose the one that felt more comfortable to her, more welcoming somehow. Looking around the masculine room she decided it was too decadent for her plain old flannel pajamas, so for the fun of it she pulled out one of the silk nightgowns she'd also packed. She quickly changed and folded her clothes neatly on top of the suitcase before grabbing her toiletries bag and heading for the bathroom. She brushed her teeth and pulled her hair back into a messy but functional ponytail. Then she crawled into the bed and scooted over until she was lying in the exact middle. She closed her eyes and was asleep within minutes.

Chapter 10

*R*eed checked his watch. It was after eleven. Hoping Caroline was already asleep so that he wouldn't have to explain his presence, he took the elevator to his apartment and let himself in using the keypad next to the door. The rooms were dark and silent. He let out a relieved breath. Relieved and... disappointed? He couldn't deny that he was looking forward to spending time with her this weekend. But he was determined to be a gentleman, and unless she'd done some snooping around the penthouse, he hoped she didn't realize he lived there.

Unsure where he would find her, Reed stepped quietly into his bedroom and stopped short. The lamp next to his bed was on, shining a low golden light across the sleeping figure of Caroline in his bed. Reed's heart pounded and his muscles tightened as his gaze traveled over her long legs and the part of her rear end uncovered by the sheet and silky thing she was wearing. He clenched a fist, tucking his fingers against his palm to stop the urge to trail them along her smooth skin.

There were extra toothbrushes in the other bathroom, and he could sleep in his boxers. He had to get out of there before he broke his promise to himself and claimed his own bed. He allowed one last look and headed for the other suite.

If she were any other woman he'd dated, he

would have crawled into bed with her. But this was Caroline, and she was special to him. Reed lay in bed with his hands stacked behind his head and puzzled through the differences. It wasn't like him to be impulsive, and yet here he was, getting ready to take a woman to meet his sister and future brother-in-law. A woman he shouldn't even be getting involved with in their present circumstances. He'd tried and failed to stay away from her. He was done fighting the attraction.

Analytical by nature, Reed took a mental step back and tried to look at the big picture. What was his goal? How did he think this would end? These were the usual questions he asked himself when he was considering a new venture, and yet a niggling little voice in his head reminded him that love didn't fit into the same mold as a business partnership.

Love? Was that his goal? Having never been in love he really couldn't say. All he knew for certain was that Caroline brought out feelings in him that were tempting and sweet, and completely addictive. The more he saw of her, the more he wanted. Without seriously considering the ramifications of a relationship with a co-worker, even a temporary one, he'd invited her to spend the weekend with him, to meet his sister. And he'd left the invitation deliberately vague, intent to let her decisions dictate their plans. He wondered what she'd made of that. Judging by her sleeping attire, he suspected she'd decided it would be something romantic. But did that mean she planned to have sex with him this weekend? God, he really hoped so.

CAROLINE WOKE refreshed and excited for the weekend ahead. She'd never spent much time alone with a man, but the idea of having Reed to herself, even if just for the four-hour drive felt like heaven. Would he be his usual enigmatic self, or would he show her his elusive playful side?

She glanced at the clock and noted that it was early yet. She had plenty of time to enjoy a cup of coffee before Reed would come for her, so she pulled her fuzzy blanket around herself like a robe and padded out to the kitchen in search of the coffee machine. She made it as far as the sunken dais in the center of the apartment that served as a living room before stopping short with a startled squeak. "Oh!"

Reed looked up from a book and smiled at her. "Good morning."

She gathered the blanket tighter and tip-toed closer. "Am I late?" He was already dressed, looking sexy in a gray Henley shirt that hugged his arms, and a pair of dark jeans.

Reed looked at his watch and shook his head. "No. We have plenty of time."

Caroline watched him watching her and suspicion dawned on her. "So, you're here because..."

He raised an eyebrow over his sparkling eyes, but he didn't respond. She could see that he was enjoying her reaction. Caroline looked around with a new eye. "I slept in your bed, didn't I?"

Another smile. "You sure did, Goldilocks."

With her eyes narrowed, she came around the

couch to stand in front of him, careful to keep herself fully covered. "Where, uh, did you sleep?"

He stared at her for so long that her skin started to tingle. "In the spare bedroom."

"I'm so sorry. You should have told me this was your place."

He tipped his head, looking curious. "Would you have stayed if you knew this was my apartment?"

Caroline shrugged one shoulder, the blanket sliding down her arm and exposing a silky strap. "Probably. But I would have let you sleep in your own bed."

Reed dropped his book and pulled her forward onto his lap. "With or without me?"

His carefree teasing expression, and the knowledge that she finally had him all to herself, did yummy things to her insides. Deliberately not answering his question, she said, "Your bed is bigger than my kitchen. You could have joined me, and I might not have noticed."

"Oh, you'd have noticed. And that's why I slept in the other room." He tipped his forehead to hers. "You're calling the shots this weekend."

"Well, if I'd known this was your place, I'd have chosen something else to sleep in." She ruffled the blanket.

He set her aside and headed toward the kitchen. "I thought it was a great choice. I'll start the coffee while you get dressed."

Too embarrassed to consider that he'd seen her

sleeping, Caroline scurried back to his bedroom to grab a quick shower and get dressed. She took her suitcase right into the bathroom with her and brushed her teeth. While she waited for the shower to heat up, she picked up a bar of soap and inhaled. She loved the way Reed smelled.

She showered quickly, feeling self-conscious knowing he was in the other room, and that he knew what she was doing. She chose a pair of comfy gray leggings and an oversize sweater and then carried her shoes out into the living room to place them by the door. She followed the smell of coffee into the kitchen and found Reed leaning against the counter, once again reading his book.

Tucking her wet hair behind her ears, she slipped past him and selected a mug from the wooden rack behind him. He didn't move aside so Caroline brushed arms with him as she poured coffee into her mug.

Tipping his head toward her playfully, he murmured, "You smell good."

She looked up at him and laughed. "Thanks. I used your soap, so I smell like you."

He leaned down and stuck his nose behind her ear. "No Caroline, you smell like you."

Determined not to feel awkward around him, she leaned back against the counter island across from him. She sipped her coffee and studied him while he leaned against the counter reading his book. He looked good this way, a hot mix of studious and sexy. She itched to photograph him this way. Women all over the world would go nuts for him.

"Do you mind if I photograph you?"

When her eyes made their way back up his lean body, she realized that he was watching her somewhat warily. Instead of commenting on her bold examination, Reed asked, "Now?"

Caroline smiled and nodded slowly. "Definitely now."

He sighed, but surprisingly capitulated. "Make it fast. I want to hit the road before rush hour."

"Yay!" Caroline bounced into the bedroom to grab her camera from her bag and hurried back before he had a chance to move. Approaching quietly, she paused and snapped a few images. In a heartbeat, the camera was snatched out of her hands and Reed held it above her head.

"Excuse me! Don't you dare drop my camera."

He gave her a challenging look. "I reserve the right to approve the pictures before you release them."

Caroline blinked at him. "Maybe the pictures are just for me, Mr. Big-shot CEO." Too late, she realized how much that gave away.

Of course, he wouldn't let that go. "You want pictures of me, just for yourself?"

"Maybe I'll print some for you too."

"In that case, you should be in them too. I don't need pictures of myself." He held the camera out to her. "Here. Does this thing do selfies?"

Caroline laughed. "It'll probably take a few tries."

She fiddled with the settings, turned the camera around and held it out in front of her. Reed put an arm around her to draw her up close in front of him. Caroline could feel the heat from his chest radiating across her back. Before she sank into a puddle of need before him, she snapped several pictures in quick succession and brought the camera close to look at the results. Reed continued to hold her close as he examined the pictures with her.

They laughed over a few shots and agreed on a couple that turned out well, then Caroline stowed her camera back in her bag and wheeled her suitcase into the foyer. Reed passed her on his way into his room and came back a few minutes later with his own suitcase and her blanket over his arm.

"Do you need your blankie?" he teased, coming close enough to wrap it securely around her shoulders like a cape.

"Funny." But she did fold it and stuff it into the tote she planned to put in the back seat.

Caroline felt nervous leaving the penthouse and taking the elevator to the underground parking garage with Reed and their luggage. It was a weekday; what if someone they knew stepped into the elevator?

As if he could read her mind, Reed reached for her hand and gave it a reassuring squeeze. "It's 5 A.M. No one comes in that early, especially on a Friday."

Caroline gave an embarrassed groan and dropped her forehead against his solid chest. "We're not doing anything wrong, so why am I afraid of being caught?"

Reed pulled her to him for a one-armed hug.

"Reed, what if this plays against our work?"

The elevator landed and the doors slid open, but Reed didn't move. Caroline turned to look up into his face. His expression was open and honest.

"People can read anything they want into this. You don't work for me so we're not breaking any rules that I'm aware of. I'm interested in you and I'd like to spend a little time with you, in a place where we won't be under a microscope." The elevator doors closed again, but neither of them moved. "Your work on this project will be finished soon and then it won't matter either way." He pushed the button to open the doors. "If you choose to treat this weekend as a business trip and use the time to get intel on me for your project, well, then I'd appreciate a heads up on that. If you'd rather get to know me, the real me, then spending a day or two with my sister will do the trick." He bent his head as if to kiss her and then seemed to stop himself. "It's up to you, honey."

Thrown off by the endearment, Caroline smiled up at him. "I'd *really* like to get to know you better. I'd like that a lot."

Creases appeared in the corners of his eyes as he took one of her hands and tugged her out of the elevator before the doors could close again. The wheels on their suitcases sounded disproportionately loud in the empty concrete parking garage. Reed hit the button to unlock his car, another noise that made Caroline jump.

Reed slanted a smile at her. "Nervous?"

"Of course not. But I'm not fully awake yet."

"You can sleep in the car." He reached for her roll-on and added it next to his in the trunk. She moved around to the passenger side and added her other bag to the backseat and then curled up in the slightly chilly leather seat. Reed slid in next to her, hit a button to turn on the seat warmer and, with a smile, produced her fuzzy blanket. She accepted it with a grin.

Reed started the car and headed out of the garage. "If we miss the traffic, it should take about four hours. We'll get there in time for breakfast."

"Perfect," Caroline murmured. Her eyes were already closed, and with the heated seat and her blanket, she was warm.

The car's radio was tuned to a mixed rock station and Reed turned the sound down low, just enough to block the road noise.

A firm hand on her knee woke her sometime later. Stretching, she looked around. They'd stopped at a gas station. "I'm going to run in for coffee and facilities. Want anything?"

"Ah, yeah. I think I'll make a pit stop too." She shifted in her seat. Reed removed his hand and already she missed its warmth. There was still an early morning frost in the air making everything feel even colder than it really was.

She stretched and jogged in place a little to get a little energy running through her. She hurried inside to do her business and grab a coffee before meeting

Reed outside by the car.

"Want me to drive for a while?" Caroline offered.

Reed gave her an incredulous look. "My car? No."

Caroline cocked a hip. "I'm perfectly capable." Secretly, she was relieved because she'd much rather be a passenger, but still, it was polite to offer.

His stance didn't change. "No."

"Hookay." She drew the word out. "Let's get moving then."

In another minute they were on the road again. They'd left the city behind a while back, so the highway was lined now with trees and the occasional pop-up small town. After a few minutes, Caroline decided to break the silence.

"So, tell me more about your family."

Reed laughed.

"What? We've got to start somewhere, right? And it beats talking about the weather."

"This weather is nice. I'm enjoying it," he teased.

She rolled her eyes and waited.

Reed caved. "You've met my dad. He's a powerhouse, and he knows everything about everything."

"I'll bet that drives your mother crazy."

Reed shrugged and rested one arm on the console between them. "She's got her own ways.

Mostly she just rolls with it. She's easy-going, not much of a temper."

"She's a saint?"

Reed's lips pressed into an almost smile. "Only now that we're all grown up and moved out."

"Ha! I believe that." She looked down at his hand. It was so tempting to reach up and entwine her fingers with his. "And you have a sister. Older? Younger?"

"I have two sisters. Angela is the oldest. She's a fashion buyer in the city."

"She dresses you?"

Reed snorted. "No. But not for lack of trying."

"My younger sister, Savannah, is the one we're going to see."

"Your favorite?"

Reed appeared to think about that. "We're just closer, that's all."

"So, what's Savannah like?"

"She's intense. When she finds something she's passionate about she's like a dog with a bone. But she's fun, too. She's a museum curator for a little Indian museum she opened up in New Hampshire. She lives in this tiny little town that sits on the edge of the reservation. She's spent most of the last year convincing both sides to play nice together."

"Wow. That's a noble goal."

Reed smiled. "She's a dreamer."

"You don't think she can do it?"

"Oh, she'll do it. I just meant that she doesn't back down from a challenge."

Caroline gave a nod. "We'll have that in common, at least."

Reed turned his head to look at her. He must have interpreted the wistfulness in her voice. "You have a lot in common. I suspect you'll get along great."

"I can get along with anyone."

He looked back to the road. "Even the man who texted you and showed up in your office the other day?" There was a note of something undefinable in his voice, almost like jealousy. Apparently not much happened in his building that he doesn't know about.

"That would be my mother's boyfriend, Tony. But we're talking about you."

"I'm pretty sure we just moved on. Your turn."

Caroline straightened in her seat and looked out the front window.

"My dad died about fourteen years ago. I don't have any siblings. My mom sort of fell apart without him to take care of her. She bounced around for a while. She was at constant loose ends until she met Tony."

"Now he takes care of her?"

She tried to consider that objectively. "They have this sort of needy relationship. It's odd, but at the same time, they're completely happy together."

"That doesn't sound so bad."

Caroline thought about that. "On the surface, no. It's not. I'm glad they have each other."

Reed must have sensed there was more. "So, why are you living with them?"

Caroline flushed, unable to define the feeling. Embarrassment, indignation? "Uh, they're living with me."

Reed directed a look at her, and she could see that things were clicking into place for him. "You're *supporting* them?"

She turned her head to look out the side window, afraid of seeing judgment in his eyes. "Pretty much," she admitted in a small voice. "I have been for some time now. At first it was a couple hundred here and there or buying them groceries. Then it was co-signing for their lease because their credit was bad. It escalated to paying their rent. Then, recently, they moved in." She gave a watery laugh. "It's cheaper for me, anyway."

Reed's voice was sympathetic, not a trace of the accusation she'd feared. "It's cheaper, but now you have no privacy. Probably no peace either."

"Not really, no." Not one to dwell on misery, she grinned playfully. "On the bright side, if I buy groceries, I have dinner ready and waiting for me every night. And Tony's great for the occasional board game or poker night."

Reed chuckled as he took the exit off the highway. "You're one up on me then."

Chapter 11

Caroline had barely gotten out of the car and was stretching out the kinks in her shoulders when she heard a squeal that made her spin around in surprise. She stepped out of the way in time to see a bouncy strawberry blond ponytail streak past her. The woman Caroline assumed to be Reed's sister gave him an effusive hug before turning her inquisitive green eyes on Caroline. Following at a more reasonable pace was an attractive man with slightly curly blond hair and a good-humored expression on his face.

Reed extricated himself from the woman and reached out to shake the man's hand. Almost in unison they turned to Caroline.

"Caroline, this is my sister Savannah and her fiancé Daniel Harrison."

Stepping instantly into her professional role as she always did when she was nervous, Caroline shook their hands. "Caroline Trumbull." She stole a quick look at Reed, unsure how to explain her presence. Reed only raised his eyebrows. Stumbling on the introduction, she offered, "Nice to meet you", in a weak voice.

Savannah looked back and forth between them and opened her mouth to speak but Daniel nudged

140

her with his elbow, cutting off anything she was planning to say. Daniel, seeming to enjoy some private joke, turned to Reed. "Is this the shadow Fred hired to make you look cool?"

"Heck of a gesture, right?" Reed's response was nearly as cryptic as Daniel's intent.

"Time will tell, I guess. Fred's always got some plan in the works." Daniel's tone was teasing but Caroline noticed that Reed's expression seemed to be saying he didn't find Daniel's comments funny. What the heck was that about?

Focusing on Savannah, Caroline watched the comfortable camaraderie between sister and brother. Savannah's openness was in direct contrast to Reed's air of privacy. Caroline couldn't wait to get Savannah alone. She suspected she'd be able to learn more about Reed in one weekend than she could by spending a whole year with him at the office. Not that she'd mind spending a year figuring him out.

Pushing aside that tempting thought, Caroline hitched a smile for her hosts. "Any chance you have coffee?"

Beaming, Savannah hooked an arm through Reed's and pulled him along. "You bet we do," she told Caroline.

Daniel indicated that Caroline should follow and then fell in step beside her. "Coffee is Savannah's favorite food group."

Caroline smiled. "I like her already, then."

As Savannah chattered away to Reed just ahead of them, Daniel seemed to be trying to get a read on her. "We set up the little cottage on the other side of the grounds for your stay, but it's a small space. If that's uncomfortable for two of you, you're also welcome to stay in one of our guest rooms."

Caroline was unsure how to respond, having no idea what Reed had told them about her, or their plans for the weekend. She opened her mouth to offer a response, but Reed beat her to it.

Apparently besides being wickedly handsome, and stoic to the point of being inhuman, he also had bat ears. "The cottage is perfect, Daniel. Thanks."

She blinked at Reed's response and tried not to show the bevy of emotions she was feeling. Surprised, anxious, hopeful.

Savannah led them into a deceptively modern, and enormous, log cabin where there was indeed fresh coffee waiting for them.

Seated at the dining table, Caroline accepted her cup with a nod and suppressed her sigh when she felt the newest hit of caffeine flood her veins.

Reed watched her with one side of his lips turned up. She frowned, hoping to discourage his nearly physical dissection of her and then turned her attention to Savannah.

"Fred tells me you created this museum yourself."

Savannah's eyes brightened with a lingering glance at Daniel. "Not entirely on my own. I had a lot of help from Daniel, Kinap, and my friend, Rachel. And from the community."

Daniel seconded that with a nod, but added, "But the vision and passion were all yours."

Savannah's expression turned sappy. Caroline couldn't help but be entertained by Reed's sister. She suspected that what you saw with Savannah was what you got.

"I wouldn't be here if you hadn't rescued me from that room."

To her left, Reed groaned in protest. "Make it stop! Next thing they'll be in a corner somewhere, kissing."

Savannah smacked the back of Reed's head, eliciting a laugh out of Caroline.

"She gets to smack you when you say something smart?" Caroline pretended to pout. She loved the banter between them.

"No. And neither can you." Reed directed his gaze at Caroline.

Savannah's eyes widened. "Reed gets smart with you?" She had her head cocked, as if that was something new.

Caroline frowned a little again, not sure why this would surprise Savannah. "It took me awhile to realize that Reed knows a language other than sarcasm."

Savannah sat back and openly studied her brother. "Huh." Her eyes flicked back to Caroline. "Ever made him laugh?"

She wasn't sure where the questions were leading, but seeing Reed's wary expression, she decided to play along.

"Laughing at me just might be his favorite pastime."

Reed huffed over that but Daniel and Savannah both laughed. Whatever she'd said seemed to have given them the answer they were looking for because the conversation soon changed. Caroline swore she could feel Reed relax as they steered onto more neutral ground.

"So, what are your plans for the weekend?" Savannah asked as she got up to retrieve the carafe from the coffee machine.

Reed shrugged. "I didn't make any specific plans."

Savannah froze and spun around, looking incredulous. "Reed Decatur without a plan! What does that look like?"

Caroline laughed. "I was wondering the same thing. In fact, that's why I tagged along. I want to see this phenomenon first-hand."

"Just so you can take pictures," Reed grumbled.

"Somebody's got to do it. Are you going to be a baby about this?"

Savannah's eyes swiveled between them again and Caroline knew they'd just confused her. She certainly couldn't blame Savannah; she was confused herself. She had a job to do, certainly, but that job didn't involve weekends in New Hampshire with the sexy CEO. She kept her expression bland as she considered the real reason she'd agreed to this spontaneous trip with a man she really wanted to get to know better.

Daniel stepped in as though no one had spoken. "This afternoon we're volunteering at a *natomuwal*."

"A *natomuwal?*" she repeated, trying out the word. "What is that?"

"It's when the tribe gets together and fixes things up for someone in need," Daniel answered.

"Ski organized this one." There was a great deal of pride in Savannah's voice when she turned to Reed. "Do you remember him?"

Reed smiled. "I remember."

Daniel sipped his coffee and murmured. "He's a good kid."

Caroline was intrigued. She'd heard about Savannah's work in Wolf Creek from Fred, and being a city girl, the idea of a community coming together to help one of their own was completely endearing. "How many people participate?"

"Not as many as we'd like," Savannah admitted. "But we're changing that one house at a time." She put the carafe back in the machine and turned around to lean against the counter. "It's tradition in the Maliut tribe to help out-to hold each other up, is the literal translation. But the tribe really struggled with some difficult social issues for so long that they'd fallen out of practice."

Daniel raised his mug to her. "That's being diplomatic." He turned to Caroline to explain. "The Maliuts and the non-natives in Wolf Creek hated each other. They've been fighting for generations."

Savannah waved that away with a flick of her hand. "It was all a misunderstanding."

Caroline noticed that both Daniel and Reed looked incredulous. Reed shook his head at Daniel. "That's got to be the understatement of the century."

"Anyway," Savannah continued over them. "A group of us thought it might help ease the tension between the two sides if we started the tradition back up again. You know, neighbor helping neighbor sort of thing."

Caroline leaned forward, her mind already running with ideas. "If the town is so segregated, how do you get people to cross those boundaries?"

Daniel nodded, "That's been the hardest part. It's not that there's really any racism going on anymore, but the community has been separated for so long that they're just sort of set in their ways now. We're trying to be intentional about bringing people together."

"We're starting small, bringing some of our own friends together to help on the reservation. Sometimes our Maliut friends come into town to help out there."

"It's slow-going," Daniel admitted.

"You have to start somewhere," Caroline added. Shooting a look at Reed, she asked, "What are we doing this afternoon? Could we help?" She looked at Savannah. "I have to admit that I love the idea."

"No plans, remember? I was going to leave it

up to you. And, knowing my sister, she would have changed any plans I'd made anyway."

Savannah pretended to look affronted. "I think you're confusing me with Angela."

"I'd never confuse you with Angela."

Savannah didn't look pacified, but she turned to include Caroline. "Angela is our older sister. She's a bit controlling."

"The fashion merchandiser, right?"

"I didn't think to ask earlier if you'd met her," Reed added.

Caroline shook her head. "No, but I know your father is very proud of all of you."

Savannah turned to Reed who was still leaning against the counter. "Daniel and I have a few wedding arrangements to make this morning, but if you're serious about helping you can meet us up here around one and we'll ride together. Mike and Rachel are going over around the same time."

Reed accepted that with a nod.

Daniel handed him a key. "We stocked the fridge with a few things and put out clean towels, made the bed. It's ready for you." He winked at Caroline before turning to Savannah. We need to get moving, babe."

Reed moved to the door, barely stopping to tow Caroline along behind him.

"See you later," she called as they headed back to Reed's car.

THE COTTAGE was situated on the other side of an enormous, renovated eighteenth century manor that Savannah had turned into a Maliut Indian museum. Though it would have been a short walk from Daniel and Savannah's house, the frigid temperatures convinced them to drive around the museum and park the car in a small lot just behind it. The cottage was tiny compared to Daniel's and Savannah's cabin, though still larger than her apartment in the city. It was easy to see why they kept it for guests. The little white clapboard building was comfortably worn. The fading wooden siding looked like it had been artfully designed rather than faded from the progression of freezing and scorching over the course of decades.

The interior was clean and bright. The furniture and decorations were new, all pointing to a beach theme, which probably fit in the summertime being that the cottage sat along the border of a fabulous black water lake, but now in the middle of November, seemed out of place.

Caroline stood at the railing of a small porch and looked out over the mysteriously dark, unfrozen water. She sensed when Reed came up behind her.

"Creepy, isn't it?"

"The water?"

Reed looked down at her with one side of his lips lifted in a smile. "It always reminds me of that scene toward the end of the *Harry Potter* series where Dumbledore takes Harry to that lake. The one where all the bodies are floating." He shuddered.

Caroline turned her back on the lake in favor of Reed. "You've read *Harry Potter*?" She hadn't pegged him as the type.

He squinted at her. "Hasn't everyone? Don't tell me you haven't, or this relationship won't go any further," he teased.

Caroline cocked her head, not breaking eye contact. "Do we have a relationship?"

Instead of answering, Reed gave her a smacking kiss and headed for the door. "I carried your things in from the car."

Caroline pivoted and followed him inside. Coming up behind him, she was tempted to reach out and smooth a hand down his back. His shoulders were so broad and strong, and she wondered how he would react if she hugged up to him and laid her head against him. It had been a long time since she'd had someone to lean on. And a man like Reed? Only in her dreams.

Shaking off the wishful thinking, she asked, "So what do you want to do this morning, Boss-man?"

Reed turned around; his dark eyes shielded. They were standing mere inches apart. If she raised her heels just a little, she'd be able to kiss him. She kept her temptation in check for the moment, but from the glint that changed his expression, she suspected he'd seen into her mind.

He dipped his head down just enough to make her instinctively lean into him. Very softly, he answered, "I thought we'd have breakfast and see the town."

Her heels hit the floor and she took a surprised, and admittedly disappointed, step backward. "That sounds good. I'm starved."

He angled his head toward her. "Are you being sarcastic?"

She collected herself and batted her eyes. "Of course not."

"Good. I'd hate to have to do to you what my sister did to me."

She shook her head, her stance steady in case he really did mean to smack her on the back of her head. "Not gonna happen."

He took a step toward her, once again placing himself solidly in her personal space and lowered his voice. "What is going to happen?" he asked, his eyes on her lips.

"Hell if I know," Caroline whispered a second before she pulled him down for a kiss. And what a kiss it was!

Caroline hadn't dated much, and she'd never been intimate with a man, but she recognized right away that what she felt for Reed was nothing short of combustible. The way his lips moved on hers, prompting her to open to him made her insides turn to liquid. If his hands hadn't been cradling her face, she would have slunk to the floor in a boneless heap.

Coming to his senses before she did, Reed lifted his head away, but mercifully kept his hands on her face. "Dress warm," he whispered.

"Okay," she breathed. Wait...what?

Chapter 12

*T*he wooded acres surrounding the lake were one of Reed's favorite places in Wolf Creek. It was only in nature that he felt total peace. In the solitude of the trees there were no judgmental glances, no one vying for his attention, no demands on his time. Out here was clean air, a breeze, and the muted sounds of a world apart from him. In his haste to get her alone for the weekend, he hadn't stopped to consider how bringing her to Wolf Creek might impact his feelings about the place. Caroline was a city girl. What if she hated it here? What if she complained the whole time? Her opinions already meant a lot to him. Would her reaction change his view, his attachment to the town, his attraction to her? He frowned, a little surprised by just how much he hoped she liked it here.

Caroline appeared at his side wearing black snow pants and a heavy coat. Her blond hair was held back in two braids and covered with a bright pink hat. She handed him a travel mug filled with coffee and gave him a concerned look.

"That's a heavy frown. Are you sure you want to go?"

He shook off his worries and forced a smile. "Of course. Exploring this area is one of my favorite

151

things to do around here."

Caroline rewarded him with one of her bright smiles. "Lead on, then. I can't wait to see it."

Reed took her hand and entwined her fingers with his, pleased by how natural it felt. They walked the narrow, snow-covered trail bordering the lake in silence for nearly twenty minutes. Reed was surprised and relieved to note how enthralled she seemed by the sights and sounds around them. Every so often she would squeeze his hand to point out some animal or tree, but mostly she seemed as content as he to walk along in thoughtful silence. Though the temperature was well below freezing, she never uttered a complaint.

Caroline let go of Reed's hand and hurried forward when she spotted two well-kept graves just off the trail ahead of them. Reed followed at a slower pace, content to watch her reaction to the site his sister had so painstakingly restored. Reed reached her side and she leaned into him, shivering a little. He put an arm around her waist, drawing her closer to his side. She cuddled in willingly, fitting herself perfectly to him like an adjoining puzzle piece.

"Who were they?" she whispered.

Reed smiled. "They're already dead. You don't have to whisper."

"It seems more reverent," she answered, no longer whispering but still speaking in a low voice.

"They are William Rogers and his Maliut wife, Mushu."

"They lived here?"

"William built the manor that houses the museum now. Mushu lived there with him for a few years."

"Why only for a short time?"

"Apparently the only way to legalize his son was to marry a white woman who would agree to adopt him."

"His son with Mushu?"

"Yes. His Indian son."

Caroline shook her head. "That's ridiculous."

Reed pressed his lips together to hold in a laugh at her outrage and then reminded her, "It was two hundred years ago."

Still looking disgruntled, she turned her head back to the marble stones. "Alright. What happened?"

"He found a woman to marry and brought her over from England. Not long after they arrived, they both fell ill and died. Mushu disappeared and the tribe was left to raise the boy."

"Talk about a plan that backfired!" Caroline muttered quietly. "So Mushu's grave is empty then?"

Reed couldn't keep the pride out of his voice. "No, she's in there now."

Caroline gave him a funny look. "You said she disappeared."

"Savannah found her."

Caroline's expression became incredulous.

"After two hundred years? How? Where?"

"Savannah and Daniel were both here researching, about two years ago now. The manor has all these secret rooms and hidden passageways. Savannah was exploring and got stuck in one of them. That's how she found Mushu."

"That must have been scary."

"For all of us," Reed agreed. "Savannah had been missing for several hours. Turns out she'd fallen down a long flight of stairs and broken her leg. Daniel and Ski, the son of a tribal elder, went looking for her and finally found her. Daniel carried her all the way back up to the top." Reed had seen the room and still shuddered to imagine his sister trapped down there with the emaciated body.

Caroline must have felt his reaction because she smoothed a hand over his abdomen and pressed closer. "What a miracle she was okay!"

Reed looked down at her, intending to agree but the way her face was tilted up to his with her cold lips so close, she was begging to be kissed. Caroline took the lead, leaving Reed shocked and aroused by the sudden and confident force of her kiss. With a groan, he wrapped both arms around her and held her until he worried she couldn't breathe. He released his hold when he felt her ease away, but he couldn't bring himself to let go of her completely. Not yet.

"Wow," she whispered. "Just wow."

"Wow what?" He prompted when she trailed off.

She blushed and turned to walk ahead of him down the path. "Wow is what it feels like to have all your attention focused on me."

Reed groaned again. "Woman, my attention has been focused on nothing but you since the first time I laid eyes on you." He shook his head as he reached her side and took her hand again. "I haven't been able to focus on anything else in months!"

"You disguise it well," she assured him, her face still pink.

"Thank God for small favors then. I'm still not sure how I'll be able to look at you the same when we get back on Monday."

She planted her gloved hands on her hips. "I can act like nothing ever happened if you can."

Reed considered that, along with the fact that her job was to transform his relationship with his staff. "Do you think we need to?"

She appeared startled by that idea and took a step closer to peer into his eyes. "Is that what you want? For people to see that we're", she faltered, "seeing each other?"

"What's the harm in it? We're both single adults. You don't work for me. Personally, I mean." He shrugged. The more he considered not having to sneak around, the more he liked the idea.

She took a step back. "Let me read my contract with Decatur Industries."

Reed nodded. He could respect that. "Let's go find my sister and let you get some pictures of me pandering myself."

Seeming to understand his motivation, Caroline

laughed and turned back to the cottage.

THEY MET Daniel and Savannah back at their house where Savannah lent Caroline a heavy old sweatshirt that she could get dirty in. Much to Reed's surprise, she seemed to love it.

"We're going to be doing some painting, a little sprucing up for one of the elders. The man is ninety, if he's a day, and he still thinks he can climb a ladder to clean his gutters. Well, things around here are nearly frozen and we're not about to let him!"

"Be warned, he can be a grouchy old guy," Daniel added as they got into his Jeep.

"Oh, he is not. He's a sweet thing."

Daniel gave Savannah an incredulous look and shook his head. "I'm pretty sure you're the only person he's nice to."

Savannah didn't seem concerned by Daniel's assessment. "Well, then it's a darn good thing you're bringing me along, isn't it?"

A few minutes later they were parked next to an older model Subaru wagon. Daniel clapped the owner hard on the shoulder. "Where's the Charger?" he asked the muscular, dark haired man.

"I'm not about to get paint on *that*," he commented as he hurried around to the passenger side to help his pregnant wife out of the car.

"Driving the mom-mobile." Daniel fist-bumped his friend. "Nice."

"Hush, Daniel," the willowy brunette admonished, but it was clear she wasn't angry.

Savannah linked an arm through the woman's and ushered her to where Reed was standing with Caroline. The men followed behind.

"Reed, you remember Rachel and Mike, right?"

Reed nodded and shook Mike's hand, and then Rachel's.

"This is Caroline Trumbull," Savannah continued. More handshaking followed.

"I didn't know you were seeing anyone, Reed. Good for you."

Reed felt Caroline look at him, so he slid her a half smile.

"He's a man of few words." Caroline spoke to fill the silence. "Thankfully I'm a woman of many. We balance each other out."

Daniel and Savannah soon set them to work scrubbing the dirt and cobwebs from the elder's aluminum siding. Giant heaters were plugged in and placed around the porch to keep them comfortable without the heavy winter clothing. The sound of the heaters and scraping on the trim was loud, and they were too far apart for easy conversation, and yet just working together side-by-side felt so comfortable.

Before long, they'd moved on to painting trim on the dreary front porch, something neither of them was apparently very good at. A few times Reed caught Caroline snapping pictures of him as he slopped paint on the cardboard covered floor. He shook his head in resigned amusement, already sure he would look completely ridiculous in whatever advertisements she had planned for him. It was a means to an end, he reminded himself. The sooner she finished this part of her project, the sooner he could have her for himself.

Chapter 13

*T*ired, but fulfilled from the activities of the afternoon, Caroline propped her arms against the railing of the cottage's back porch and looked out into the expanse of darkness ahead of her. The wind was biting, and the air froze in her nostrils, but she breathed deeply anyway. Nothing was this fresh and clean in the city. It was never this quiet either. She watched snow fall on the open water until the sound of the sliding door reached her ears.

"This is unbelievably peaceful," she said softly. "Chilly," she laughed, "but beautiful."

Reed stepped up behind her and gently pulled her back against his chest. The contrast of the cold air and his warm body made her shiver. His hands reached around to rub her forearms to generate warmth. Going with the moment, Caroline laid her head back against his sternum and relaxed. He squeezed her tighter for just a moment. They stood together in silence, watching the snow fall against the dark backdrop of a lake surrounded by trees.

Caroline could feel Reed's heart beating steadily against her shoulder blade. He was relaxed, and yet she instinctively knew he was still waiting for her to communicate her decision. Would this be a business trip? Or the beginning of a relationship? In her heart there was no decision. From the first moment she'd seen him in the lobby of Decatur Industries she'd wanted him. She was finished denying herself.

For one weekend he was offering her the chance to let go of her trappings. Two glorious days to forget about her mom and Tony. No worries about her living situation. If she remembered to take a few pictures, she could even set aside thoughts about work. Not only was Reed offering himself, he was offering her an escape. A true vacation!

Caroline turned in the circle of his arms. "Let's go inside."

Reed's eyes heated as he looked down at her. "I built us a fire."

"Sounds like heaven."

"It could be." There was a question in his eyes.

"I have no doubts." She leaned on tiptoes and pressed her lips to his knowing he wasn't going to make the first move, not this first time anyway. She let him take the lead with kissing while she stepped him back to the sliding door and fumbled behind him to get the door open. Her success brought a wave of warm wood-scented air. Over the threshold Reed held her closer with one arm and closed the door with the other.

He backed her up against the smooth cold glass and pressed in, pulling her leg up around his waist. Caroline could feel how much Reed wanted her but her mind puzzled though the logistics of getting naked in yoga pants and a bulky sweatshirt. This wasn't exactly how she imagined her first time with

Reed.

Feeling a little awkward yet determined to make the scene play out the way she'd planned, Caroline gently removed herself from Reed's embrace and peeked up at him. He raised his eyebrows. No judgment, just that burning question.

"Can I have a few minutes?"

Reed reached out to hold her upper arms gently, as if he couldn't stop himself from touching her. He brushed his lips lightly against hers and then stepped back. "Take all the time you need."

Caroline gave him a grateful and embarrassed smile and scurried into the bedroom to locate her suitcase. As quickly as she could on shaky legs, she changed into the short silky white nightgown she'd packed in anticipation of this exact moment. She pulled the band out of her hair and shook it out around her shoulders. She looked at her reflection in the mirror and smiled. She opened the door quietly and stood there a moment, happy for the chance to observe Reed unnoticed.

He was sitting on the couch looking at the fire. He'd pulled up his shirt sleeves and rested his forearms on his thighs. Seriously, how was he so tan in the middle of November?

She shifted in the doorway, drawing his attention. His face reflected awe and something else, something very like possessiveness as he watched her approach.

"Sorry for making you wait," she said to break the silence.

Reed shook his head once. "You're worth the wait."

As soon as she was close enough, he reached forward and guided her down to his lap.

"Good answer," she teased. She lowered her voice and didn't bother to hide the uncertainty she was feeling. "I hope you still think so later."

Reed's hands stilled on her hips and he cocked his head at her. "We don't have to do anything you don't want to do."

"Oh, we're doing this!" She put her hands on his forearms, more to steady herself than anything else, but she also wanted to touch him. "I'm nervous. But I had this fantasy and I kind of wanted to make it happen."

With a sound like a groan he brought her up against his chest and kissed her. Hard. With one hand he pulled a blanket from the back of the couch and tossed it on the rug in front of the fire. "Tell me if I get it wrong."

"You're nailing it so far." Caroline tugged at his shirt, desperate to see the body that until now she'd only felt beneath layers of expensive fabric. She could feel him chuckle against her lips when she nearly tore the shirt off his shoulders. She leaned back just enough to examine her prize. "Wow."

Reed's eyes showed tender amusement. "You're going to make me blush."

"Shush. This is my fantasy."

"Yes, ma'am."

Caroline pulled Reed down to the blanket and knelt before him. "Where did you get this tan?" She put her lips to the tip of his shoulder. She felt his shrug.

"I guess I just have that kind of skin." He brushed his palms up the backs of her arms to settle on her shoulders. "I like yours better."

She continued with her exploration of his body, trailing her fingers down his chest to his abs. "When do you find time to work out?"

His focus on her was razor sharp. "Usually when reporters and gossipers assume I'm with a woman somewhere."

Caroline appreciated his ironic tone and dropped back on her heels, faking a look of shock. "You mean you don't date models?" She let her gaze travel from his knees to his eyes. "I'm no longer interested."

Evidently understanding her remark for the joke it was, Reed growled and snatched her back to her knees, pressing her along the length of him. "Do you need convincing?"

"Mm. Yes, please," she whispered.

Reed angled his head to kiss her and stopped. "Am I stealing away your fantasy?"

She shook her head. "You are my fantasy, and you're leading me right where I want to go."

Solemnly, Reed looked into her eyes for just a moment before lowering his head to capture her mouth in a kiss. His lips on hers, his tongue moving against hers sent a zing all through her core. It was as if he felt reverence for her and she loved him even more for it.

His hands slid from her shoulders to skate down her back and settle on her hips. With a touch so light it could have been a breeze, he lifted the hem of her nightgown and raised it up higher while he continued to explore the skin he was systematically baring. When he reached her breasts, his touch tickled so much that she broke off the kiss with a laugh.

Reed used the opportunity to lift the gown over her head and toss it onto the couch behind him. He held her away at arms-length and examined his prize. "God you're perfect."

Embarrassed over his honest praise, she reached out and placed her palms on his pecs. His skin was hot from the fire. She shivered, her nipples tightening almost painfully. Reed noticed and covered her breasts with his hands again. She closed her eyes to the sensation. Reed's lips on her startled her into resuming her exploration of his body, moving down his abs to the fly of his pants.

His hand over hers stopped her before she could touch him. "You're sure?" he whispered against her lips. "Because if you're not, we have to stop now."

Caroline lifted her face away and pierced him with a determined look. "My choice, Reed. I chose you. I choose now."

He nodded in understanding, and maybe relief before scooping her in close so that she felt the length of him pressed against her pelvis. She snaked a hand between them and unfastened his pants and then used both hands to pull them down to his knees, rubbing her breasts against him in the process. The contrast between them made her tingle in a delicious way. He was hard and smooth, and his skin was so hot all over.

Reed laid her back against the blankets and twisted to pull his pants the rest of the way off before settling beside her. On his side, he loomed over her, studying her the same way she was looking at him. Memorizing, savoring.

Staring turned to kissing, which quickly escalated to touching. In the space of their quickened heartbeats, Reed was cuddling and rubbing a path from Caroline's neck to her breasts, pausing to trace her belly button before settling between her thighs. He groaned when he slipped a finger inside her and found her ready for him. Then it was her turn to moan when he removed that finger to add a second one before sliding them up into a magical spot she didn't even know existed. In the next moment she saw stars.

Before she had time to fully comprehend what had just happened to her, Reed sat up to retrieve a condom. She watched in lazy fascination as he expertly rolled it on and returned to her. His full weight on her was one of the most heavenly things she'd ever felt. Impatiently, she rubbed her pelvis against him, but he caught her hips to hold her still. He eased into her slowly, something she quickly decided she was thankful for because they were a tight fit. As she wiggled to adjust to the feeling, she also discovered that his cock brushed that same spot his fingers had just awoken. She couldn't stop herself from chasing that glorious display of fireworks and sensation.

Somewhere in the back of her consciousness she knew that Reed was letting her take the lead and thought she probably shouldn't be so wanton, but in that moment she flat out didn't care. All she knew was that what he was doing with her felt amazing and she wanted to experience every single second of it.

Reed was right there with her as the flashes of light and sizzling shocks took over, and once she could think clearly, she realized that he was still holding her close, petting her softly and tickling soft kisses along the side of her face and neck. She blinked up at him. "Wow."

Reed chuckled, his chest hair tickling her. "That's kind of what I thought, too."

SOMETIME LATER they dozed on the blankets in front of the fire. Caroline was tucked in beside Reed, her head in the crook of his arm, one arm petting the sprinkling of chest hair beside her face.

"I feel really lazy," she mumbled.

Reed smiled. "Not lazy. Relaxed. Think of this as a vacation."

"Hmm. No wonder I didn't recognize the feeling." She tipped her head up to rest her chin on his chest. "Is there another way to relax without feeling lazy?"

"I'm sure there are lots of ways to relax."

Caroline rolled her eyes. "How do you relax

when you're on vacation?"

"You mean before I had you to entertain me?"

She smiled. "Yes, before me." She liked the way that sounded.

"I like to read."

"Oh, me too. I brought a book along in case I found some quiet time."

Reed moved to sit up. "Go grab your book and I'll grab mine and we can meet back here. I'll show you my second favorite way to relax." He stood and then leaned down to help her up.

Caroline tucked the blanket around her and stood. "If reading is your second, what was your first?"

Reed snaked an arm around her waist and pulled her in close. "What we just did is my new favorite. Everything else has just shifted down a notch." He let go and swatted her backside. "Go!"

Caroline returned to the bedroom to grab the romantic suspense novel she'd packed and realized two things immediately; she'd left her nightgown in the living room, and Reed had apparently put his things in another room. Interesting.

Back in the living room she quickly pulled on the nightgown and got comfortable on the sofa. She thought through their altered status as she waited for Reed. Caroline had never spent the night with a man before. Would she be able to sleep? Feeling intimidated by the unknown of what came next, she pulled the blanket back around herself like a protective cocoon and huddled on one side of the couch.

Not long after Reed returned wearing a pair of jersey knit pajama pants and a carrying his own paperback. "Is there room for two under that blanket?" He didn't wait for an answer before settling beside her.

She pulled a corner of the blanket out from under her and spread it across both of them. Reed stretched out and settled his feet on the ottoman before them. He pulled Caroline's feet across his lap and rested his book on top of her legs. "Perfect fit," he teased.

Caroline got a glimpse of the cover of his book. "Mystery. Huh. I kind of figured you for the nonfiction or biography type."

He pinched her toes. "I have more of an imagination than that."

She smiled. This was the side of him she had hoped to see this weekend. They shared a long look and Caroline knew they were both thinking of other uses for their imaginations. She blushed and Reed looked away with a knowing grin before opening his book to a page he'd marked.

For the next hour they stayed that way, cuddled up together, the only sound that of the wood popping and hissing in the fireplace. Between making love and the peaceful quiet between them, Caroline finally understood why people looked forward to vacations. And why on earth didn't people do this every chance they could?

Hearts in Training

When Caroline yawned for the third time, Reed lowered his book and looked her over. "Ready to head to bed?"

"Ye-ah." She ended on another yawn. "It's been an eventful day."

His expression turned tender. "Yes. It has." He tossed his book on the table beside the couch and scrubbed a hand over his face. "There is only one bedroom, but the couch also pulls out."

Caroline slid her legs to the floor and sat beside him. She laced her fingers together and looked at them. "I've never slept with anyone before."

She could feel Reed suppressing laughter beside her.

"I think we've established that, honey."

She elbowed him. "I mean literally sleeping." She looked at him and noted the smirk still on his face.

"I know babe. But you don't sound nervous anymore." He put his hand over hers. "It really is okay either way. We've covered a lot of distance today, both literally and metaphorically. I understand if you need some space."

Caroline's heart felt uncomfortably large, but she narrowed her eyes at him. "Are you for real?"

He frowned for a split second. "I think so?" His words came out like a question, making her laugh. "The bed is plenty big enough for two, and we can put pillows between us if you're uncomfortable."

Caroline looked in his eyes and spoke her most pressing concern. "What if I snore?"

Reed laughed and pulled her up to follow him into the bedroom.

They took turns using the bathroom to get ready for bed. Reed let Caroline go first, which meant that she had a few minutes while he was in the bathroom to regroup. It had been an amazing day in so many ways. She sat on the edge of the bed and chewed her lip to keep herself from smiling.

Reed came out of the bathroom and placed his folded clothes on a chair beside his suitcase. Caroline couldn't help but stare. He was wearing only a pair of dark gray boxers and his body was amazing. Catching her staring, he straightened and walked around the bed toward her.

"What's that look for?"

Caroline shook her head. "I was seriously just wondering how I got so lucky."

Reed pulled her to her feet and hugged her tight. He kissed her softly and then turned her lose. "You're tempting me, but you've got to be exhausted after all the scrubbing and painting."

"And love-making?" She gave him a flirty look. "I've got a little energy left." As if to make a liar out of her, she yawned wide.

Reed gave her a knowing look. "Maybe just enough energy to crawl into bed. Which side do you want?"

She looked down at the double bed and shrugged. "I tend to sleep in the middle of my bed at home, so I guess it doesn't really matter."

Reed moved to the side closest to the door and plugged his phone into the outlet. Caroline dug her charging cord out of her bag and handed it to Reed with her phone so that he could plug hers in beside his. Her phone chirped a message just as he was plugging it in. Reed picked up her phone, tapped the screen and read the message aloud.

Hope you had a wonderful day. We looked him up on the internet and he's a good-looking young man. Good night, Carrie. Love Mom and Tony.

Caroline closed her eyes and flopped on the bed, face down with her head buried in the pillow. Maybe she should be glad her mother hadn't said anything worse, but this was embarrassing all the same. Reed's parents hadn't texted to check in with him as if he was a child. They treated him like the grown man he was and let him live his life.

She felt the bed dip beside her and a second later she felt Reed's hand massaging her backside. "That was nice of your parents to check on you." He paused, then added, "Carrie."

Caroline groaned making Reed laugh. She rolled over and stared up at the ceiling. Reed's hand was a heavy warm weight, now on her belly.

"I really do think it's nice. You're in another state with a man they've never met." He wiggled his eyebrows. "Doing heaven knows what. They were worried." He rubbed her stomach and reached for her phone. "Do you want to text them back, Carrie?"

Caroline sat up and took the phone from him. "Call me Carrie one more time and you will be sleeping on the pull-out."

Reed laughed again while he pulled the covers back and settled in bed. Caroline sent her mother a quick text to say goodnight and handed her phone back to Reed to plug in again. He turned off the bedside lamp and reached out to pull her down beside him. Caroline snuggled in close and sighed. Reed's skin was warm, and he smelled so good. Reed pressed a kiss behind her ear and whispered. "For the record, I like the name Carrie on you. But I promise not to use it in public."

Caroline thought about that in silence for a few minutes. She sort-of liked that Reed knew about her nickname and evidently planned to use it. "Does that mean we'll spend more time alone like this?"

She felt Reed pull away from her in the dark. "You're kidding, right?" He settled back in and held her close again. "I'm addicted to you. I'm pretty sure you'll tire of me before I ever tire of you."

She smiled knowing he couldn't see her. "Mm. Wanna bet?"

Chapter 14

Caroline stretched and flopped over onto her back. The unfamiliar ceiling caught her by surprise. In a flash she remembered the evening before and tipped her head to see Reed lying on his side, his head propped on the heel of his hand, watching her with a tender and amused expression on his face.

"Good morning." His voice was husky, and he so looked good. Unfair.

She scooted up to the headboard and rested back against it. "Good morning to you."

His other hand reached out and caressed her abdomen as if he couldn't stop himself from touching her. "You didn't snore."

Caroline covered her face and laughed. "Oh, my God." She lowered her hands and shook her head at him. "Well, now we know, I guess." She laughed again. "Didn't you sleep last night?"

His eyelids lowered a fraction and he shook his head slowly from side to side. "I didn't want to miss a thing."

"Watching someone sleep can't be all that exciting. Are you a pervert?"

Reed smiled. "I won't always get to see you like this. I wanted to memorize every cell."

"Every cell, huh?"

"Every cell, Carrie."

She rolled her eyes but smiled. "What's the plan for today, Boss-man?"

Reed moved to sit up beside her and gave her the side-eye. "How about we make a deal. I won't call you Carrie in public, if you don't call me Boss in private? Away from the office we're equals," he lowered his voice, "lovers, and I don't want you, or anyone else, to see it any differently."

The request playful, but Caroline understood its importance to Reed. "Deal," she winked and added, "babe."

Reed laughed. "We could try skiing, or ice skating. Or maybe Christmas shopping."

Caroline thought about that. "Or all of the above?"

"And then warm up in front of the fire." He wiggled his eyebrows.

"Mm. The same way we did yesterday? Because, honestly Reed, that is my very favorite way to warm up now."

"Absolutely. Breakfast?"

"The conversation just went from sex to food."

Reed laughed. "Are you surprised?" He raised a hand. "I'm a man."

"I'm delightfully aware." She was very aware "What's for breakfast?"

Hearts in Training

"Well, we can see what my sister stocked for us in the kitchen, or we can hit Beans and Bagels."

"Ooh. Yes. Assuming those beans are coffee beans, I'm all over it."

He rolled off the bed and stretched, showing off a set of abs so well-defined he could put Thor to shame. "Race you to the shower."

Caroline tipped her head toward the door. "I'll give you a head start. The view is pretty damn good from the back."

Reed leaned down and snatched her off the bed and over his shoulder. "Let's go shower, princess."

BEANS AND BAGELS was so much better than Caroline expected. Being from New York City, she was spoiled by the quality and quantity of coffee shops available to her. Beans appeared to have all the sophistication of a New York coffee chain, with the charm of a small-town hang-out. And, judging by the crowd, it was indeed a small-town hang-out.

As they waited in line, Caroline looked around at the patrons. They were a mix of retirees and harried workers, along with a handful of young mothers whose toddlers were chasing each other around a table near the back.

Seeing the easy camaraderie squeezed Caroline's heart a little. She loved the energy of the city, but it often came at the expense of familiar, friendly faces. She wondered what it would be like to be any of those young mothers sitting in the corner, meeting up to talk while their children played in a safe place.

Reed's hand on her lower back ushered her forward, bringing her back to present.

"Hey Reed. Visiting your sister this weekend?" A pretty brunette was leaning on the counter, apparently waiting for a refill. She straightened and held out a hand to introduce herself to Caroline. "Bailey Adams."

"Caroline Trumbull. This is a great place."

Bailey nodded. "It really is. One of my favorite places to be in the morning."

Before Caroline could respond, the barista was ready for their order. Reed ordered first to give Caroline time to look at the menu hand-written in chalk above them. After giving her own order, they stepped off to the side to let the next patron order. While another employee waited on the next customer, the owner leaned on the counter across from Bailey. "I'm Stacie Porter." She pointed to herself, "I do breakfast." She pointed at Bailey, "She does dinner."

Caroline looked between them. They were clearly good friends.

Reed explained while Bailey snatched up her phone to check a message. "Bailey owns Bailey's Restaurant across the road there." He pointed out the wide front windows to a two-story brick building across Main Street. "Stacie gets the breakfast crowd and Bailey gets the dinner crowd."

"Ah. I saw the restaurant when we came through town yesterday. Maybe we can eat there tonight?" Caroline looked at Reed, not sure what his plans were. Well, apart from skiing, skating, shopping, and sex.

Reed looked down at her, either not noticing or not caring that he now had Bailey and Stacie's attention as well. "We can do whatever you want."

Caroline could literally feel the silence after Reed's quietly spoken offer. She flashed him a quick smile and then looked over at the women, taking in their surprised expressions. "What am I missing?" Caroline asked no one in particular.

Stacie playfully fanned herself and looked at Reed in wonder. "Just never seen him in action before, that's all. Potent."

Bailey agreed solemnly and glanced at her phone again. "Luke's back. Gotta go!" She hopped off her perch and headed for the door with an absent wave.

Stacie waved after her. "Her husband does search and rescue. He's been gone a few days and she tries to be there to meet him when he gets home."

"Wow. No kidding." Caroline thought about that for a moment. "I'm not sure I could handle that."

Stacie bobbed her head slowly. "Me either. But she handles it well. She handles Luke well. I always say everyone has a perfect partner. They're a good match."

Caroline smiled. She liked the idea of that. "A perfect partner." She nodded. "I think so too."

Stacie moved over to let an employee slide their orders across the counter. "It was nice to meet you. Good to see you again, Reed. I hope you have a relaxing weekend!"

Reed nodded and ushered Caroline to a table in front of the windows overlooking the sidewalk. He pulled out a chair for her, and then took the seat across from her. She sipped her coffee and sighed.

"Well. What do you think?" he asked quietly.

"Mm. This coffee is amazing."

Reed was silent for a minute. Caroline looked up when he didn't answer. He was watching her, his eyes serious. "I meant about perfect partners." He looked down at his cup, gave it a half turn and looked at her again. "What is your perfect partner like, Carrie?"

Caroline put her coffee down and looked beyond him for a few beats. Such a personal question. Oh, she knew the answer. But would she scare him away if she offered the absolute truth? She pretended to consider the question.

"Well. My perfect partner would be a man."

Reed gave an exasperated laugh. "After last night, I would hope so."

Caroline gave a shrug and a tiny smile. "You never know."

"Enough, Carrie. Out with it. I want to know."

"He would be quiet. Smart. Calm." She thought about Reed in various meetings with his employees. "Alpha when he needs to be."

"Alpha?" He leaned forward.

"You know, in charge. Forceful, decisive."

Hearts in Training

"Decisive, huh?"

"Definitely. I don't want a partner I have to take care of." Caroline sipped her coffee.

"Like your parents?"

She conceded that without speaking. "And perceptive."

Reed grunted. "That's a tall order, Carrie."

She laughed at the almost forlorn way he said that. "Oh, there's more."

"I can hardly wait," he mumbled.

She gave him a sharp but teasing look. "Hey, you asked." She dropped her gaze from his face to his wide shoulders currently cased in a T-shirt and unbuttoned flannel shirt, down to his abs, hiding beneath that soft, fuzzy fabric. "He's also hot. Like abs, thighs--" she gave a fake sigh "--butt. Tall, dark and handsome. The whole package."

"Seriously?" Reed said a little too loudly making Caroline laugh.

They watched a minivan stop at the corner and then turn left onto Lilac Street. Caroline took a bite of the cinnamon muffin she'd ordered. Heavenly.

"Want to know what my perfect partner is like?" he offered quietly.

Yes! Her heart screamed. But outside she managed a funny, worried look. "I don't know. Do I?"

With a wicked smile, he leaned toward her and gave her a decisive nod. "You do."

Recognizing he was teasing her for her alpha comment, she laughed and waved a hand. "Go ahead. Tell me."

"She is highly organized. Maybe to the point of obsession." He paused and then smiled as if at some memory. "She's not intimidated by my attitude. Or by my position. She tells me what I need to hear instead of what she thinks I want to hear. She's refreshingly honest."

Caroline huffed a laugh. She might not soften the truth for him, but she was still intimidated by his presence. Reed Decatur was just so...much.

"My perfect partner sees me as a knight in shining armor sometimes, and as a shoulder to cry on at other times."

Dang it. That did it. Caroline could feel the prickling pressure of tears gathering behind her eyes. "You want a weepy woman?" she joked, hoping like hell she could keep her own tears at bay.

Reed's explanation was as straightforward as his expression. "I have a lot to offer, and not many chances to offer it. I like that I can be useful. Needed."

"I'm surprised women don't take advantage of that."

"Oh, they've tried." He seemed to think about that, or maybe how to explain. "I've gotten pretty good at telling the difference between clingy and someone who legitimately needs me." He leveled a look at her. "A woman who thinks she needs to face the world alone, I want to show her that she doesn't."

She nodded, unsure she could respond without giving away the perilous state of her emotions. The idea that Reed could offer support, even just a sounding board was so attractive that her heart nearly hurt from wanting it. She took a sip of her coffee and hoped it looked like she was considering his comments while she worked on keeping her voice steady. "Weepy and needy. Oh, and honest and bitchy." She shook her head. "Are you sure you can't do better than that?" Her translation was meant to tease him, but honestly, he was describing her, and she knew he could do better. He could have any woman in the world, a woman that wasn't saddled with the baggage of her own insecurities and her parents' poor decisions.

Reed studied her. "So sassy." He sat back and looked out the window for another moment. "Not that it would matter, but leggy blondes are sort of my thing."

Caroline smiled, pleased with the turn to something less emotional. "Legs, huh? See many leggy blonds in northern New Hampshire?"

"Only the one I brought with me. But this way I don't have to share her with anyone else."

She shook her head. Time for a change in subject before things got any deeper. At this rate, parting with him at the end of the weekend would be painful. "What should we do next?"

"Let's go check out the nature preserve. We can try out the skating and skiing. And then, when you're really good and cold, I'll take you back to the cottage and warm you by the fireplace." He wiggled his eyebrows.

"Mm. That sounds nice." She paused to sip her coffee. "I'm seriously going to miss having the use of a fireplace when we go home."

"I don't have a fireplace either." He lowered his chin. "Maybe I should find a new place."

Caroline laughed. "Don't be ridiculous. You have a nice place. I'm sure you can think of other ways to warm up."

He tilted his head. "I have a jacuzzi tub."

"There you go." She pursed her lips. "I have a radiator."

Reed laughed. "Nice." He appeared to think about that and nodded. "I could work with that."

Caroline rolled her eyes, but she appreciated the way he downplayed the chasm between their lifestyles. They gathered their trash to deposit on their way out. It felt completely natural when Reed's hand sought hers to twine their fingers together. They strolled along Main Street, peeking in the windows of the various shops and stopped to read the menu for Bailey's Restaurant.

"You could do a little Christmas shopping here. You're not going to find anything like this in New York." Reed leaned in to whisper in her ear.

"True." She paused in front of Fresh Cuts and looked at the poinsettias in the window. White and green and red, they preened in the limited light of the overcast day.

Hearts in Training

"I'm pretty familiar with the shops in town. What do you want to get your parents?"

Caroline pursed her lips. "Do they have jobs around here?"

"Sorry?"

She shook her head. "No, I'm sorry. That was rude of me."

Reed tugged her hand to stop and pulled her into the circle of his arms. "Neither of them work?"

"Nope. Neither of them."

"You're supporting both of them?"

Caroline blushed and looked away. "No, not totally. They both get assistance. But they tend to spend it faster than they receive it. So, I help."

He nodded and she was relieved to see that there was still no recrimination in his expression. She had enough for both of them.

"What were their careers?"

Caroline made a sarcastic sound. "My mom never did anything. She stayed home when I was little and then, when my father died, she didn't really bother to try the workforce."

"And Tony?"

"Um, I think he was a mechanic at the taxi garage."

Reed smiled. "Wouldn't they love to find jobs under the tree for them?"

"Yep. But I'm sure they'd rather have a fat

stocking full of cash."

He pulled her in close and hugged her. "Hmm. I like my idea better." He released her and pulled her along to check out more shops.

REED THOUGHT about Caroline's description of her perfect partner as they drove to the nature preserve that bisected Wolf Creek from the Maliut Indian Nation. He knew she felt the strong chemistry between them, but for him, it was more than attraction. He loved the way she instinctively knew what he needed. He loved the way she stood up to him. He loved the way he felt when he was with her, like he was ten feet tall and bullet-proof. He loved *her*.

He stole a glance at her in the passenger seat, looking out the window with a silly smile on her face. Her cheeks and the tip of her nose were still pink from walking around town. She had to be cold, but she never once complained. That was the thing about Caroline, she was tough. He hadn't been kidding when he'd said she needed him. Without a partner to share the load, she would go through her life taking on everyone else's burdens. Oh, she avoided talking about her family, but he knew they were a huge pressure on her.

He wouldn't have considered a perfect partner as someone who needed him, because she was right, needy wasn't really his thing. But Caroline was different. She needed a man who could take on her burdens, help her let them go, and be strong enough not to lean on her, too. If she wasn't careful, she'd follow in her mother's footsteps, loving a man that she would have to take care of. Reed shook his head. He would never be someone she had to take care of.

As if their future together was a foregone conclusion, he put the conversation aside and reached for her hand again. She was wearing gloves, yet her hand was still tiny in his. She looked at him and smiled, seemingly as content with the silence as he was.

He pulled into the parking lot and found a place near the large, lighted pond used for ice skating in the winter. There were a few couples and several children trying their hand at skating. Some were quite good, while others were doing some chaotic skate-walk moves that propelled them along in a choppy fashion.

"Skating first?"

Caroline looked at him with a challenge. "I'm game if you are."

"Oh, I'm always game." He winked.

Ten minutes later they were skate-walking along with the other couples, staying near the rail for safety. It didn't take long for Reed to see that Caroline was a natural on skates.

"Have you done a lot of skating?" he asked, holding her hand, now more for himself than to keep her on her feet.

She shrugged. "Some. My parents would bring me to Rockefeller at Christmastime when I was young. And I've done some roller-skating, too. But I used to dance, remember? This isn't that much different."

"I suppose not. Did you dance for a long time?"

Her expression turned wistful. "Yes. I started when I was five and danced all through college."

He calculated that. She couldn't have been out of college all that many years. "So, you've only recently stopped dancing?"

She shrugged again. "It's been a few years. I loved it, but it doesn't pay the bills. And it's so competitive."

Reed dismissed that. "You're one of the most driven people I know. That's not an excuse."

She stopped so suddenly that Reed slipped and landed not-so-gracefully against the split rail fence. "Maybe not. But it really doesn't pay the bills unless you're at the very top. And I couldn't do that and still be there for my mom when she was struggling."

Reed pulled her down on the fence beside him. "You've made a lot of sacrifices."

Caroline looked away, out toward the children spinning and laughing on the center of the ice. "I've made sacrifices. Yes. But I weighed them. I never did anything I didn't want to do. Sometimes it would be nice to have a little less," she paused, her head tipped to the side, "responsibility. But I get by." She smiled up at him. "Too much about me. Ready to try out skiing?"

Reed raised one eyebrow. "I'm a decent skier."

"Great. Then you can rescue me when I hit a tree halfway down the bunny hill," she told him, making

Hearts in Training

him laugh.

Caroline didn't exactly hit a tree, but she did need to be rescued after all. Three hours later they were once again in Reed's car and headed back to their cottage after dinner at Bailey's Restaurant. He'd noticed that Caroline favored her left foot as they'd walked back to the car.

"Are you sure you don't want someone to look at your leg?" Reed asked in the quiet darkness.

"I'm fine."

"Carrie." He tried a warning voice, but she only laughed.

"Really, Reed. I just twisted it funny when I fell. Nothing is broken and I'm sure I'll live."

He resisted the urge to roll his eyes the way she always did and tell her that she didn't have to be so strong. But then, he understood her. She probably didn't even realize she was doing it. She didn't yet know him well enough to realize that he would pamper her anyway. One way or another he'd see for himself whether she needed to see a doctor or not.

"I sure hope you live," he teased. "I'm getting kind of attached." When she didn't immediately respond, he added some levity. "Besides, it's going to be hard to explain your death at work."

She chuckled.

Parking beside the door, Reed told her to stay put and hurried around to her door in case she didn't listen to him and tried to get out by herself. Thankfully, she appeared to be in an accommodating mood and waited for him to help her out of the car. With a flourish and hoping to heavens that the small front porch wasn't slippery, he swept her up in his arms and carried her to the door. Even bulked up in heavy winter clothes, she hardly weighed a thing.

He unlocked and opened the door with one hand and then pushed it closed behind him with his foot before plopping her carefully on the couch. In a few minutes, a tiny fire was licking at the bottom of fresh logs and kindling. He was thankful he'd forgotten to turn the manual thermostat down before they'd left that morning, so the cottage was already a comfortable temperature.

"Put your foot up on the ottoman. I'm going to bring in our packages and lock the door. Then we can look at your injury."

"I'm fine," she called after him in a singsong voice that made him smile on his way back into the cold to retrieve their purchases.

Five minutes later he was back and freezing. It felt good to lock them in the little cottage. They were cozy and warm and had the whole night ahead of them.

Caroline had taken off her boot and was bending over her leg, prodding the skin around the inside of her ankle. He took a seat on the ottoman beside her elevated foot and gently took her foot in his cold hands. Her ankle was slightly swollen.

"Hurts now, doesn't it?" he whispered.

She was still bent toward her foot, bringing them nearly nose to nose. "It does now that my boot is off.

Your hands feel good."

"Ice would feel better," he reminded her.

"Your hands are like ice. Same thing."

He chuckled. "Want ice?"

She shook her head. "I'd rather have you."

Reed couldn't resist. He closed the last few inches between them and kissed her. Hard. He was so damned proud of her. "We have all night."

"We only have tonight," she whispered against his neck where she rested her head against his collarbone.

His heart landed somewhere down around his stomach. "I know." He listened to their mingled breathing for a few minutes. "It doesn't have to end when we go back."

Caroline inhaled and seemed to hold her breath for a minute. "But it won't be the same. We can't be ourselves together. We'll have to pretend that nothing has changed." She caressed the side of his face. "I don't know how I'm going to do that."

Reed thought about it. She was right. Until her contract was finished, they really shouldn't be seen as a couple. This weekend was a moment in time, a perfect moment that they would have to keep as a memory. But not something they could relive anytime they wanted.

"We can still be together sometimes in the evening. Or you could stay with me on weekends."

Caroline was already shaking her head. "Not

while I'm working for you. Someone would see us eventually and report it."

Reed's indignation was hot and instantaneous. "You don't work for me. Not technically."

"I know. But that isn't how it looks, and most of your employees won't know the difference."

"You live farther away. I'll come to your place." Now that their window of time was closing, he felt the same desperation she seemed to be feeling.

"My parents moved in with me, remember?"

"Damn." He put his forehead to hers. "We really do need to get them jobs for Christmas. Or an apartment."

She laughed again. "My contract is almost done. It won't be that long. A few months maybe."

Unacceptable. "I can't stay away from you that long!"

She leaned in and kissed him. "We have one more night."

"I'll take it."

Chapter 15

*R*eed woke before Caroline and was content to spend a precious few minutes just looking at her while she slept. Even with her hair spread around her and her mouth slightly open, she was the most beautiful woman he'd ever seen. In any other situation, he'd have said 'screw it' and gone public with their relationship. But he knew Caroline was right. The timing was wrong. Her career was very important to her, and an affair with a client could be detrimental for getting future contracts. As much as it would kill him to put their new relationship on the backburner, he would do whatever she needed to ensure her reputation was intact.

With two fingers, he gently smoothed her hair away from her cheek and caressed her jaw. Her eyes fluttered open and immediately cleared. She smiled and stretched and then reached out a hand to rub her fingers against the stubble on his face.

"Hi." Caroline scooted closer and pulled a leg up over his thigh.

"Hi yourself." He rubbed her thigh. "How's your ankle?"

"Hmm. Kinda hard to feel any pain right now," she teased.

Reed moved his arms around her back and pulled her tight against him. "Oh, I don't know. I'm feeling a little pain."

Caroline started to move away, and Reed tightened his hold. "If you move, you'll just make it worse." He nudged his erection against her belly.

"Ah, I see." She wiggled against him and then rolled fully on top of him. "Just one way to fix that, huh?"

He smiled. There were, in fact, many ways to fix that, and he'd take any of them as long as they involved being in bed with Caroline. Bringing his hands down to her hips, he let her have her way.

AN HOUR LATER they met Savannah and Daniel for breakfast at Beans and Bagels. Just like the day before, the conversation was easy and entertaining. It was impossible to feel uncomfortable around Reed's sister and her fiancé, but much too soon they were on the road, headed back to New York and their separate, busy lives.

They spent the first hour in silence, the radio playing quietly in the background of Caroline's thoughts.

Reed reached over and rested his hand on her thigh. "Should we talk about what comes next?"

Caroline tensed, hating to trade the peace of the weekend for thoughts of the future. "What comes next?"

He squeezed her thigh before returning his hand

to the steering wheel. "Well, for starters, are you planning to see other men? Keith? Ridley? Any of number of other men I've seen hit on you?" His hard voice gave her an idea what he thought of that.

Caroline turned to face him. The idea of spending time with any other man was ludicrous and made her feel a little ill. She imagined him out with another woman and her heart broke a little. Was that what he wanted? What he expected?

"Um. Well, I don't exactly have time to date. So", she dragged out the word, "that would be no for me." Reed frowned at her and turned back to the road. She knew her answer had been evasive, and he deserved something more. She swallowed her pride and admitted the truth hoping it wouldn't scare him away. "I don't want to date anyone else." She drew in a breath and put a hand on his arm. "But I also know that you have to attend a lot of events and you can't very well attend them alone. I don't expect you to live like a monk just because we spent the weekend together, Reed. I understand if you want to go out with other women."

Reed turned incredulous eyes on her. "I don't want to go out with other women, Carrie. And you know I'm perfectly happy skipping all those events."

"You can't do that! It's your job to represent the company. You happen to be the hot new CEO, remember?"

He rolled his eyes. "A description I didn't choose." He shrugged. "Then I'll go to things alone. It's really not a big deal."

She thought about that. Would it play for or

against him to attend public functions alone? "Decatur Industries really needs a publicity department, Reed."

He squinted at her for a second. "Where did that come from?"

"I'm trying to decide if it would be better for your image to show up with a date or alone. If you had a publicity team, they could give you direction."

"On my personal life?" He frowned again. "I don't think so, Carrie. My personal life is off-limits."

Caroline sighed. "Do you know you only call me Carrie when you're irritated with me? They won't control your personal life. They'll just give you pointers to help you manage your reputation."

"I don't need someone to give me pointers." He sighed too. "And I call you Carrie when we're having a personal conversation. It's a pet name."

"A pet name you only use when you're irritated," she mumbled. She really needed to get the conversation back on track. "I'm just saying that I understand if you need to invite a woman to an event." When he frowned again, she rushed to add, "I won't like it. But I'll understand."

"Well, let me go on record and say that I won't understand if you show up with another guy."

Caroline bit her lip to prevent a smile. His jealousy was flattering, and completely unnecessary.

"I'm sorry," he added. "I should be all noble and say I understand, but I won't. I'll be jealous as hell, and I don't think I'll be polite about it."

Despite his dark mood, the image of him confronting her date made her laugh aloud. She shook her head while he gave her the side-eye. "I kind of like that, actually. *So* alpha."

Reed seemed to relax beside her. He put his hand back on her thigh. Caroline covered it with her own. "Let's just take it one day at a time, okay?" She looked out the window, her mood sinking the closer they got to the city. "We'll see where this goes," she whispered. He must have heard her because he squeezed her thigh.

REED DOUBLE parked in front of Caroline's building and turned to face her, resting one wrist on the steering wheel, his other hand snaking behind her neck in a move she'd already become accustomed to. "Last chance to change your mind." He lowered his voice. "Come home with me."

Caroline was sorely tempted by the invitation, but she knew her reasons for keeping their relationship private were good ones. "You know that's a bad idea."

He brushed a thumb across her cheek and then hauled her in for a heated kiss. "Then let me carry your bags inside."

Before she could remind him that her mom and Tony were probably inside, he was helping her out of the car and hauling her bags out of the trunk. Bags over his left shoulder, he wrapped his right arm around her to help her hobble to the elevator.

"You know I can manage, right?"

Reed slanted her a glance. "I'm being gallant here. You really should have it X-rayed. Maybe get crutches, too."

Reed let Caroline lead the way to her apartment on the third floor. She paused before reaching the door. She could already hear her television blaring from the hallway. Her mom and Tony were in her apartment.

Reed tipped his head toward the door. "Sounds like they're home. No hanky-panky by the radiator tonight, huh?"

She shook her head, feeling more miserable by the minute. There was no way he'd leave without meeting her family. Humiliation washed over her. He had such a nice, normal family. How could she explain her own overly dependent, unfiltered, shockingly unsophisticated family?

She closed her eyes and whispered. "I had a great time this weekend." She opened her eyes and met his gaze. "Truly. It was life changing for me." She gave a short, quiet laugh. "For more than the obvious reasons." She brushed her hair back and reached for the larger of her bags. "I've got this. You should get back to your car before it gets towed."

Reed stared at her and she knew she wouldn't be able to change his mind. "Not a chance," he told her. He opened the door with his free hand, leaving Caroline no option but to follow him into her apartment.

"I guess we're doing this," she muttered.

"We sure are," he told her solemnly.

"THERE YOU are!" Heather chirped, and then choked on a startled breath. "Oh!"

Tony looked up from where he was lounging sideways on Caroline's loveseat, and swung his feet down with a thud. With a grunt, he rolled to a standing position and tucked in his shirt. Caroline's mother stepped forward, a wide grin spreading across her face. "Carrie, who's this?"

Reed offered his hand to her mother. "Reed Decatur, ma'am."

Heather positively beamed now. Caroline said a silent prayer that her mother would remember her filter.

Heather clasped Reed's hand in both of hers and held tight. "Heather Trumbull. Caroline's mother," she added unnecessarily. Tony ambled up beside her and held out a hand as well.

"Tony DeLuca. Carrie's step-father."

Caroline frowned at him. "Not exactly," she mumbled. Marriage had not been part of his relationship with her mother.

Tony smiled, unconcerned by her correction. "Close enough, Carrie, close enough."

Reed released the older man's hand and took a subtle step back to stand beside Caroline. "It's nice to meet you both."

"I suppose you've heard all about us." Heather paused, but Reed didn't respond. "We're so proud of Carrie. I bet she's turning your company on its ear!"

Caroline tapped her foot on the floor lightly, wishing it would open up and swallow her now. Reed, she noticed, seemed content enough to witness her embarrassment.

"She certainly keeps me on my toes."

Tony nodded in understanding. "She's a feisty one." Tony winked her at her. "With her fancy degree and all, we figure she's earned it though."

Caroline wanted to shove Reed out the door to spare him from any further description of her. Or better yet, shove her mother and Tony out and keep Reed there. Assuming he still acknowledged her after this embarrassing display.

"Well, I hope your weekend was everything you hoped it would be." Heather told him with a theatrical wink.

"It was a business trip, Ma," Caroline lied.

"It was very nice to meet you." Heather waved a hand and pulled Tony back to the living room to give them some privacy.

"Likewise," Reed answered.

Caroline stepped closer to Reed, giving her mother and Tony her back. Keeping her voice low but professional in case her mother and Tony could still hear, she looked up at Reed. "Thank you for carrying my bags up."

Reed's eyes softened as he looked down at her, reflecting the same emotions she was feeling. She wasn't ready for their time alone to end.

"And for this weekend." Her eyes tracked

toward the couch where Heather and Tony were once again seated in front of the television. "I'm sure you can see now how different that was for me."

Reed squeezed her hand. "We'll talk tomorrow."

She nodded. Right now, she was wishing she'd accepted his offer to go back to his place instead.

"Goodnight Carrie," he whispered.

She growled at the use of her nickname and closed the door behind him. She could have sworn he heard his answering chuckle. She rested her forehead against the closed door for a moment and then let out a frustrated breath and turned around. She hitched her bags over her shoulder and stomped through the living room to her bedroom.

Chapter 16

Caroline made it to the office an hour earlier than usual. She knew she'd regret it at the end of the day when everyone else was leaving and she was still there, but there was no way she was ready to deal with her mother and Tony that morning. She'd gotten ready as quietly as possible and snuck out of her apartment before the sun had even come up.

She grabbed a large coffee and headed to her office. She didn't strictly have anything that needed to be done this morning, so she leaned against the window and gazed out over the hazy Brooklyn skyline. A text dinged on her phone.

You're early today. Wanna come up?

She should have anticipated that Reed would already be in the office. One of these days she was going to remember to ask how he always knew when she was in the building.

Need me already? She texted back.

The dots that indicated he was typing a response seemed to play forever before just a single word came through. *Yes*

She snatched up her laptop, phone, and coffee and rode the silent elevator to the eighteenth floor. Even the canned music didn't start this early. Jamie wasn't in yet, so Caroline let herself into Reed's office. He was standing behind his desk watching the sun rise over the same buildings she'd just been looking at.

Hearing her approach, he turned and examined her. "How's your ankle?"

It was still sore, and she knew her choice of shoes would make it nothing short of agony by the end of the day. Instead of sharing all that, she shrugged. "It's fine."

He didn't look like he believed her, but he let it go. "Want to talk about last night?"

A million responses flooded her mind, but she settled on the truth. "Not particularly."

A smile touched his lips. "It wasn't so bad, was it? I enjoyed meeting your family."

Caroline tried not to gape at him. He looked serious. "They're ridiculous!" She closed her eyes and tried for some tact. "Thank you. They are very different from your family. I should have prepared you."

Reed squinted at her. "They're not aliens. Did I embarrass you?"

"Of course not."

"I meet all kinds of people. Our differences are what make life interesting."

She considered him for a moment. "Thank you for not judging me."

He pulled her closer and leaned down to whisper,

"Consider me a judgment-free zone."

Caroline melted against him, loving the feel of his hard chest beneath his tailored suit. She loved the fact that she now knew what lie under his perfect wardrobe. Seen, tasted, touched. Unconsciously, she slid two fingers between the buttons on his shirt, seeking the heated skin beneath. She could feel Reed's heartbeat and his indrawn breath.

"Two can play at your game, you know," he whispered into her hair.

"Not at the office," she breathed as much to remind herself as him. She tried to take a step back, but he held tight.

He lifted her onto the edge of his desk and moved her knees apart to stand between them. "Not while we're working. No." He made a show of checking his watch. "But it's not business hours yet."

Caroline smiled in response to his own impish smile. Making love on his desk was one of their mutual fantasies. Was it time to check that one off the list?

Letting her shoes fall to the floor, she hitched a leg behind Reed's knees and drew him closer. She could already feel the evidence of his interest, but she wanted him to experience hers. With one hand she released the single clasp holding the bodice of her sapphire wrap dress closed letting the silky fabric gape across her chest, and then leaned back on her elbows knowing that Reed would happily take it from there.

Like a child offered a gift, Reed gazed at her,

from her eyes down to the cleavage exposed by her gaping dress. His interest was so intense that she could feel his eyes on her. Slowly, so slowly, he moved aside the fabric to expose her breasts, covered in a lacy black bra. He touched her reverently, as if it had been years since he'd seen her like this, rather than mere hours.

Continuing his exploration, he untied the silk tie that fastened her skirt and let the fabric fall away. She was exposed from head to toe, only her black underwear barring her from being completely nude. Amazingly, she didn't feel embarrassed laid out on his desk before him. No, what she felt was adored. Treasured. Reed's hands heated a path from her breasts to the juncture of her thighs, paused a moment to tease before starting a path back up to her shoulders. He pulled each strap down gently, kissing and massaging as he unclasped her bra and paused to look at her.

"So perfect," he whispered.

A second of clarity made Caroline pull Reed up from where he was kissing a path down her ribcage. He looked at her questioningly.

"The door?"

He hovered over her and planted a kiss on her lips. "Locked the second you walked in. Now, where was I?" Levering away again he moved back to continue his assault against her senses.

Thirty minutes later they were redressed and seated across from each other, once again collaborators on a business project. Reed smoothed a hand across his desk. Caroline raised an eyebrow in question.

One side of his lips quirked upward. "I'll never think of my desk the same way again."

"Neither will I."

Reed rested his forearms on his desk and leaned forward. "About your family." Her light-hearted mood faded. "Anything I can do?"

She tilted her head. "Maybe look the other way if you see me camping on the sofa in my office."

He seemed to consider that for a second. "I have no doubt you'd really do it. I can't imagine my parents moving into my apartment and making themselves at home." He tapped a few keys on his computer. "I'll get you a key to my penthouse." He held up a hand to halt her when she tried to interrupt. "I understand your worries that we'll be found out. If it helps, consider it as just for emergencies."

Caroline stared at him, so many emotions going through her, but first and foremost was love. "Thank you."

Worried that she'd get carried away and speak the thought aloud, she cleared her throat and brought them back to business. They reviewed the list of training and classes she'd developed with HR. Reed added some suggestions and helped her prioritize which should be offered first before signing off on the project. As she stood to leave, she saw Reed hit the button to unlock the door. Not a minute later, Jamie poked her head in to say good morning. If she was surprised to find Caroline already there, she didn't comment on it. Caroline decided that one day she'd find the courage to ask Jamie just how much she saw and heard. But then again, maybe she didn't want to know.

"Good morning, Jamie." Caroline smiled at the older woman and turned back to Reed. "I'll update my report with your suggestions and have it ready to present to the committee. I can probably have it for them later today so that it's ready for your next meeting."

Reed tilted his head toward Jamie. "Can you get a meeting scheduled for this afternoon to review Caroline's report for the training department?"

Both Caroline and Jamie gaped at him. Caroline spoke first. "It doesn't have to be today, Reed."

He looked at her, his brows drawn down. "The sooner the better."

It would have been unprofessional to roll her eyes, so Caroline resisted the urge. Instead, she smiled at Jamie. "It really can wait until later in the week. I know Mondays are hard to schedule."

Jamie looked back and forth between them, her knowing expression conveying that she understood the unspoken dynamics between them. She nodded. "I'll see what I can do. It may not be today, but I'll get something on the calendar for early in the week."

Reed pursed his lips but nodded his agreement. "Thank you."

"I need to get going on this," she indicated her laptop, "so I'm heading down to my office." Caroline took a few steps toward the door, following where Jamie had just left.

"Carrie, wait." Reed's voice was low. He met her at the door and pushed it nearly closed, shutting them off from the larger outer room beyond.

"Reed. You can't call me Carrie here." She kept her voice low, hoping Jamie couldn't hear them.

He ignored her reminder and pulled her tight against him for a lingering kiss. Caroline let herself relax against the hard planes of his chest, savoring his smell and the comfort of his arms before easing away. She looked up at him and smiled. She brushed her thumb against his lips to wipe her lipstick from his mouth. Oh, this game was dangerous!

"See you later," he told her with a crooked grin.

Caroline spent the rest of the morning in meetings with Human Resources, interviewing candidates for various positions in the new department, as well as some quiet time spent updating her training proposal and creating a proposal for a publicity team. By afternoon she was feeling quite accomplished. If she could get the right people in the new training roles, it was possible

her contract could be finished by Christmas. She turned to her windows and smiled.

Her smile faded as she considered what the completion of her contract really meant for her life. She'd need to find a new contract. Normally at this stage, she'd already have another job lined up, ready to shift straight into a new project. Without something waiting in the wings, would she be able to afford not only her rent, but supporting her family as well? She had savings, but it would be tight-even tighter than it was already.

Hearts in Training

On the other hand, there was Reed. With her contract for Decatur Industries finished they would be free to have an actual, normal relationship. The idea was a huge bright spot on her horizon. But she wasn't exaggerating when she said she didn't have time to date. When she was working on a project, she gave it her all and that meant long hours and near mental exhaustion. Could she still give her job one hundred percent and still have something left to offer a man like Reed Decatur? The idea both thrilled and scared her.

Her desk phone rang, bringing her back to the present. Her caller ID showed that Jamie was calling her.

"Hi Jamie. What can I do for you?"

"Hi Caroline. Reed asked that I make an appointment for you at a nearby clinic."

Caroline's heart jolted. "Ah." She swallowed, unsure how to respond without giving too much away. What must Jamie think of her now? "Did he say why?"

She could hear in Jamie's voice that she was suppressing laughter. "To get your foot X-rayed, of course. He said you mentioned that you injured it over the weekend. I noticed you were limping a little this morning, so I took the liberty of getting you an appointment with my favorite doctor."

"Oh! You are so sweet, Jamie." She breathed a sigh of relief. "I did twist it this weekend and I haven't had time to have it looked at."

"Well, I emailed you the time and location. I'll

make sure there's a car downstairs to drive you." Jamie paused, and when she spoke again her voice was motherly. "And for the record, dear, Wolf Creek has an excellent physician. You really shouldn't have waited so long to have it looked at."

Jamie outright laughed at Caroline's indrawn breath.

"Does everyone know where I was this weekend?" Caroline wondered.

"I certainly hope not!" Jamie laughed. "But I follow Savannah on some of her social media and she posted some pictures this weekend of the both of you."

Caroline's stomach took a dive. She hadn't considered that people at Decatur Industries would know Savannah. "Oh."

"Oh, don't worry. Besides, I've known Reed pretty much his whole life. There isn't much he can get by me." She paused. "You're good for him and, not that you need it, but I approve wholeheartedly of you two seeing each other."

Tears sprang to Caroline's eyes. She cleared her throat. "Thank you, Jamie. We both feel it's best to keep things quiet until my contract is up."

"I understand." Instantly, Jamie's voice was all business again. "Make sure you get to that appointment. It won't do you any good to pretend your foot isn't bothering you. Neither of us are going to let it go."

Caroline laughed. "I believe you. I'll be there."

"Good."

CAROLINE MADE good on her promise to go to the appointment and headed down to the lobby a few minutes early. As Jamie had told her, a car was waiting for her by the curb. She instantly recognized Reed's driver when he got out to help her into the car. She smiled and nodded a greeting to the red-haired executive, Elizabeth as they passed on the sidewalk. Elizabeth nodded, but her greeting wasn't exactly friendly. Barely civil might have been a better way to describe it.

"Hi Mason." Caroline greeted the man as he slid behind the wheel and prepared to pull out into the afternoon snarl of Lower Manhattan traffic.

"Hi there, Miss Trumbull."

She laughed. "Just Caroline. I feel old when people address me so formally."

He gave her a half-smile in the mirror. "No one is going to mistake you for being old."

"Thank you." She smiled back and turned her attention to checking emails on her phone. More bills from her mother and Tony, several Christmas ads, nothing exciting on her personal email. She switched over to her company email and perused those. She tried to give some serious thought to drumming up a new contract, but her heart just wasn't in it. The truth was that she loved this company. The people were wonderful, and the new program was one she was particularly proud of. This was a place she could see herself in twenty years from now.

Before she could delve into the images of herself and Reed, twenty years older and working side-by-side, she felt the car slow and pull up to the curb of an attractive brick building.

"Here we are, Caroline." Mason half-turned to address her. "Just stay put for a sec, I'm going to help you out."

Caroline reached for the door handle. "I got myself to work this morning just fine, Mason."

He shook a finger at her. "Maybe so, but you didn't do it on my watch."

She laughed. "Okay then."

He was out of the car and helping her to the sidewalk in no time. He even ushered her up the four steps and through the front door. He handed her a card with his name and number. "Text me when you're wrapping up and I'll come around and get you again." He gave her a stern look before heading back outside to find a place to park.

One X-ray and lots of poking and prodding revealed that her foot was sprained. The doctor showed her how to wrap it properly and then a technician fitted her for crutches. An hour later, Mason had her back in the car and on their way to the office.

"Sure you don't just want me to take you home, Caroline? You could put that foot up and get some rest."

She was shaking her head before he'd even finished. "I'm good. I've been walking on it for two days already. I'll live."

Mason looked at her in the mirror. "You're a tough one. I'll give you that."

The crutches caused a stir back in the office and Caroline spent quite a bit of time explaining them to co-workers as she hobbled from the lobby to her office. As soon as she was seated behind her desk, she kicked off her shoe and sighed. She would have to take a taxi home now because there was no way she'd be able to use the crutches to walk the ten blocks to her apartment. She was thankful for the care, but the taxi was an expense she couldn't afford right now.

An instant message popped up on her computer from Reed.

What's the prognosis?

She was surprised he didn't already know. *Hasn't your network of spies told you? Full amputation at the knee.*

Three laughing emojis floated across her screen. *You would still be sexy as hell.*

She smiled. *Just a sprain. Alternate heat and ice and keep it wrapped. Use crutches. Oh, and I've been banned from skiing.*

The doctor banned you from skiing?

I banned me from skiing. It's very clearly bad for my health.

OK, from now on nothing but sitting in front of a fireplace for you.

She sent a winking emoji. *Yes, that's much safer.*

Caroline worked another few hours on the

classes to be offered in her training division. Deciding it would be better to catch a taxi before it became too late, she packed up her stuff and headed for the elevator.

Ten blocks and too many dollars later, Caroline maneuvered her bag and crutches out of the tiny taxi and out onto the sidewalk in front of her building. Two men huddled near the stairs, smoking. Alert, but not concerned, Caroline sorted out her crutches and hiked her bags more securely on her shoulder. The taxi peeled away in search of another fare, leaving Caroline on the stoop.

Out of the corner of her eye, she saw one of the men drop his cigarette and stub it out on the sidewalk and then hurry past her to stand in front of the door. She gave him an absent-minded smile. It was nice of him to get the door. She awkwardly climbed the steps and stood to the side to let the other man join the first at the door. She made eye-contact and hitched in a breath. What she saw looking back at her was nothing short of pure evil. She glanced around quickly, noting with a sick feeling that she was alone outside the building.

She reached for the door handle and so did one of the men. His hand collided with hers and settled there, firm and unmovable.

"Excuse me." She tried to pull her hand away, but he held tight.

"You Tony DeLuca's daughter?"

Panic gripped her, but she was able to answer truthfully. "No."

Hearts in Training

He waved that away. "You know 'im, right? He's livin' with you."

She focused on breathing normally and staying aware of the man standing just beneath her on the stoop. She shook her head in answer.

The man gave her a frustrated shove. "Don't lie to me! I know you know 'im. Don't even matter what the relationship is. He owes us money and we're here to collect."

The danger nearly equaled Caroline's frustration. "How much does he owe you?"

The man's grip lessened on her hand just a little. "Thirteen grand."

She kept a poker face while she took that in. Thirteen thousand dollars! Even if she wanted to bail Tony out, she didn't have that much. What on earth could he have gotten into for that kind of money?

"I know where he lives. Let me go see if he's home. If he is, I'll send him out." Caroline knew it was a long shot, but short of screaming for help, she couldn't think of any other way to get him to let her go.

"Good try, sweetheart. But I ain't got a guarantee that you're even gonna talk to him for me."

"I can try to call him."

The man looked her up and down. She wished she was wearing pants instead of a dress. She felt vulnerable. And scared.

"Maybe we can work out our own deal."

213

She exhaled slowly and worked to contain her growing dread. "I don't think so."

Anger made the man bunch up. He was instantly taller, and much more menacing. Caroline felt the man on the step below crowd closer to her. Fear gave her a strange sort of clarity. She braced herself on one crutch and prepared to take a swing at the men with the other. It would be a paltry defense, but it might buy her time to get her cell phone, or yell for help.

She spotted the older man that lived below her in 2B coming down the sidewalk with a bag of groceries. She feared for his safety, but at the same time wondered if she could count on him to call for help.

The nasty little man on the step below her made a grab for her so she swung out her crutch as hard as she could. It connected with his sternum, knocking him down several steps onto the sidewalk below. Just as she was bringing the crutch back around to take a swing at the man blocking her from the door, his fist connected with her cheek just below her eye. She fell back, hitting her head against the brick corner of the doorway. Before she lost her balance, she was able to get one good smack on the guy with her crutch.

She heard her neighbor run toward them. "I've called the police!" He shouted. The two thugs took off and the downstairs neighbor leaned over her and helped her to sit up. Caroline straightened her dress around her legs and pulled her coat closer around her. The cement steps were freezing and so many different parts of her were hurting that she couldn't take stock of them all.

"Thanks." Her teeth chattered so hard she wasn't sure the gentleman could hear her. She cleared her throat. "Did you really call the police?"

"I didn't have time. I can call them now though. I wanted to be sure you were alright first."

Caroline nodded. "I'm fine." She nearly smiled at that. She'd been fine after a sprained foot, too. Maybe Reed was right. She didn't have to be strong all the time. She dropped her head into her hands and took deep breaths until some of the shaking subsided. She was so angry that she didn't think she could face Tony right now, and so scared that she wasn't sure her apartment would feel safe, either. The urge to cry overwhelmed her and she gave in to it.

"Are you sure you weren't hurt?" The man patted her knee and indicated her crutches. "Seems like you were already pretty banged up."

"No. I really am fine. I just need to sit here a bit longer."

He nodded as if that made perfect sense. "Is there anyone I can call for you?"

She started to say no, felt the throbbing in her face and changed her mind. She was going to have a bruise by morning and no matter how much she tried to downplay it, she knew Reed would never let it go. "I have a friend I can call."

The neighbor got to work retrieving her bags as well as his own bag of groceries while Caroline dialed Reed's number. As if he had a sixth sense, he seemed to know something was wrong.

"Are you okay?" he asked in lieu of a proper greeting.

"No-yes. I'm okay. But can you come get me?" Her voice cracked. The pressure of holding herself together suddenly seemed impossible. "Please hurry."

"I'm already on the elevator, Carrie. Are you at your apartment? What's happened?"

She took a breath. He was on his way. "Yes. I'm in front of my building. I was attacked by some-" She hesitated, not wanting the neighbor to hear her explanation. "I'll tell you later."

"Are you hurt?" She could hear the concern in his voice.

"I'm not hurt badly. I just…I just want to go somewhere safe." She didn't even care that she was crying in front of both Reed and her neighbor now. She was freaked out and cold, and every single part of her was sore. "I just need a safe place to go."

Reed made a sound like a groan. "I can't get there fast enough. But I'm on my way. Are you safe right now?"

She nodded and then realized he wouldn't be able to see that. "Yes. My neighbor ran the guys off. He's here with me now."

"Tell him to wait until I get there," Reed ordered.

Caroline looked around at the neighbor who was watching her silently from a few feet away. He was holding her laptop bag and purse, clearly attempting

Hearts in Training

to give her some privacy for her conversation. "I don't think he's planning to leave me."

"Good. I'm just a few blocks away now. Hang tight."

Caroline nodded to her neighbor. "My friend is on his way to get me."

The gentleman nodded and stepped forward to set her bags on the bottom step near her feet. "I'll be happy to wait here with you until your friend gets here," he assured her. "It's chilly outside tonight. Are you warm enough?"

She attempted to smile but that made her cheek and scalp hurt. "The cold is probably good for me. It's like putting ice on a wound, right?"

The man chuckled and sat down beside her. "That's a good way of looking at it." He squinted at her in the dim light. "Are you sure you don't want me to call the police? I didn't get a good look at those losers, but maybe you can tell a little more?"

"Not much. They were here looking for someone they thought I knew. When I refused to cooperate one of the men lost his temper. You pretty much saw the rest." She closed her eyes and let out a breath. "I'm so thankful you got here when you did. It could have been much worse."

He nodded again. "It sure could have."

They both looked up in time to see Reed's car slide up to the curb and come to a quick stop. He nearly bolted from the driver's seat in a rush to see for himself that she wasn't injured.

With a polite nod to the neighbor, Reed crouched in front of Caroline and touched her chin. With two fingers, he tilted her face to both sides. She knew when he spotted the bruise blooming under her eye. His face went cold and angry. He stood, and together with the neighbor, helped Caroline stand on her crutches. Knowing that Reed was watching her, she tried not to flinch as she took a few steps toward his waiting car. She knew the car would be warm and safe and so she left her things on the step for Reed to carry and picked her way across the sidewalk to the passenger side of the car.

She saw Reed offer her neighbor his card and then shake his hand. The man gestured to her bags, so Reed flung them over his shoulder and stowed them in the trunk before making sure she was settled. Once her seatbelt was hooked, he sped back to the Decatur building. They didn't speak during the drive, but several times Caroline could feel his worried gaze on her. He reached over and took her hand, holding it gently until they pulled into his spot in the underground parking garage.

"I should have asked before. Do you need to go to the hospital?"

"No." She tipped her head back against the headrest. Her muscles were shaky, and she was tired. "I'm sure I'll be-"

"Don't say fine." Reed turned off the car and came around to help her out. He pulled her crutches from the backseat and handed them to her. She took a few steps with the crutches before Reed stopped her. "Leave them here and I'll come back for them.

Hearts in Training

I've got you." He took the crutches and leaned them against the back of his car. Turning back to her, he picked her up and carried her to the elevator. Inside, he set her down but pulled her back into his arms so that she could lean against him. Caroline didn't complain. She was exhausted and letting Reed take care of her felt good.

The elevator didn't stop between the parking garage and the penthouse, for which Caroline was grateful. She was sure she looked like hell, and there was no way she'd be able to stand on her own without crutches. She was still shaking too badly.

When the elevator doors slid open, Reed took her back into his arms and carried her through his bedroom into the attached master bath, with its huge sunken jet tub. He set her gently on the tiled side of the tub and stepped back to look at her. She stared back at him, too tired and shaken to care about her appearance.

"I'll go down and get the rest of your stuff and I'll be right back. Are you okay in here?"

She nodded. He leaned in and kissed her lightly. "Be right back."

Caroline waited until she heard the door close and then stood and slowly limped to the mirror above the sink. Her face was a mess. Her makeup was smeared, but worse than that was the bruise on her cheek. Nothing short of Hollywood makeup was going to cover that up for a while. She gingerly checked her scalp where she'd hit her head on the building to see if it was bleeding. Her skin was tender, but she didn't find any blood.

She untied the tie at her waist, letting the dress slide from her shoulders to the floor. Would she ever be able to wear the dress again without thinking of tonight? She wasn't sure. She turned to examine her back and shoulders in the mirror as best she could. She could see faint bruises around a scrape on her right shoulder where she also hit the corner brick.

Reed came in as she was twisting in front of the mirror. He stood back for a minute and then circled around her, his fingers brushing here and there where he found bruises. "Your elbow is scraped." He put a finger lightly above the spot to let her know. "And your backside. Here." Another touch. He stood behind her and put his arms protectively around her, folding them over her chest. He rested his chin on her head. Their eyes met in the mirror.

"Want to take a bath?"

Caroline knew he could feel her shaking, but he didn't comment on it and she was glad. "That would be nice."

"I'll get you something to wear." He paused in the doorway. "Have you eaten?"

"No."

He gave her another once-over. "I'll give you a little privacy. We can talk later."

Caroline filled the tub with hot water and located a bottle of Reed's body wash. It had a masculine scent, but she didn't care. In the morning she would deal with the fact that she'd come here without a change of clothes, or even without anything but her laptop and purse. Maybe she could get up early enough to sneak out of the building before other employees started to arrive. She got into the tub and groaned. The warm water felt heavenly after sitting on the frozen sidewalk outside her apartment building. She leaned back and closed her eyes, letting the water lap against her chest and neck.

A light knock on the door startled her eyes open. "Just checking on you."

Caroline sat up and turned to look at him. He was standing in the doorway, far enough away that he couldn't see her naked body. It was unnecessary since he'd already kissed every inch of her, but she appreciated the gesture anyway.

"You can come in." She tried to give him her usual teasing smile. "There's nothing here you haven't seen."

He was at the side of the tub in two strides. "True, but that pleasure is still new to us. I won't assume that means I can walk in on you whenever I want."

Caroline thought about that. "Thank you." They held eye contact for several seconds.

"Want some bubbles?" Reed asked playfully.

"You have bubbles?"

With one corner of his mouth tipped up, he pressed a button to activate the whirlpool jets. The sensation of water rushing around and over her sore muscles was exactly what she needed at that moment. She closed her eyes and sank lower into the water with another groan.

Reed chuckled and rubbed the top of her head. "If you keep that up, I'm liable to join you, invited or not."

"Would we both fit?" Caroline opened one eye to look at him.

Reed stood and moved toward the door. "Don't tempt me. You've had a long day and I'm trying to be noble here. I have dinner ready for you."

Now that the terrible shaking had stopped and she was once again warm and safe, she realized she really was hungry. She let the water drain and toweled off. Reed had left her a T-shirt and a pair of jersey knit pants. They were too big, of course, but they were clean, soft, and they smelled like him. She pulled the light fabric over her head and hugged it to herself.

She padded into the main room of the penthouse and spotted Reed sitting at the kitchen island, a book in one hand and a long neck beer in the other. "Something smells good," she remarked.

He put the book down and swiveled to look at her. "Nice. I think I like those clothes better on you."

She chuckled. "Thanks." She smoothed the T-shirt down over her waist. "Maybe I'll keep them. To remind me of you." She took a seat beside him at the counter and peered into the containers spread in front of her. "You had Chinese delivered?"

"There's a little place across the street that I love. It's my version of comfort food," he admitted.

"Mine is nachos, but this is great, too." She loaded a plate with selections from each of the cartons. "Thank you." She dipped her head for a second. "I've been saying that a lot today."

Reed was silent until she looked at him. "You don't need to thank me. I'm glad you called me. I'm proud of you."

Caroline laughed. "Believe it or not, I thought about your reaction to seeing these bruises as I was sitting there on the sidewalk and I knew I had to call you first."

He nodded once. "You did the right thing." He let her eat for a few minutes, but she knew he was dying to question her. Just thinking about it made her queasy. She pushed her plate away and turned to face him.

"When I got out of the taxi there were two men hanging out by the door to my building."

Reed stood and pulled her over to the sofa and then settled her down beside him. Once she was cuddled up to his side, he waved a hand for her to continue.

"I didn't think much of them at first. They were kind of huddled in a corner, smoking." But as soon as I reached the door one of them blocked me. He asked if I was Tony's daughter and when I said I wasn't, he threatened me. Apparently, Tony owes someone a lot of money. I guess they thought if they roughed me up, he'd pay up."

Reed must have felt her worry for he squeezed her tighter against him. The arm around her shoulders dropped to her waist to caress her hip. "Did they know you? Did they use your name?"

She thought about that. "No. They didn't even know for sure that I was related to him."

"Did they say how much he owes?"

She swallowed and whispered, "Thirteen thousand."

Reed let out a breath. "Wow."

Caroline let her head drop down on his shoulder. "Yeah. Wow."

"Do you know what he's getting into? Gambling? He's not doing something illegal, is he?"

"No, I don't think he's doing anything illegal. Gambling is a good guess, but I honestly can't say. I've always tried to keep him at arms-length, you know?"

They sat quietly for a few minutes. When Caroline started feeling sleepy, she moved out of Reed's arms. "I'm falling asleep on you. If you want to point me to a room, I'll get out of your way."

Reed gave her a tender smile. "What if I point you to my room?"

Caroline yawned. "Are you sure? I'm not going to be exciting company tonight."

"You might be more comfortable knowing you're not alone tonight, Carrie. I know I'll feel better having you near."

"Then, I'll take it. As tired as I am, I'm not about to be picky."

Reed pulled her onto his lap and stood. "Then I'm doubly glad you called me tonight." He turned off lights as he went through each of the rooms, at last settling Caroline on the huge bed in his room. Pulling the blankets up around her, he tucked her in and bent to kiss her forehead. "I'm going to clean up the kitchen and make a few calls. Go ahead and get some sleep, sweetheart."

Chapter 17

*R*eed closed the door quietly and returned to the kitchen to pack away the leftover food and clear the dishes. Once that was complete, he grabbed his cell and called his sister.

"Angela, I need your help."

His sister was silent for so long that he thought she'd hung up on him. "Ang?"

"Reed? What's wrong? Do you know what time it is?"

He checked the clock on the nearby coffee machine. "It's nearly eleven. Did I wake you?"

"No."

He could hear her sigh over the phone. "What do you need?"

"I need woman's clothes and a Christmas tree."

"Um?" She laughed. "I'm afraid I need more detail than that. I have so. Many. Questions."

Reed hesitated. His older sister wasn't known for her discretion. She was, however, a buyer for a major Manhattan department store and the only person Reed knew could do what he wanted.

"Look, it's a long story, but I have a woman

staying with me that needs a few days' worth of clothes. And it would be nice to decorate this place for Christmas."

Angela's voice sounded suspicious. "Is this some kind of *Pretty Woman* thing? Where did you find this friend?"

Reed shook his head. Maybe he should have called his mother instead. "She really is a friend. You'd probably like her. Anyway, she was roughed up in front of her apartment building tonight and called me, so I picked her up and brought her here. She wasn't in any shape to pack and I just didn't think of it." He ran a hand through his hair. His blood burned again just thinking about it. "Now she's stuck here for a while, so I want to make the place look cozy, and I don't want her walking out tomorrow wearing the same thing she wore today." He lowered his voice. "Plus, she works here too so people would talk."

"Reed! You're having an affair with an employee?"

"She's a contractor." He growled into the phone. "And this isn't an affair."

"Interesting. Okay. So, what's her style? Size? Colors?"

"Colors? What the hell are colors?" Reed was quickly regretting calling Angela.

Angela seemed to understand his frustration. "Don't worry, Reed," she told him earnestly. "I know what I'm doing."

He sighed. "I know. That's why I called you. I

can tell you her style, but how do I know her size and colors?"

"Go look at the tags in her clothes. Unless they're handmade they'll tell you the size."

Reed opened his bedroom door quietly and stepped inside. Caroline was sound asleep, sprawled on her stomach and taking up nearly half of his king-size bed. He smiled knowing he would join her soon. Remembering Angela was waiting on him, he hurried through to the bathroom to find her discarded dress. It took him a few minutes to locate it stuffed in the trash under the sink.

"This says six 'P'."

"Ok, perfect. Now, do you have any pictures of her?"

"Yes. Hang on. I think I have some on my phone. I know Savannah took some too, so maybe you can find some on her social media."

"You took her to Wolf Creek and introduced her to Daniel and Skids?"

Damn! "Yes."

"So, she's more like a *special* friend. What's her name? Have Mom and Dad met her yet?"

Reed rolled his shoulders and tipped his head back to glare at the ceiling. Damn his sister for being so perceptive. He never took anyone to Wolf Creek, most especially not a date. "Her name is Caroline. She's a contractor the Board hired to develop a training division in the company."

Angela started laughing. "So, Dad hired her?"

Reed gritted his teeth. "Probably."

More laughing. "Nice. I can't wait to meet her."

It was no secret that their father loved to meddle in his children's lives. When their sister, Savannah, was first setting up her museum in Wolf Creek, their father had been instrumental in throwing Daniel and Savannah together, and now they were happily engaged and building a whole world together.

"Just get Caroline some clothes, please."

"Sure thing, just as soon as you tell me her style."

Reed thought about that and nearly smiled. "She dresses like me. Only feminine."

"Business suits?"

"No, but we often dress alike."

Angela laughed again. "On purpose? Like, twinsies?"

Reed growled. "No. But if I wear a black suit, white shirt and black and white tie she'll wear a black and white dress. Or, if I wear blue, she'll wear something that complements blue. It's kind of funny, but I noticed it right away."

"Okay, so she's formal."

"Classy," he corrected.

"Got it. Send me a couple of pictures and I'll get a few things together. When do you need everything?"

"In the morning."

"What?" Angela drew out the word.

"She'll want to go to work tomorrow and she can't exactly show up wearing my pajamas."

"Aww. That's cute though. She's wearing your pajamas?"

Reed made a rude noise. "I'll send you a couple of pictures."

"I can do the clothes, but I'm hiring someone else to deal with your tree."

"You're the best, Ang. See you in the morning. Oh, and Angela? Bring makeup, too." He hung up and dropped his cell on the bathroom counter. His sister would come through for him, or rather, for Caroline, but he wondered how painful it was going to be dealing with his sister in the morning. He stripped down to his boxers and brushed his teeth and then turned off the lights.

He climbed into bed and pulled Caroline close. She rolled onto her side and cuddled up to him with a contented sigh. Reed squeezed her tighter and closed his eyes. In a twist of fate even his meddling father couldn't have orchestrated, he didn't have to part with Caroline after all.

Sometime during the night, Reed woke her from a nightmare. She clutched at him, squashing herself as close as she could get. He held her close while her breathing returned to normal.

"Make love to me," she whispered against his neck. "Help me chase the bad stuff away."

Reed didn't have to be asked twice. He'd thought of nothing but making love to her since the moment she stepped out of the bathroom in his pajamas.

Hearts in Training

Truth be told, he'd been thinking of her in his bed since she'd left it the previous morning. She was a surprising addiction. Oh, he'd been interested in her from the start, but the more time he spent with her, the more he wondered how he'd ever leave her.

He kissed her mouth first, making love to her with his tongue before gently examining all her sensitive spots. He came across the bruise on her hip and fury tore through him. His Carrie was sweet and innocent, too vulnerable for her own good. Kissing that spot gently, he forced the image of her being shoved into a building from his mind and concentrated on making her feel nothing but ecstasy.

Remembering that sex was still new to her, he forced himself to go slow. He savored every movement, every sound she made until he knew neither of them could prolong the moment any longer. He took her over the edge and followed her there, holding her as tightly as he dared and wishing he never had to let her go.

Caroline relaxed into sleep almost immediately, but Reed laid awake for several hours afterward. He thought about his reaction to her. She was special, yes. He considered the feelings he'd had for former girlfriends, even Melanie with whom he'd once considered marrying. Had he ever felt this possessive toward any of them? Had he felt the same uncontrollable jealousy he experienced when he saw his employees hitting on Caroline? Never. He thought about how desperately he'd wanted her to stay with him instead of taking her home after their weekend in Wolf Creek. He rolled to his side and watched her sleep. Was it selfish that a tiny part of him was glad she'd been forced to call him tonight? Oh, he'd never have wanted her to come to him because she was hurt and scared. But she was here now, and he was going to make the most of his opportunity to keep her just a little bit longer. He had two more startling thoughts before he drifted off to sleep. He was in love with Caroline. And this was the marrying kind of love.

REED WOKE Caroline early the next morning by raining kisses on the unbruised parts of her face and neck. She rolled over and stretched, then snuggled back into his side.

He rubbed her unbruised hip, shaking her awake again. "You might want to get up, babe. My sister is bringing some things over for you."

Caroline bolted up and bonked Reed in the nose. "Savannah is coming here? Now?"

Reed rubbed his nose and sat back against the headboard. "My older sister, Angela. She lives here in Manhattan. I gave her a call last night and asked her to bring some clothes and other girlie things over for you."

Caroline blinked at him. He was starting to think he should have led with coffee. He dipped his head down into her line of vision. "Hey, are you okay? Awake?"

"You thought to get me clothes?"

"Well, yeah. You can't very well walk out of my apartment wearing the same dress you wore yesterday. And you definitely can't wear my pajamas in public either." He looked at her in his T-shirt. He wouldn't mind seeing her in his clothes every single day, but this wasn't the time to bring *that* up.

Caroline smoothed down the cotton shirt, her eyes never leaving his face, her voice teasingly defiant. "Some people wear pajamas in public."

"They wouldn't start a riot. You're not leaving my apartment dressed like that. You'd be mauled for sure."

She laughed. "So, what should I be wearing when your sister gets here?"

"A robe?"

"Super. Do you have one?"

Reed smiled at her smart reply and rolled off the bed. "I'll be right back."

"Bring coffee," she called after him.

Five minutes later, Reed had located his robe in the back of a spare closet and returned with it and a steaming hot cup of coffee. Caroline was in his bathroom, examining the bruise on the side of her face. "I'm not sure what to do about this." Their eyes met in the mirror. "I don't have any makeup." She poked at the yellow and purple skin. "I'll have to make up a great story."

Reed pulled on a white v-neck T-shirt and leaned back against the counter; his arms folded over his chest. "I did ask Angela to bring you some makeup, but I have an even better idea. Why don't you take the day off instead?"

"Are you taking the day off, too?"

"I can't. I have a couple of meetings that can't be rescheduled."

Caroline nodded. "I can't justify taking the day off either, Reed. I'm not sick, and I'm not going to lie around all day."

Reed almost laughed. He'd known that would be her response. "Which is why I asked Angela to bring you the clothes and makeup."

Caroline stepped up to him and laid her head on his shoulder. "So very thoughtful. Just one of the things I love about you." She sighed.

Reed's muscles tightened. Had she just admitted that she loved him? He opened his mouth to ask her about her comment when he heard the penthouse door open. The purposeful sound of heels filtered in from the front hall. Damn! "Angela is here."

"Oh goody," Caroline whispered. She ran a comb through her hair, pulled the robe on and followed Reed out of the bathroom.

WHERE SAVANNAH was all soft edges and relaxed familiarity, Angela was no-nonsense. She looked more like Reed with her dark hair and tall stature, and she was beautiful in a way that would make her look dressed up no matter what she was wearing.

Spotting Caroline, Angela stepped up to her and offered a hand. "Caroline Trumbull, I presume. Angela Decatur. Nice to meet you."

Caroline shook the woman's hand, suppressing a

smile at the formality while she was clearly wearing Reed's pajamas. "And you. I hear you're going to be my hero today."

Angela tipped one side of her mouth in a smile and looked at Reed. "Well, I think my brother would rather claim that title, but I did bring you some clothes. And makeup." She studied Caroline's bruise. "That must hurt."

Caroline dipped her head once. "It does. I'll probably avoid smiling for a while."

"This would be a good time to work on your resting bitch face."

"Excuse me?" Caroline wasn't sure whether it would be appropriate to laugh. Angela had sounded so matter of fact.

"Your resting bitch face. That's where you don't smile, and you sort of look pissed at the world."

"But I'm not."

Angela nodded her agreement. "No, I know. And I can already tell that you're pretty easy-going. But a good RBF will keep people from questioning you all day. It's like a signal warning people to stay away."

The pieces were coming together now. "Ahhh. I see where you're going with this."

Between them, Reed laughed, causing both women look at him with nearly identical expressions indicating his hilarity wasn't appreciated. "Sorry," he muttered. "I just can't picture Carrie trying to mean mug people in the office all day." He stared at

Caroline for a second and then cracked up again. "Nope. I can't see it."

Caroline glared at him. He stopped laughing.

Ten minutes and one cup of coffee later, the women were set up in Reed's bedroom so that Caroline could try on the clothes Angela had brought. Caroline was impressed with Angela's skill. Going only on what Reed had apparently told his sister about her, Angela was able to match her style and size perfectly.

Caroline gestured at the row of dresses now hanging in Reed's closet. "I'm just blown away by this, Angela. You're seriously a miracle worker."

Angela smiled. "It's what I do best." She looked in Reed's closet and then looked around his bedroom. "So, ah, are you living here too?"

Caroline's heart gave a little jolt. "No!" She released a breath. "I mean, no. Reed's a good friend. Last night after I was attacked, I was a little freaked out, and I called him. He picked me up and brought me here. I don't have any designs on moving myself in." She laughed at herself. It all sounded so old-fashioned.

Angela made a humming sound. "Too bad. You'd fit really well in here." She handed Caroline a dress from the selection to try on. "Are you seeing each other?"

Caroline wished Reed was here to deflect these questions. She didn't know Angela and didn't want to put Reed in an awkward position with his family.

Angela gave her a look at the pause. "I know he's

taken you to his favorite hideaway. And you met Savannah and Daniel." She shrugged. "I assume you've met our parents."

"Actually, it was your dad that hired me for this project." Caroline thought about that. "I met your mother just briefly at a company event. I didn't get a chance to speak with her."

Angela looked thoughtful. "She'd like you. I'll have to tell her to pop in and take you to lunch one day soon."

Awkward didn't begin to describe how Caroline was feeling at that moment. "That's kind of you, but I don't want to put her to any trouble. And as busy as Reed is, he probably wouldn't appreciate the distraction right now."

Angela chuckled. "You're good! But I know when I'm being handled. Our mom knows how to navigate an executive's schedule." She watched Caroline apply makeup and tapped a finger on her lips. "It would be a bit of a giveaway though, wouldn't it, if she came to the office to meet you." She handed Caroline a tube of concealer. "I'll have Mom and Dad come here instead."

Caroline dropped the tube and gaped at Angela in the mirror. "Here? Why?" She righted the tube and used a tissue to wipe up the smudge on the counter. "What I mean to say is, it isn't really necessary to ask your mother here just to meet me. I'm sure we'll cross paths at some point before I move on to my next contract."

Angela narrowed her eyes. "Well, our dad's been singing your praises, and now that Reed's taken you to his secret hideout to meet Savannah and Daniel, well, I think the writing's on the wall."

Caroline's stomach clenched. Was Reed truly serious about her, or was Angela simply reading more into this than was warranted? "There's no writing on the wall," Caroline reminded her. "We're friends and he's helping me after a scary incident."

It was clear that Angela didn't believe her, but at least she refrained from mentioning it again. Minutes later Reed was back with two large coffees, one in a disposable cup. He handed it to Angela.

"Time to go, Ang. Thanks for your help."

Angela raised the coffee in a salute to her brother. She looked over at Caroline. "It was nice to meet you. And so illuminating! Good luck with this guy."

Caroline looked from Reed's frown to Angela's conspiring smile. "It was really nice to meet you as well. Thank you for loaning me the clothes. You really are my hero today."

Angela blew them both a kiss and let herself out of the suite and then out of the apartment.

Reed took a sip of the coffee he held and then offered it to Caroline. She took a few gulps and handed it back.

"Your sister is..." How to describe what she felt about Angela's comments? "Determined."

Reed laughed. "What's she trying to convince you to do?"

Caroline turned her back to the mirror and faced

Reed. "She wants me to meet your parents."

Reed frowned. "But you've already met my dad."

Caroline pulled the robe closer around herself. "No Reed. I mean she wants me to *meet your parents*."

"Ah." Reed took another sip. "My mother is going to love you."

Caroline made an exasperated noise and turned to finish her makeup. "That's exactly what she said, too."

Reed stepped behind her and gently lifted the hair away from her neck to leave a trail of kisses from her ear to her shoulder causing goosebumps to break out all over her skin.

"We're going to be late." She sighed, letting him take her weight when she leaned back against him. Reed wrapped his arms tightly around her and hugged her. Their eyes met in the mirror and Caroline smiled.

"I can be ready in a few minutes. Do you want breakfast?"

Caroline shook her head. "I can grab a yogurt when I go to my office." She started to say she would hurry, and then realized that they couldn't really leave or show up together anyway. "I'll go in a little later, if you don't mind my being here alone. We can't very well show up at the same time."

Reed gestured to the apartment. "What I have is yours."

"Thank you." She watched him turn to leave the room. "Hey, don't forget your coffee."

Reed stopped in the doorway and grinned at her. "That one is your coffee. I left mine in the kitchen so that you wouldn't drink it."

Playfully, Caroline threw a cotton ball at him. "You've been drinking my coffee?"

Reed chuckled and headed to his closet.

"You owe me six ounces of coffee!" she hollered after him.

"You can punish me later, Carrie," he called back from the bedroom.

He hadn't been kidding about being quick to get ready. Less than ten minutes later he was fully dressed and ready to take the elevator to his office one floor below. Caroline had just finished her makeup and followed him to the door, still wearing his robe.

"What do you think? Can you still see the bruise?" She'd spent much longer than usual on her makeup, trying to conceal the marks as well as possible.

Reed took her chin between his fingers and tilted her head from one side to the other. "I know it's there, Carrie. No amount of makeup is going to make me forget what those bastards did to you."

Caroline groaned. "Let me ask this way. Will other people be able to tell my face is a watercolor under all this makeup?"

Reed smiled and kissed her lips softly. "Probably not."

"Thank you."

Hearts in Training

He pulled the door open and stopped on the threshold. "Don't go home without talking to me first, okay?"

Caroline's first reaction was indignation that he'd given her an order, followed quickly by fear, and then curiosity. "Are you afraid they'll be back?"

Enigmatic as usual, Reed answered, "I'm afraid of a lot of things, but I don't want you to return to your apartment without telling me."

"I promise. I'll tell you if I leave the building. You need to go." She gave him a small push toward the door. "You've got a Board meeting in half an hour. I'll head down to my office as soon as I'm dressed."

Reed looked at her in his robe. "Take your time. Or don't come down at all. I kind of like the idea of keeping you all to myself up here." He gave her a lecherous smile and disappeared into the elevator.

Chapter 18

*A*n hour later, Caroline was stumping her way to a meeting on her crutches, alternately wincing and giving thanks for the many elevators in the building. She'd scheduled the meeting to present some class ideas and to brainstorm with the heads of several departments for additional training opportunities. For that reason, she was surprised to see Fred Decatur waiting for her near the door.

Caroline smiled at the older version of Reed. "It's good to see you, Mr. Decatur. Are you joining us?"

The senior Mr. Decatur beamed at her. "Fred, please. And yes. I won't get to participate in fun stuff like this for very much longer."

Caroline nodded her thanks when he held the door open for her. "Well I'm glad you're making the time. I imagine you're going to have a lot to contribute."

Fred's eyes crinkled at the praise. He moved around to the head of the table and pulled out a chair for her. "Plus, I wanted to see for myself how you were doing today." He paused and studied her face. "You look better than Angela let on. My wife, Gail, is really looking forward to meeting you, by the way."

Caroline tipped her head back, the mystery of why he was checking on her solved. "Ah yes. Angela was a godsend to me today. Be sure to tell her thanks again when you talk to her."

Fred gave a little head shake as if to say it was no big deal. To Caroline, though, it was a big deal. A very big deal. Was this what it was like to have a family, she wondered? As if she'd telegraphed her thoughts, Fred squeezed her shoulder and set her crutches against the wall directly behind her chair as she took her seat.

Caroline looked around the room to bring the meeting to order and stalled at the smug and slightly unnerving look on Elizabeth's beautiful face. Shaking off the sudden anxiety caused by that look, Caroline went through the agenda and slides for their current class offerings before opening the floor for discussion. Several ideas were tossed out, and then molded and refined until they had more solid ideas. As predicted, Fred had plenty of insight to share, and it was abundantly clear that, like Reed, he knew exactly what went on in his company. In some ways, he also reminded Caroline of her own father.

"Before we wrap up, does anyone have any questions?" Caroline scanned the group and noted a few people who looked like they had something to say.

"Who will be heading up the new division?" a director named Ken asked.

Caroline acknowledged the question, but before she could respond, Elizabeth quipped, "Whoever gets to Reed first, and I don't think you have the ah, qualifications." There were a few awkward chuckles, but most of the group seemed to understand the veiled joke for what it was. Spite. Caroline couldn't believe Elizabeth would say such a thing in front of Fred.

"With all your knowledge and experience, you'd be a shoo-in for it, Caroline. Any thoughts of throwing your hat into the ring?" Alan asked. Caroline smiled at the man and avoided making eye contact with both Fred and Elizabeth.

"This really is a great company and whoever is hired is going to be very lucky. I really haven't given any thought to applying though."

"You mean it hasn't come up over dinner?" To Caroline's mortification, Elizabeth winked at her and added, "Or breakfast?"

Caroline's heart beat frantically, and she willed her face to remain impassive. It was impossible not to sneak a glance at Fred now. In an expression she often saw on Reed, she knew he was also controlling his features. Only the subtle tic of his jaw hinted at what he was feeling, though whether it was directed at Elizabeth or herself, she couldn't tell. Her stomach churned uncomfortably. Not only was her reputation on the line, but if she and Reed continued a relationship beyond her contract there, she wanted to make a good impression with his father.

Hoping she wouldn't regret opening up the conversation, Caroline used her politest voice, "Excuse me?"

Elizabeth gave a fake chuckle. "Oh, sorry! I totally thought your relationship was common knowledge."

Several directors leaned forward in interest, gazes swiveling between Elizabeth and Caroline. Fred's eyes, Caroline noted, never left Elizabeth's face.

Caroline feigned confusion. "My relationship with whom?"

"With Reed, of course." She waggled her cell phone in front of the group. "I'm friends with Savannah on social media. I've seen the pictures."

Caroline opened her mouth to defend herself, but Fred surprised them all by laughing. "You mean the publicity shots she took for the ad campaign?" Fred shook his head and laughed some more.

Elizabeth's confidence seemed to crack just a little. "In cozy little Wolf Creek, New Hampshire?"

Fred dipped his head, his eyes still sparkling. "Savannah's idea. She's always looking for ways to cross-promote her work in the town." Fred turned mischievous eyes on Caroline. "But Elizabeth's assumptions prove the point you made the other day, Caroline. We do need a formal publicity team." He looked around the table, a stern look on his face now. "I'll be sure to share this example with Reed when I see him next." His gaze cut over to Caroline and she nodded her gratitude. Fred was clearly no slouch.

Elizabeth, evidently not ready to concede defeat, got in one last prod as the group gathered their things to leave. "The selfie of the two of you on his computer background is adorable, though. Was that taken in your apartment or his?"

Fred chuckled again and muttered, "Caught! That's what you get for testing the camera settings.

Let the rumors abound." He gave Caroline a surreptitious wink and led the rest of the directors from the room.

Elizabeth hung back while Caroline unplugged her computer from the screen and gathered up her notes. "Doesn't matter what kind of cute spin Fred puts on your little romantic getaway. It still comes down to the fact that you're screwing the boss." There was a warning in her tone that made Caroline look up from the table and froze. Reed was standing behind Elizabeth and it was clear from his expression that he'd heard enough.

"Who is screwing whom?" Reed asked in a pleasant voice as if merely asking for the latest gossip.

Elizabeth whirled around and Caroline could no longer see her expression. "You two! You're having an affair."

Caroline's fingers dug into her computer, but Reed didn't look affected by the accusation. He looked at Caroline. "Are you married?"

Caroline frowned at the question. "No."

Reed transferred his gaze back to Elizabeth. "And neither am I. So, there can't be an affair." He looked thoughtful. "Still, an affair sounds better than, what did you call it? Screwing?" He nodded. "Definitely more polite than to say she's screwing the boss. And yet", he continued over her sputtered interruption, "neither description is quite what it should be."

"And what is that?" Elizabeth asked tightly.

Hearts in Training

"None of your damned business." He looked at his watch then at Caroline. "Our one o'clock appointment is waiting in my office."

Caroline swept past both Reed and Elizabeth and managed to catch the nearby elevator just as the doors were closing. The lift already had several occupants, but Caroline let out a ragged breath. As far as she knew she and Reed didn't have a one o'clock appointment, but she recognized an escape opportunity when one was presented to her, so she took the elevator to his office in case he wanted to talk.

Caroline stepped off the elevator and stopped short.

"Carrie!" Tony came off his chair and hurried toward her, concern on his wrinkled face. "Are you okay, girl? We worried when you didn't come home last night. What's with the crutches?"

"What are you doing here, Tony?" she asked quietly. She could only imagine what he'd said to Jamie while he'd waited up here.

"Yer young man called me this morning and asked me to come down." He leaned closer so he wouldn't be overheard, though Caroline expected that Jamie could hear him anyway. "Think he's fixing to ask me if he can marry you?"

Caroline leaned away and shook her head, dread filling her chest with lead. Would he say that to Reed? God, she hoped not. "No, I don't think so, Tony."

A minute later Reed stalked past. "Come with me, please."

Jamie gave Caroline an encouraging smile as she followed the men into Reed's office. Reed gestured for Tony to take one of the chairs across from his desk. Caroline moved to take the other chair, but Reed put a hand on her back and guided her around his desk to take his chair. He moved his hand to settle on her shoulder and gave it a reassuring squeeze before folding his arms over his chest. Direct and to the point, Reed tipped his chin at Tony. "What are you into for thirteen grand?"

Both Caroline and Tony looked at him. Tony appeared shocked. Inwardly Caroline groaned. She should've guessed that Reed would get involved. Had she really told him her perfect partner had an alpha side? Dumb.

"It's nothing bad. Honest. I wanted to raise some funds, but it didn't pan out."

Reed studied him for a minute. Caroline watched Tony squirm, feeling just a little bit sorry for him.

"Caroline was roughed up last night on her way into the building, by a couple of guys looking for your thirteen grand."

Tony half stood. "What?" He sat back down and leaned across the wide wooden desk to take a better look at Caroline. "My God, girl! Are you okay? That's why you didn't come home? Your ma was so worried, but I told her you probably just stayed over with your man here, and that calmed her down." His gaze took in her face, seeming to linger on the bruised side of her face. So much for her makeup job. "The bastards hit you? Anything else? Is that what you got them crutches for?"

Hearts in Training

Caroline shook her head. "The crutches are from a skiing accident. But I whacked them with one of my crutches and got knocked off the stoop. I'm okay." She looked up at Reed and noted he was frowning at her.

Tony looked ill. "Why didn't you call me, Carrie? I was right upstairs, and I could have dealt with it."

Caroline could see the guilt and worry in his face, and for the first time appreciated that he really saw her as a daughter. "I couldn't lead them to you, Tony. None of us would have been safe."

Tony moaned and dropped his head in his hands. "I messed up, Carrie-girl. I put you in danger."

Beside her, Reed straightened. "I agree, and this could keep happening until the issue is resolved. So how are you going to make this right?"

Tony moved hands from his face and set up straight. He thought for a minute and seemed to come to some decision. "I'll get a temporary place for you and Heather to stay, a hotel maybe, so there'll be security. Then I'm going to find these guys and work out a plan to pay them off." He capped his speech with a nod.

Caroline knew he was upset, but still she had to ask. "Do thugs offer a payment plan?"

Reed huffed a laugh. "I will loan you the money and you'll work out a plan with me to pay it back."

Both Tony and Caroline objected immediately. "This is a family issue, Reed. We can work it out without your charity," she told him.

Reed's eyes burned into hers in a silent battle of wills. Little by little his expression softened until she understood what he was telling her. Here was a way he could be her knight in shining armor, a way that he could show her he cared. "I'm going to do this," he whispered.

"I know," she whispered back. His answering smile showed he was proud of her.

Turning back to Tony, he slid his hands in his pockets. "I'm going to help you out of this mess," he announced. Tony started to thank him, but Reed continued. "But I have conditions that you will have to agree to." Reed stabbed him with a hard look. "These are non-negotiable."

Tony nodded, his attention solely on Reed now. "Carrie stays with me until I feel it's safe for her to go home."

Tony quickly agreed. Reed, she noticed, didn't ask for her agreement.

"I will pay for a hotel room for yourself and Heather for two weeks, until I'm satisfied this has blown over and you're holding up your end of the bargain. Third, I want you to get help for your gambling addiction. Lastly, I'm going to give you a job."

Tony sat back, looking thunderstruck.

"While you're working for Decatur Industries, you and Heather are also going to take a money management class together. Carrie will review your work in the class." Reed looked down at her, the next comment aimed at both of them. "From this day forward, Carrie will not give you a single dollar, except on your birthday or Christmas." He looked from Caroline to Tony. "Not a cent."

Tony's eyes were misty. "Why are you doing this for us?"

Reed shrugged; his expression once again shuttered. "Because it's in my power to give you a chance to make things right."

If Caroline hadn't known she loved him before this would have clinched it. What Reed was offering Tony wasn't just a way out, it was a way forward. A chance to reclaim his pride and build a life for himself and her mother. Caroline waited for Reed's eyes to connect with hers and then told him everything her voice couldn't share. His answering look told her he understood.

Reed cleared his throat. "I'm going to take you down and introduce you to your supervisor and show you around a little. Once we're finished my secretary will have all the necessary details worked out for the hotel and money transfer."

Caroline reached for her crutches and Reed held the chair steady as she arranged herself and hobbled around the desk to walk with them to the door. Tony put a beefy arm around her shoulders and squeezed her into a one-armed hug. "I've never meant to hurt you, Carrie-girl. Thirteen thousand is how much we've borrowed from you, and I was trying to get it back. You work so hard and we can see what it's doing to you. Yer man here is a good man. Let him take care of you for a bit, yeah? Yer not any less strong for accepting a helping hand."

Caroline nodded, shocked at Tony's perception. "Take care, Tony. And congratulations on the new job."

Tony shook Reed's hand and beamed. "Heather's going to be so proud of me!"

While Tony headed for the elevator, Reed paused inside the door and cupped a hand around Caroline's neck. "You look tired."

"I am." She squinted up at him, hating to admit it. "It's been an awful day."

Reed's smile was understanding. "Go upstairs."

"For what?"

"To wait for me."

Caroline laughed despite her mood. "Kind of hard to disobey an order like that, Mr. Alpha."

Reed dropped his head and laughed. Leaning close, he whispered. "You can be the boss later."

"Deal," she chirped.

Caroline waited by Jamie's desk for the next elevator, not wanting Tony to know where she was headed. As soon as the doors closed on the men Jamie handed Caroline a key card.

"Your very own ticket to the penthouse, Miss Trumbull."

Caroline turned startled eyes on Jamie. "Thank you." She turned the card over in her hand. "I don't know whether to be slightly embarrassed or completely mortified!"

Hearts in Training

"Because I know you're shacking up with the CEO, you mean?" There was a twinkle in Jamie's eyes.

Caroline dipped her face and then laughed to herself. "I guess so." She took a seat beside Jamie's desk. "Awkward doesn't begin to describe how today went."

"Fred might have mentioned something about a meeting with Elizabeth an hour ago."

"If the employees didn't think I was a slut before, they will now. Does Reed often give women a key to his apartment?"

Jamie made a face. "Never. And what you're saying is nonsense. No one thinks you're a slut, and no one who's seen you and Reed together would think badly of you."

"Thank you, Jamie. I am so grateful Fred was there. I didn't invite him, so it was pure luck he showed up."

Jamie smiled. "Not pure luck. I knew Reed was tied up, so I sent Fred. I sense that Elizabeth thinks she has some sort of claim on Reed, and I didn't think it would be a good idea to leave you alone with her."

Caroline sat back and eyed Jamie with new respect. "My guardian angel, huh?"

Jamie shrugged. "I sent Reed down as soon as he was free."

"He arrived right on time."

"You really do look tired, Caroline. Why don't

you go lie down for a bit?" She winked. "Even Superman takes some down-time now and again."

Caroline thought about her throbbing ankle and the various other parts of her that felt worse for the wear.

"I believe you're right, Jamie. I think I will go lie down for a few minutes. If Reed's looking for me-"

Jamie interrupted her with a laugh. "No worries. I know where he'll look first."

Caroline nodded. "Thanks."

She let herself into the penthouse and leaned back against the door with a sigh. The place was warm and quiet, truly a safe place to relax. She adjusted her crutches and was about to go to Reed's bedroom when she spotted the tree in the living room. Moving into that room to get a better look, Caroline leaned in and took a deep breath. There weren't any lights or decorations, but the tree itself was a gorgeous Douglas fir.

She went into Reed's bedroom, tossed the crutches on the bed, and hopped the rest of the way to the bathroom on one foot to the huge, sunken jet tub. She clicked on the romantic playlist of songs on her phone and filled the tub with hot water.

Five minutes later she was up to her earlobes in hot swirling water, her phone playing her favorite swoon-worthy songs. She closed her eyes and laid her head back. Here, in Reed's apartment she felt a world away from her life. It was both a problem and a blessing, for she knew that once the danger had moved on, she would move back to her own space.

Of course, if Tony stuck to his agreement and no longer needed Caroline's help, perhaps she could afford a better place. Nothing as extravagant as Reed's penthouse, of course, but something in a safer area would be nice.

On the heels of that thought came the reminder that she still hadn't lined up a new contract. Alan's question from earlier floated back to her. She'd sent out a few feelers and a couple of resumés, but she hadn't followed up on any of them. She hadn't really considered applying for the new director position either, though in truth, she knew she could do the job. She'd created the position, after all. Caroline considered the pros and cons of working for Decatur. She was passionate about the role. And the pay and benefits were great.

She thought about what it would be like to see Reed every day. Always lurking in the back of her mind was the reminder that she really didn't know their status. He'd been jealous over the idea of her seeing anyone else, and he'd made it clear he wasn't going to see other women. He'd never explicitly said they were a couple, but she supposed by definition they were. If things went south between them, she'd still be there, still seeing him. She might even report to him. When he moved on, she'd likely see that, too. She tried and failed to imagine what it would feel like to see Reed with another woman now that they were intimate.

"Mind if I join you?" Reed's voice cut through her inner monologue, startling her.

Her eyes snapped open, her heard pounding.

"You scared me!"

Reed was sitting on the ledge of the tub, his shirt already unbuttoned and a grin on his handsome face. "What are you thinking about so hard?"

Caroline watched him slip off his shirt and reach for his fly. "I was just daydreaming."

He stood and shucked his pants and boxers to stand before her completely nude. "Anything I can participate in?" Reed motioned to her and she scooted forward to let him settle behind her. His arms immediately came around her, seeking out her breasts and massaging them in the hot water.

Caroline settled back against his chest and sighed. It was decadent the way he made her feel. She thought of her daydream and chuckled. Pushing aside worries for the future, she knew she had him for the moment. He pinched her nipples and prompted, "Share?"

"I remembered that I haven't put much effort into lining up a new contract. That thought led to another and I was day-dreaming about my perfect career."

"Oh boy. Is this going to be like your perfect partner? Something I can never live up to?"

Caroline tried to turn around, but Reed held tight. "You're joking, right? I described you!"

Reed hugged her again before loosening his hold. "I described you, too."

Caroline sighed. "I know. I called you last night because I remembered how much you wanted to save somebody."

"You. Caroline. I only want to save you."

"You did. Big time."

"So, tell me about your perfect career." Reed continued to caress various parts of her body while she spoke. His touch was gentle and subconscious, not meant to be a turn on, but rather a comfort.

"I imagined a shorter commute, for starters."

"Definitely a plus. What else?"

"Something more permanent. Not contract based like I am now. Something that doesn't require much travel."

"I'm with you so far." Reed sounded as relaxed as she felt.

"Something nine-to-five. With vacations."

"Vacations that involve making love in front of a fireplace?"

"Of course." She laughed. "Or a hot tub." She hesitated and wondered if her next comment would spook him.

He squeezed her tush. "Spit it out, Carrie."

"The kind of job that would let me have a family."

"You have a family," he reminded her. "Two of them if you get married."

She elbowed him in the ribs. "Babies, Reed. I want babies!"

Reed chuckled behind her. "Right now? Cuz,

yeah, we could work on that."

Caroline froze. Reed continued rubbing her, working on her forearms now. "Relax. I'm teasing. Sort of. Go on. What would you be doing in this perfect career?"

She drew in a breath. Would it sound like she was using her position, literally, to lobby for a job? "I want to head up a training division," she whispered. "I would love that."

Reed was quiet for a few minutes. Caroline could feel his heart beating harder. She was starting to think she should have kept that to herself.

"I know you would. And you would be brilliant."

"But I can't work for you." She couldn't hide the regret in her voice.

Reed leaned to the side to look in her eyes. "No. I can't *hire* you. Executive Directors are vetted and approved by the Board. As long as I recuse myself it's all above-board."

"What? You checked?" Caroline turned around on her knees to face Reed.

He brought a hand up to brush her damp hair away from her face. "Actually, my dad did. He sent me an email on it this morning." He dropped his hand with a splash and turned the jets off. "He offered to recuse himself as well, if it came to that."

Caroline was speechless. When the possibilities became too much to contain, she launched forward and kissed him. Hard.

"The position is posted. It would be up to you to apply, interview, the usual drill. But, if you're interested, I say go for it."

Caroline moved to sit on the edge of the tub while Reed opened the drain. "Wow," she whispered.

Reed eyed her. "Wow, is right." He got out of the tub and handed her a fluffy white towel. "Are you ready for bed?"

Caroline patted her face dry and then wrapped the towel around herself and grabbed her phone. "It's the middle of the afternoon!"

"Yes, it is."

"So, it's not bedtime," Caroline reminded him.

Reed hooked a finger in her towel and propelled her forward. "We're not going to sleep, sweetheart. Not for a while." Before Caroline could take a single hop toward the bedroom Reed had swept her up into his arms, pushed her crutches onto the floor, and deposited her on his bed. Her phone, still playing a romance mix, landed beside her. Reed tugged the towel out from around her and dropped both towels on the floor before covering her completely with his body.

"About today," Caroline whispered.

"Later," Reed mumbled against her lips before sliding his tongue in to rob her of her senses.

After a bout of lovemaking and even a bit of a nap, Caroline cuddled into Reed's side and listened to his deep, even breathing. Every stolen moment with him felt like a blessing, even if he was sleeping. She knew the assaults on her reputation and integrity wouldn't stop anytime soon. She thought again about working for Decatur. She and Elizabeth would be equals. They would report to the same Board, one of whom Caroline was in a relationship with. Would the snide comments and veiled insults end then?

Beside her Reed's phone chirped a message. Instinctively, Reed clutched her tighter and rolled over to snatch up his phone. "My mom wants to know what you like on your pizza. They're bringing us decorations for the tree and dinner."

Caroline bolted upright and clutched the sheet nearly to her chin. "They're coming here now?" She took a slow breath to calm her racing heart.

"Here," Reed confirmed. "Probably in an hour. Unless it takes you that long to answer the question." He raised his brows a her.

It took a moment to remember what he wanted to know. "I don't know. I'm not picky."

Reed gave her a look like she was crazy. "Seriously?" He shook his head. "How can you not have an opinion on pizza? That's downright un-American."

"Seriously," she confirmed. "Are you going to eat little fishes on it?"

"Gah! No."

Caroline shrugged. "Okay then. I can just pick off what I don't like."

Clearly not believing her, Reed texted his mother and then leaned back against the headboard. "We have time for a quickie."

Caroline wrapped the sheet further around her and shook her head. "Not hardly! Not when I know your parents are on their way. I've never even met your mother. And your dad! He hired me."

"My mom will love you. And clearly my dad already approves."

"He approved of my resumé. He didn't approve of me seeing his son." She sat back with a thud. "What am I supposed to wear for pizza with your parents?"

Reed shrugged, obviously not seeing the concern. "I don't know. What do you wear for pizza with your parents?"

"I can't wear a T-shirt and leggings to meet your mom!"

Reed rolled to his side and spread an arm across her waist. "It's pizza, Carrie. Just pizza."

"What if she judges me?"

Now Reed looked confused. Caroline felt like a teenager going on her first date. Worried. Excited. Nervous.

"I'm missing something here. What would she judge you for?"

Caroline envied the black and white way Reed's mind worked. "I don't know who she expects me to be, so I'm afraid I won't pass the test."

Reed pulled her under him and locked her there, piercing her with a serious gaze. "First, she will like you for you. Since I know her and you don't, you'll have to take my word on that. Second, it's just pizza. My dad will probably turn on the news and eat on my couch. Third, and most importantly, it doesn't matter what she thinks of you. *I* like you and that's all that matters, right?"

She nodded. "Thank you for what you did for my family today. I never could have-" He stopped her with a quick kiss.

"But I could, so I did."

Knowing she was wading into deep waters, she had to ask. "Why?"

With another smacking kiss, Reed rolled over and got out of bed. "Let's find something appropriate to wear for non-judgmental pizza with the parents."

Chapter 19

Reed's mother, Gail, adored Caroline, just as he'd known she would. Nearly from the moment his father introduced them Reed could see they'd each found a kindred spirit. Where his mother was reserved, Caroline was outgoing, but both possessed the same iron strength of will, patience, and positive outlook. Both had the qualities necessary to handle a Decatur man. Reed nearly smiled over that, which considering he was supposed to be watching the financial news with his father, would have seemed strange. The idea that Caroline was just the woman to handle him, made him happy. It wasn't an easy thing to find a partner who saw past the trappings of his position and wealth to understand the man beneath. But Caroline had done that from the start. She sensed his mood, knew what he needed without being told, and never hesitated to stand up to him when he was wrong. He knew she was sensitive about her relationship with her parents, but she didn't need to be. Not with him. With time and patience, she'd understand that. He knew that it was time to tell her how he felt, and she'd teed up the conversation perfectly earlier, but he couldn't follow through. Not yet.

Her position with the company did present a

problem for them. If she were anyone else, he'd have proposed, moved her in, anything to bind her to him immediately. But Caroline had a career and a professional reputation to uphold. It would be selfish to put his wants before her future. And he knew that if he came clean about how much he loved her, he could be taking her own decisions about her future away from her.

Even without Jamie's ears listening for gossip, he knew his executives speculated about their relationship. For his own part, he didn't particularly care if people talked, as long as it didn't impact their job performance. But it hurt to know that Caroline was being treated with less than the respect she deserved. Would any of that change if Caroline became a permanent employee? It could help, certainly. Without the speculation people would move on. And Reed knew he could put her in the new director position without anyone's assistance. But a move like that wouldn't be fair. She'd never be taken seriously if she didn't get the job on her own merit. He ran a frustrated hand through his hair.

"What's going on, son?" Fred asked in a low voice.

Reed had been so lost in his own thoughts that he'd inadvertently tuned his father out. "Nothing. Sorry."

His father huffed. "I wouldn't say she's nothing." He glanced over to the tree where Gail and Caroline were hanging ornaments and laughing. "I suspect she's actually a whole lot."

Reed stole a glance too and then nodded. "How

Hearts in Training

did you handle the business and a family at the same time?" Reed thought back to his childhood. "You were always there. How did you manage both?"

Fred blinked, a half smile on his face. "Are you having a baby?"

"What? No! Sorry. No. Just thinking about the future."

Fred looked over Reed's head for a minute. "I wasn't there as much as I wanted to be, but I worked at it. Your mother helped. She kept my priorities straight, reminded me what was important."

Reed glanced back at Caroline and made eye contact. She aimed a huge smile at him which he returned.

"Are you worried you'll be too distracted to be a good husband?"

Reed thought about that. "No. I think we could manage if it were just the two of us. But she wants children."

"You don't?" Fred frowned at him.

"I do. We both do." He corrected. "But we're so busy. Mom didn't work. Or rather, raising us was her job."

His father nodded. "That's how it worked for us. You'll make it work for you. That's the thing about kids, Reed. You're always just flying by the seat of your pants, making decisions with the information right in front of you."

"Great," Reed muttered, feeling slightly ill. Flying by the seat of his pants was not a comfortable position for him. He looked at Caroline again and was filled with warmth and appreciation. But that feeling was normal for Caroline. They'd work it out somehow.

"Caroline's the one, huh? So, does this mean you're going to pop the question?" Fred asked quietly.

Reed frowned. "She's got to figure out her career situation. I don't think it would be wise to do anything while she's considering her next move."

Fred leaned forward and thumped a hand on his shoulder. "Well, we support you, son. You'll do the right thing. Good luck." Fred stood and called over to Gail. "Well, my dear, shall we go? These kids have to work tomorrow."

Reed stood and followed his father toward the door. His mother and Caroline joined them to say goodbye. Gail hugged Reed then Caroline.

"Thanks for dinner and the decorations, Mom. It was good to see you."

Gail reached up and put a hand on his cheek. "You're very welcome. We always love seeing you." She turned to Caroline. "I'm so happy to have met you. I can see why all three of my children are taken with you." She paused to smile at Caroline's surprised expression. "Take care, dear."

Caroline stepped up to Reed the instant the door closed on his parents. She wrapped her arms around his waist and pressed a cheek to his chest. Loving the contact, Reed squeezed her in return.

"That was nice. You were right, I did really like

Hearts in Training

your mom. I can see how she managed you guys. She's clever and subtle."

Reed laughed. That was the perfect way to describe her. "I don't want to talk about my parents right now." He dropped his hands down to her hips to keep her tight against him. "I think we should talk about us."

"Uh oh." Caroline tipped her face up to his. Her eyes were still shining from their impromptu dinner party, but he could see the worry there too.

"Is this where you say, 'it's not you, it's me'?

Reed tightened his fingers on her. "That's not what I had in mind."

"Worse?" She cocked her head. "Better?"

He gave her hips a little shake. "Shush."

She leaned away. "Seriously? Shush?"

He watched her expression change from sunny to worried. "We haven't spent much time talking about the future, but I think we need to."

Caroline took a breath and moved to take his hand. Leading him to the couch, she murmured, "Maybe we should sit down."

She took a seat in the corner, tucked her feet up under her and pulled a pillow onto her lap. Reed sat next to her, giving her enough space to lessen his temptation to touch her, but also to let her know he would take her seriously.

"Your contract with Decatur is nearly up. I assume you're looking for your next job?"

Caroline drew her brows down, looking a little confused. "We just talked about this."

"I know. But I want to discuss it some more."

"Normally I would have had another contract lined up by now. I've been so distracted that I've gotten behind. I've sent out a few feelers, nothing concrete."

He reached for her hand and turned it over in his. He rubbed his thumb along her knuckles, enjoying the contrast of her soft small hand against his. "Will you get by? Without an income, I mean." Even predicting her reaction to his question, he felt the instant zing of anger shoot straight from her hand up his arm.

Caroline tried to pull her hand away, but he held tight, continuing his sweeping rhythm across the back of her hand.

She sighed. "I still get a salary. It's just less, and you know, my parents-" She trailed off.

"We've taken care of that, right?" He wanted her to remember that she was no longer responsible for their income.

"Right. So yes, I'll be okay. With my crazy hours I don't spend that much time in my apartment, so I don't need something better right away, and I don't have that many expenses."

Reed could relate. Until Caroline started staying with him, he was never home much either. He squeezed her hand. "Until we know that things are calmed down with Tony, I don't want you going back there."

Hearts in Training

"Two weeks, right?"

Reed was tempted to say 'forever' but he knew they weren't there yet. "As long as it takes to know you're safe."

She looked troubled by that. "That could extend past my contract here."

Reed suppressed a groan. "Your contract isn't here." He gestured around his apartment. "Your contract is with the same company I work for. What happens here is between us. And I want you to stay as long as you'd like."

"People will talk," she warned him.

"Honey, they're already talking. Who cares?" He let go of her hand and put an arm around her, fitting her into his side.

"I'm creating your public image as this young, handsome, good-works-doing CEO and you're shacking up with an employee!" She tried to get up, but he held fast.

"I am a young, handsome, good-works-doing CEO." He hated saying that aloud. "Who is spending quality time with his girlfriend." He paused, taking apart what she'd said. "Wait. You're not trying to make me out as some kind of playboy, are you?" Dread formed a hollow knot in his gut.

"That wasn't my angle." She shrugged. "But you are single. And you are hot. You're totally magazine cover material. People will see that."

Reed stood and paced away from her. He took a breath and stomped back to the couch. "Hot is

269

subjective. If I'm hot, as you say, I can't help it. And I'm not single." He cut a hand through the air. "I won't go along with that."

Caroline stared up at him. He didn't know if her frown was the result of his outburst or his denial of being single. Frankly he didn't care. The last thing he wanted was to be a sex symbol. And if he had any say in it, he wouldn't be single for long. He shook his head. "Think of something else."

"I can't stop what the press does with your image. But I can help protect you from the bad stuff at work." She stood and took a few steps toward Reed. "Just like you protect me from the bad stuff out there."

Chapter 20

*I*n keeping with her promise that she wouldn't go home until he was certain things had been resolved between Tony and his creditors, Caroline made herself at home in Reed's penthouse. He had done the noble thing and offered her the choice of using the guest bedroom or sharing his bed. Though it would certainly cause heartbreak when she returned to her own home, in Reed's arms was where she wanted to sleep. She had seen the pleasure and relief in his face when she declined the guest room. Stepping up to him and sliding her arms around his waist, she laid her cheek against his chest.

"Right here is where I want to be." She squeezed him. "This close."

Reed rested his chin on her head. "Then we're in perfect agreement. That's exactly where I want you."

Over the course of the next week, Caroline worked with the HR department to draft a proposal for a publicity team. She also sent out resumés for various positions, some of which were on the other side of the country.

The idea of leaving New York, especially of leaving Reed caused a physical pain in her chest. But she knew she had to be realistic as well. If things didn't work out between them, she would need a fresh start. Maybe once her mom and Tony were self-sufficient, she would feel free to live somewhere else.

She immediately thought of Wolf Creek. She'd never seen herself as a small-town kind of woman, but she could see herself fitting in there, walking around town, grabbing a coffee at Beans and Bagels, dinner at Bailey's. She frowned. Savannah and Daniel were there, which meant that the rest of the Decaturs would also be there every now and again. No, if she needed a fresh start she'd have to go farther away.

Two days later Caroline received a call from Steiner and Rohmann, a company in Los Angeles that every Transition Coordinator would kill to work for. The company was on the leading edge of technology and innovation. She swallowed to keep her coffee from burning a path back up her esophagus and swiveled to look out the window. A few months ago, she would have jumped at the chance to work all the way across the country. L.A., in the land of sun and smog. Now, her heart constricted. It was nearly a six-hour flight to New York, not exactly an easy commute.

For a split second she considered turning down the interview. But of course, she couldn't. The opportunity to pitch her agency's services to a company of their renown didn't come along every day. This kind of visibility would go a long way for her career and for her agency. Her computer announced a new email, the travel itinerary for the interview just as the company's administrative assistant had promised. She drew a shaky breath and opened the email. The flight was scheduled for tomorrow's red-eye. How was Reed going to react to her news?

She checked his schedule. His day was full, and there was no way she was going to tell him over instant messaging. She would have to wait until tonight. Caroline checked her calendar for the next two days and worked on rescheduling her meetings. By six o'clock she'd done everything but pack for the trip. She researched the company, familiarized herself with their key players, and jotted notes on their likely goals. Apart from talking to Reed, she was ready.

She slid her computer and phone into her bag and headed for the elevator. She slid the keycard into the slot indicating the top floor and waited for the doors to close. To her horror, the doors were nearly closed before opening again to let Elizabeth and another employee join her. Caroline worked to keep her facial expressions neutral while Elizabeth and the other woman moved in beside her, eyeing her from the side. Inside, Caroline wanted the floor to open up and drop her. Could she cancel the penthouse stop? She scanned the buttons, but she couldn't see a way to undo her keycard entry. The elevator would take her to the top before taking the other woman to the ground floor. Damn, damn, damn! Without a better excuse, Caroline pulled the printed travel itinerary from her bag and held them as if bringing important papers to Reed for his review. Would it work? She doubted it, but she wasn't about to step out of the elevator without a plausible work excuse for being there.

She tried not to notice Elizabeth's knowing look as she brushed past the other women, papers in hand, and exited in the penthouse lobby. Thank God the elevator didn't open directly into Reed's apartment!

"Have a great evening, Caroline." Elizabeth tittered. The other woman laughed softly.

Caroline kept her back to the elevator until the doors were closed. She knew her face was flaming red. Stepping up to the heavy wooden door, she dropped her forehead against it and thunked it against the door a couple of times. The door opened on the third thunk and she fell forward, into Reed's startled arms.

"What the heck?" He pulled her inside and looked into the lobby before closing the door behind her. "What's wrong?"

Caroline let her bag slide to the floor and stood in Reed's embrace. "Bad day."

"Ah." Reed pulled her in closer and held her tight. "Wanna talk about it?"

"Not really," she mumbled against his chest. "I'm pretty sure it's contagious."

He chuckled and led her to the kitchen island. She took a seat while he busied himself getting down a wine glass and pouring some wine for each of them. He slid her glass across the granite. "I'm pretty tough. Try me."

Caroline stared into the glass and wondered if he

really would brush this off. Not able to look him in the eye, Caroline took a sip of her wine and traced a finger along the surface of the countertop.

"So, the good news is that I have a job interview the day after tomorrow."

She could sense Reed leaning on the counter across from her. "That's great! What's the company? Anyone I know?"

"Steiner and Rohmann," she squeaked. She took a fortifying sip of wine, but she still couldn't look at him. She saw him move and chanced a peek at his face. His expression was impassive. He had his arms folded across his chest and his dark eyes were focused on her face.

"You know that's in California, right?"

She nodded, miserable.

"So, you're thinking of taking a job in L.A.?" He turned toward the sink and then back again. "Across the whole U.S.A. from here?"

She looked down into her glass. "I applied before...us. Honestly, I'd forgotten all about it until today."

Reed shook his head, his eyes narrowed, and suddenly she could see why people considered him a person to be wary of. If she didn't know him better, she would be tempted to be afraid of him.

"Why didn't you turn them down?"

Her mouth fell open. "It's an amazing opportunity. People in all levels of my field would kill for the opportunity to try for this job!"

She looked at Reed, but he wasn't swayed. He was angry, she could see it in the set of his jaw. "I don't have a job, Reed. Once I'm done here, I don't have anywhere to go."

The minute the words left her mouth she wanted to take them back. She could see the storm raging in his mind.

"You belong *here*." Reed's quiet voice was in complete contrast to the simmering anger in his eyes. "Have you applied here?"

Her stomach churned. "No. I haven't."

He paced into the living room and then stomped back and grabbed her hand, towing her along to the couch.

"We're going to talk about this, aren't we?" As she'd hoped, Reed showed a glimmer of humor at her attempt to lighten the moment. For some reason, he preferred to talk on the couch.

"Why haven't you applied yet, Carrie?"

Caroline picked at a spot on the pillow beside her. "I don't want the job to be handed to me, Reed. I want to know that I earned it. I want to know that I was good enough to beat out all the other contenders."

Reed frowned at her as if he couldn't believe what he was hearing. "You would. How can you doubt that?"

"How can I know that? I'm the president's girlfriend."

"Relationship aside, Decatur Industries would be

honored to have someone of your caliber, with your creativity, heading up our training department." He shook his head. "Don't ever doubt that." He reached out and took her hand again. "If that was the good news, I'm not sure I'm healthy enough to hear the bad news."

Despite the anxiety making a hurricane in her stomach, Caroline gave a small laugh. She scooted forward and let Reed pull her into his lap. "The bad news is that Elizabeth and another woman just saw me get out of the elevator on this floor."

Reed stopped rubbing her back for just a split second. "That's your bad news?" He pulled her in closer again. "I think your priorities are out of sync, babe."

Caroline leaned back to look at him. "You're not worried that having witnesses to my being here is going to hurt you?"

Reed shrugged. "Not anymore. Why are you worried about it?"

Caroline sputtered, unable to settle on just one reason. "People already think I'm some kind of whore, Reed."

Reed clutched her tighter. She could feel his anger zap through her. "The hell they do! Elizabeth is jealous. Everyone else we interact with approves or is respectful enough to keep their thoughts to themselves."

"Of course, they are! They value their jobs."

Reed held her by her shoulders. "Who isn't treating you with respect?"

Caroline shrugged his hands off her shoulders where they landed on the tops of her thighs. She petted the soft dark hair on his forearms. "You can't fight all my battles for me, Reed." She looked in his eyes and saw the determination there. "Believe it or not, I managed my life pretty well before you came on the scene."

Reed looked down at her hands. "I overstepped, huh?"

She put a hand to the side of his face, scraping her fingers across his stubble. "Your heart's in the right place."

Reed tipped his face into her hand and looked at her. For a few seconds, Caroline thought he was going to tell her he loved her. Instead, he asked softly, "When does your flight leave?"

"Tomorrow night's red-eye. I'll probably stay the night and be back on Friday."

"Will you come back here?"

Caroline smiled. "If you still want me."

Reed growled and pulled her back into his lap. "I always want you."

She wrapped her arms around his neck and tipped her forehead to his. "Always is a long time."

"Always," he repeated.

There was a kind of desperation to their lovemaking that night, and Caroline wondered if Reed felt it too. Afterward she lay wrapped in his arms, listening as his breathing evened into sleep. She laid awake most of the night thinking through her circumstances.

Using the same thought process, she followed on projects, she examined her goals, her resources, and giving her heart a little voice in the matter, she considered her wishes.

She weighed the pros and cons of taking the job in L.A. if it was offered to her. She did the same with the idea of working for Decatur. The list of pros was much longer for staying in New York, though in a way, riskier too.

Rolling over in his arms, she watched Reed sleep and tried to imagine a future without him in it. She couldn't. The fact was, she loved him, even more than she loved her career. And she was relatively certain Reed loved her too. No, he hadn't said the words, but he'd shown her in ways that spoke every bit as loudly.

If she didn't get another job in New York right away, Reed would support her. She had no doubts about that. But could she let him? She honestly didn't know. Just as it was in Reed's nature to take care of everyone he loved, it was in hers to take care of herself.

She moved on to consider what it would be like to live and work with Reed. They wouldn't be together most of the day, and as an executive she would answer to the entire Board, so she wouldn't strictly answer to him either.

She thought about the rumors, the bad feelings some of the women had directed her way. Would they go away? Probably. Would it damage her reputation with the company? If she had her dream job and her dream man, did it even matter what other people thought of her? She thought about how Reed would react to that and smiled in the dark.

Time and again he'd fought for her like the modern-day knight she'd described as her perfect partner. What had she done to fight for him? Nothing, that's what.

Snuggling back against Reed's chest Caroline made a few decisions and then fell into a blessedly deep sleep.

Chapter 21

*W*ednesday dawned cold and snowy. Caroline rolled over to find that Reed had already gotten out of bed. She pulled on one of his T-shirts, a white v-neck, and followed the smell of coffee into the kitchen. Reed was sitting at the island staring into his cup. She padded up behind him and pressed a kiss to the side of his neck. He gave her a half-smile as she poured her own cup and leaned on the counter across from him.

"Good morning, sunshine." She studied his tired face. He was in serious need of cheering up.

"Hi yourself." He raised his eyes long enough to check her out in his shirt.

She sipped her coffee and watched him for a few minutes, trying to decide on the best plan to cheer him up. "What do you have on your plate today?"

He shrugged and glared at the counter. "Couple of meetings, then driving my girlfriend to the airport."

She gave him a sympathetic glance. "Is she coming back?"

Reed heaved a sigh and pushed his mug away. "God, I hope so!"

She came around the counter and straddled his

lap. "Don't you think she's going to miss you?"

Reed's hands immediately settled on her hips, but his expression didn't change. "How the hell would I know? Suddenly I have no idea what's in your-her head."

Caroline stroked her hands down his muscled shoulders. "Maybe she's going to miss you terribly, but she still has something to prove to herself. Something important to her." She stopped at his elbows and leaned forward to put her forehead to his. She could feel his breath on her face. "Do you trust the way you feel about her enough to let her discover this one last thing?"

"I l- ". She smashed her fingers against his lips.

"Yes or no." She removed her fingers and replaced them with her lips, drawing him in for a long, slow kiss.

He made eye contact and answered solemnly. "Yes."

"Then I imagine there's a lot to do today before her flight leaves." Knowing he was every bit as dazed and turned on as she was, Caroline slid off Reed's lap and snatched up her mug before heading back to the bedroom. She paused and looked over her shoulder. "Oh, and I'll need to borrow a suitcase."

Another decision made last night; Caroline rode the elevator to Reed's office with him. If Reed didn't care who saw them together, she wasn't going to worry about it either.

The doors opened to his floor and he kissed her goodbye in full view of Jamie before stepping into

Hearts in Training

the outer area of his office. Embarrassed but happy, Caroline gave Jamie and Reed a little wave before the doors closed and whisked her down to her own floor.

Fulfilling another decision, Caroline submitted her resumé for the training director position and then worked on responding to emails for the rest of the morning. She texted her itinerary to Reed's phone and called her mother to check in and let her know about the trip.

True to form, Heather spent the first twenty minutes of the call gushing about the hotel and how wonderful Tony's new job was. She spent another ten minutes talking about the money management class they were taking, making sure to praise Reed for such a smart idea. Once all her own issues had been discussed she settled in to hear about Caroline's upcoming trip.

"I'm flying out tonight and I should be home on Friday."

"How exciting, Carrie. California! Is Reed going with you?"

Caroline shook her head even though her mother couldn't see her. "No, Ma. He's much too busy. And besides, I'm pitching my company's services to a new account."

"A new account?" Her mother parroted. "You have a perfectly good job right here in New York. Why on Earth would you want to leave?"

Caroline could hear an edge of worry in her mother's voice and she understood. California was too far for a quick visit or to meet for lunch. "I don't want to leave, but my contract here is nearly up. I have to keep my options open and being invited to pitch for this company is a huge honor."

"Well, I don't have any doubts that you've earned the honor, but don't forget you have people here who love you, and who will miss you horribly if you move away."

"I know you love me, Ma." Caroline began, but her mother interrupted.

"Yes, but I meant Reed."

"Reed?"

"Yes, silly. What will he do without you?"

Caroline's heart cracked a little. "He'll be fine, Ma." A noise near the door made Caroline look up and freeze.

"I'm not so sure about that," Reed told Caroline in a low voice.

Her breath left her for just a moment. "I love you, Ma. I'll bring you something from L.A. and call you when I get back." She barely waited for her mother to say goodbye before disconnecting the call.

Reed folded his arms and moved farther into her office, his gaze never leaving hers. Caroline hitched a smile on her face but really, she wanted to sink into his arms and let him make everything all better.

"What's up?" she asked.

"I missed you already." Standing an appropriate distance from her and with his back to the door, no

Hearts in Training

one would have reason to speculate about their conversation. But Reed's expression, combined with the tone of his voice, felt more intimate than an embrace.

"I'll be gone two days." She thought about that. "What will it be like when I move back to my own apartment?"

Reed shrugged and slid his hands into his pockets. "I'm trying not to think that far ahead."

Caroline acknowledged that. She didn't want to think about it either. Especially right now. "Don't you have meetings this afternoon?"

"Jamie rescheduled them." He was still watching her.

"You have the afternoon free?"

"I thought we could run over to your apartment so that you could pick up whatever you need for your interview."

"Wow. That's-" She stopped and laughed. "You just don't want to loan me your luggage."

Reed smiled just as she'd intended. "My feelings for you only go so far, you know." The twinkle was back in his eyes.

"Oh, I know. You're stingy with your feelings." She wanted to touch him so badly. From his expression she suspected he felt the same way. "Thank you. I would feel more comfortable in my own clothes."

Reed called Mason on the way to the elevator so that he was waiting in front of the building by the time they'd crossed the lobby.

They didn't speak much on the way to Caroline's apartment. She reached for Reed's hand and he held hers in both of his, his grip the only outward indication of his present mood.

Caroline was relieved to see that nothing had been disturbed in her apartment while she'd been staying with Reed. She flipped quickly through her mail, pulling out the items that needed attention and stuffing them into her messenger bag. Reed followed her through to the bedroom and lounged on her bed while she decided what to take to California.

"The company Christmas party is Friday night," Reed reminded her while she was sorting through her business attire.

"I can't wait! Jamie told me so much about it that I can practically picture it. An actual ball!"

"I've never asked if you were going. I guess I just assumed you would go with me."

She stepped out of the closet and laid her selections over the end of the bed. "I assumed that too. Or, if nothing else, that we'd each go separately." He shook his head. "I know- we're not really hiding anymore. But my point was that I wouldn't miss it for anything." She turned back to her closet, looking at her dress options. "Should we coordinate our outfits?"

At that, Reed laughed aloud. "Don't we always?"

She chuckled, knowing how often they dressed in matching colors. "I guess we do." She moved aside a few options but none of them felt quite right.

"I had planned to find something in the next day or two, but obviously that's going to be tough now. Maybe I'll call your sister tomorrow. Think she'd be willing to find me something for the ball?"

Reed's eyes shone. "She'd be thrilled. She'll make sure I match whatever you choose."

"It's pretty short notice. She won't mind?"

"She won't mind at all. She thrives on pressure."

Caroline bustled around collecting other clothing to pack. "I know your parents always attend, but what about your sisters? Do they come?"

Reed stretched his arms behind his head and stared at the ceiling. "They try to come. Savannah and Daniel will be there this year. They'll stay for a few days so that we can celebrate Christmas as a family before heading back to Wolf Creek." He was quiet for a minute. "And this year, your family will be there too, since Tony is an employee now."

"Oh! You're right. I hadn't even thought of that. Both of our families will be in the same place at the same time." Caroline watched as Reed worked to maintain a straight face.

"Should we introduce them?" he asked.

Caroline pictured that and laughed. "I'm pretty sure we can't avoid it. I should apologize in advance to your family."

Reed laughed and pulled her down beside him. "They love you and want the best for you. There's nothing wrong with that."

"I know. You're right." She patted his face and

gave him a quick peck before rolling off the bed to grab a few more things from her bathroom.

"We need to mark this occasion," Reed told her.

She peeked her head around the bathroom door. "Our families meeting?"

"No. You said I was right. Can I call Jamie and have her draw that up in writing?"

Caroline laughed.

Reed rolled off the bed when Caroline zipped the case shut and then took it from her to roll it to the door. He stopped in her living room and looked around. "You don't own much, do you?"

Caroline stopped behind him and tried to view her place through his eyes. "I'm not much for clutter."

He looked over his shoulder at her with a playful expression. "That's smart, you know."

"Why?"

"This is New York, honey. Square footage is expensive."

Caroline stepped around him to pick up her bag and keys. "Are you trying to impress me? My entire apartment could fit in your master suite."

He followed her out the door and held her bag while she locked up. "Are you impressed by the size of my...apartment?"

Caroline rolled her eyes but stepped up close to him. "Yes. In fact, I'm only interested in your huge," she paused to kiss him, "apartment."

THEY STOPPED for take-out and took it back to Reed's place for a late lunch. Seated at the island, Reed peeked at Caroline as she dug into her pasta. If she was nervous about the trip or the pitch, she didn't show it. Then again, she was used to this. In so many ways Reed was impressed by her. He knew he had a terrific job, but he'd known from his teen years that the company would one day be his to run. He'd never had the kind of insecurity that Caroline had in her career. He knew that, given the choice, Caroline would stay in New York. But he also understood that she had a job to do, and her need to continually prove herself is what drove her to follow through on this pitch, even if she no longer wanted the account.

He also knew he'd been a jerk for making things more difficult for her. She'd become the sunny spot in his life, and he couldn't imagine his life without her now. The choice was hers to make and he needed to respect that.

"So, did you make any plans for your free time in L.A.?"

Caroline shrugged. "I might do a little sightseeing. You know, see the Hollywood sign, take a celebrity home tour or something."

Reed laughed, but he could picture her in a little tourist van with a colorful map spread out in front of her. "You could hit Rodeo Drive and do a little Christmas shopping."

Caroline gave him a startled look. "Christmas is less than a week away and I haven't gotten you anything." She leveled a look at him. "Any chance you wrote a note to Santa this year?"

If he had, she would have been at the top of his list. Instead, he teased, "You know that Santa-child communications are strictly confidential."

"Hmm. Well, that's no help." She gave him a beseeching look. "What's on your Christmas list?"

Reed thought about the cologne and clothing he'd received from women in the past. "Nothing you'll find on Rodeo Drive, that's for sure."

She gave him a frustrated sigh. Being completely honest, he answered, "Having you with me this year is enough."

All too soon it was time to leave for the airport. Knowing he wouldn't be able to see her to the gate, he opted to drive her himself so that they could spend the time alone.

The closer they got to the airport the faster Caroline chattered. "You have my flight and hotel information, right?"

"You sent it to my phone and email this morning."

She nodded. "Good." She checked her phone. "And you'll have someone pick me up on Friday, in plenty of time to get ready for the ball?"

"I'll be there, honey." Reed couldn't imagine asking her to take a cab all the way downtown. Minutes later he pulled up to the temporary parking section for her airline and parked to help her with her bags. Cars honked at him to move, but Reed didn't care, and Caroline didn't appear to either. Wrapping her tightly in his arms he kissed her and turned her loose.

"Call me when you get to your hotel room, okay?"

She nodded and reached for the handle of her suitcase. He watched her take two steps toward the doors and look over her shoulder.

"I love you. I'll call you in the morning when I'm settled." And then she was gone.

Reed had a lot to think about as he drove the length of Manhattan to his building. Knowing he wouldn't be able to sleep until Caroline's flight landed, he stopped in his office to pick up a few files he should have read earlier in the day. Checking the time, he decided to put in a call to his sisters as well. As he dialed, a plan began to formulate in his mind.

Chapter 22

Caroline was exhausted when she finally checked into the suite Steiner and Rohmann reserved for her. The rooms were beautiful, but she still preferred the simple elegance of Reed's apartment. Thinking of Reed, she texted him a selfie in her suite and then added a note that she was going to take a shower.

Reed's response was immediate and short. *Send pictures.*

She sent three laughing emojis and set to work unpacking her bag and then grabbed a hot shower to revive her. As soon as she was out of the shower and dressed, she checked Reed's schedule on her phone and confirmed that he was just heading into his first meeting of the day. She texted him a quick note that she would call him later and received two hearts and the words, '*Break a leg*'.

Heaven help her, she'd only just left the crutches behind. Pulling the silliness aside, she settled on the couch to review her research notes on the company and check her emails for any last-minute changes.

Finding no changes, Caroline headed to the concierge to meet the car that would take her to the meeting. While she waited, Caroline spotted a couple that reminded her of Daniel and Savannah. Thinking of them gave her an idea for Reed's Christmas gift. The more she thought of it, the more excited she became. She checked Reed's calendar and then sent Jamie a quick but thorough message. Jamie would be the perfect person to get the details worked out. Feeling a sense of peace, Caroline got into the hired car and enjoyed the passing scenery.

The offices of Steiner and Rohmann were impressive, an imposing figure of glass and steel. The administrative assistant she'd been corresponding with met her in the lobby to escort her to the conference room.

Caroline reviewed her presentation in her head as they walked. She'd done this dozens of times in dozens of locations. Normally, she enjoyed the buzz of adrenaline she got from selling her company's services to a prospective customer. Today should have been no different, except this time all she felt was tired. She wanted to go home. She nearly laughed aloud. Home to Reed's apartment. Home to her little windowed office on the fourth floor of the Decatur Industries building.

Returning to present with a renewed sense of purpose, Caroline delivered a fantastic pitch. She beamed at the group seated around the table. She knew that she'd impressed them.

"Before I wrap up, does anyone have questions?" She answered a few questions and dodged a few others about contract negotiations, leaving that for her company's leadership team. Mindful of the two-hour window they'd scheduled, she had time for just one more question.

"Will you be handling the account personally?" one of the older gentlemen asked. The whole group seemed to hang on her answer.

She smiled in what she hoped was total confidence. Before her contract with Decatur, that kind of question would have sent her into cloud nine. "No decisions for which of my highly capable associates will win the opportunity have been made, but I'll certainly be available to consult." She paused and looked at the individuals sitting around the table. "I'm truly honored for the opportunity to pitch our services to you, and I wish you all the best in your decision."

An hour later Caroline had dropped her computer off at the hotel and took a car into the heart of the city to do some sightseeing. Los Angeles was so much more crowded than it appeared on television. There were homeless people everywhere, so much more than in Manhattan and she wondered if that was because the weather was fairer here.

She stopped to admire the handprints outside Grauman's Chinese Theater and studied the stars on the sidewalk in front of fancy stores and cheap tourist stores alike. Just like in Times Square there were costumed actors and street peddlers trying to catch the attention of wide-eyed tourists. She put her head down and passed through the crowd until the sidewalks were less congested. Here, there were upscale shops and cute little bistros.

Peeking into a few store windows Caroline decided to do a little last-minute Christmas shopping. She stepped into a store that sold items for couples of all forms. Thinking of the times Reed snuck some of her coffee she bought a set of travel mugs labeled *His* and *Hers*. She also bought a set of matching lumberjack plaid flannel pajamas for Savannah and Daniel.

In another shop she bought a set of picture frames for Reed's parents and a gorgeous silver necklace for Angela. She bought her mother a leather-bound bill organizer and a wallet which she would fill with gift cards to their favorite restaurants. She came across a small boutique selling lingerie and decided to buy herself a gift as well. Maybe she'd even wrap it and put it under the tree for Christmas morning. She grinned as she imagined Reed's face when she opened it.

Knowing that Jamie was taking care of the rest of Reed's gift, she stopped in another small boutique and selected a gift for Jamie as well.

She found a coffee shop and settled her packages on the seat beside her. Checking the time, she realized that Reed would be out of work. She also hadn't spoken with Angela about a dress for the party. She sent Angela a quick text and then dialed Reed. He answered on the first ring.

"Carrie. How'd it go?"

She smiled into the phone. "Great. I think we'll get the contract."

"Congratulations." He sounded genuine.

"They asked if I would be handling their account." She told him, still savoring the experience.

"That's a huge compliment."

She tried to picture his expression. "Yes, I think so too."

"What did you tell them?"

"I told them I would be available to consult but that my company would select the right resources to work with them." She could nearly feel Reed's relief through the phone.

"You wouldn't take it if they offered?" he asked quietly.

"No." She shook her head even though he couldn't see her. "It just doesn't feel right, you know?"

"I know." He was quiet for a moment. "So, you're coming home?"

"My flight leaves tomorrow afternoon," she reminded him, wishing it was sooner.

"I guess that will have to be good enough. What are you planning to do tonight?"

"Well, I went Christmas shopping this afternoon. As soon as my car arrives, I'm going to head back to the hotel, and then try to get a reservation at a swanky restaurant. See if I can rub elbows with some famous people."

Reed laughed. "Sounds like you've had a productive trip already." He lowered his voice. "What did you get me for Christmas, Carrie?"

"Hmm. You'll have to wait until Christmas. It's a surprise."

Reed groaned and then turned serious. "I can't

Hearts in Training

wait that long to give you your gift. Would it be okay if I gave it to you a little early?"

Caroline saw the hotel's car pull up to the curb, so she left some cash on the table and gathered her packages. "Can't keep a secret that long?" she teased.

"Something like that."

"My car's here. I've gotta go. I love you, Reed."

"Carrie, I-" Reed faltered.

"I'll call you later tonight if it's not too late. I keep forgetting there's a three-hour time difference."

"That's okay, honey. Call me whenever. Go catch your car and I'll look forward to seeing you tomorrow."

Two hours later, Caroline had a table for one at a popular seafood restaurant. She placed her order and then looked around, scanning the faces for celebrities. Everyone looked familiar in that way strangers often do when you're away from home, but she didn't see any A-list stars dining with her that evening. She guessed that was one thing she couldn't cross off her list on this trip.

She wondered if Reed ever travelled to L.A. for business. If so, maybe she could tag along and see more of the area. Apart from the shocking homeless population, she loved the bright atmosphere and comfortable temperatures.

She returned directly to the hotel after dinner, not feeling brave enough to experience the city alone at night. She checked the time and added three hours. It would be the middle of the night on the East coast.

Disappointed, she took a shower and got ready for bed. She tucked herself in and found a romantic Christmas movie to fall asleep to. She watched the couple on T.V. share a long look and decided it really would kill her to move back into her own apartment. Having Reed beside her, holding her all night had spoiled her for ever being able to live alone again. She hugged the pillow beside her and let the low sound of the movie lull her to sleep.

The next day she woke too early due to the time difference and made herself coffee in the in-room machine. She took it out to the little balcony outside her room and waited for the sun to come up. Caroline reflected on how much she used to enjoy business trips. She used to think of them as an escape from the life that tied her to New York City and her family, such as it was. Now, she realized, leaving New York left a hole that the excitement of a new location couldn't fill. She was headed home today, and she was ready.

Once the sun had come up and she knew Reed would be awake she sent him a quick text to say good morning and got a response back right away. She knew he'd be extraordinarily busy today wrapping up everything that needed to be done before the next week. She hoped he didn't notice that Jamie had moved a few items from next week to today. She smiled. He'd either love his Christmas gift, or he'd be angry that she interfered. She dearly hoped it was the first one because it was too late to back out now.

Next, she texted Angela. Angela immediately sent her some pictures of dresses to choose from for the party. She flipped through them, expanding and examining each dress before deciding on a tea-length red satin gown with a fitted bodice that settled into a deep V in the front and back. Angela approved of her choice and promised to leave the dress and matching shoes at Reed's place later that evening. Caroline sat back in her chair and stretched her arms high above her head. Everything was falling into place.

Caroline ordered breakfast from room service and then packed quickly so that she could enjoy her food on the balcony. Excited as she was about going home, she wanted to soak in every bit of the temperate California weather before she returned to the December tundra of Manhattan.

Her flight left early, putting her back in New York just before five P.M. The ball started at seven-thirty so she would be cutting it very close. Perhaps she should have asked Angela to bring her dress straight to the venue. But no, after travelling all day she would want to freshen up before the party.

With the snarl of L.A. traffic Caroline barely made her flight, but once the plane took off, she allowed herself to relax, even managing to sleep for most of the leg to Minneapolis. Her layover in Minnesota should have been short, just forty-five minutes, but she departed the plane to find a snowstorm over Michigan delaying all the connecting flights headed East.

Praying her luggage containing Christmas gifts found its way to the right place, Caroline hitched her purse across her body and set out in search of lunch and a quiet place to call Reed. She settled on a Tex-

Mex restaurant and found a corner booth where she could prop her feet on the bench seat across from her.

She was quickly greeted by a waitress and placed her order before calling Reed, for once not checking his schedule first.

"Carrie?" His voice was hushed.

"Reed. Did I interrupt anything important?" Her voice cracked and she knew he'd notice.

"Nothing is more important than you. I'm just meeting with Alan."

"Please apologize for me." She really liked Alan.

"He'll understand. What's wrong, honey?"

"My connecting flight is delayed. I'm grounded in Minneapolis." She could hear Reed growl into the phone.

"That's not convenient, is it?"

She wanted to cry. "This sucks. What if I don't make it back in time for the party? I don't want to miss it." Her voice cracked again making her glad Reed couldn't see her face.

"I don't want you to miss it either, Carrie." He was quiet and she knew he was thinking. Planning and executing were two of his strongest skills. She trusted him to figure this out. "I won't be able to pick you up from the airport." His voice was apologetic.

"I know. That's okay. You need to be there to greet your employees."

"I didn't want to do that without you," Reed

admitted.

She almost, *almost* laughed at that. "I'm so sorry, Reed. I know you hate peopling. Hopefully it's just a couple of hours. I'll rescue you the instant I get there."

"Text me when you know your arrival time and I'll send Mason to pick you up at the airport. Angela took your dress and whatever else up to my place. I'll tell him to bring you there and wait for you."

"Okay. Thank you for being here for me. Again," she whispered, seriously close to tears.

"Always, Carrie. I'll see you soon."

Her food came just as she was hanging up with Reed. She'd no sooner put a forkful of chicken enchilada in her mouth than her phone rang again. Caller-ID indicated the number was Decatur Industries. She swallowed her bite too quickly, hoping it wouldn't give her indigestion later and answered the call.

"Caroline Trumbull."

"Caroline? This is Bill Burns from Human Resources."

"Oh! Yes. How are you, Bill?"

"I'm good. Ready for the party tonight, and then a long relaxing week off with my family for the holidays."

Caroline looked longingly at her food. Bill was a talker. "That sounds wonderful."

"So, that's why I'm calling, actually. I'd like to

wrap up a few things before my vacation. Not that you're a thing." He stopped and laughed at himself. "I apologize. Let me start over."

Caroline forked up a bite and wondered if she could chew it before she'd need to speak again. Just in case she decided to go for it, she held the bite in front of her mouth.

"The Board here at Decatur would like to offer you the position of Executive Director of Training."

Caroline let the fork fall back on her plate. "Excuse me?"

Bill cleared his throat. "I'm sorry. Sounds like this hit you as a bit of a surprise. We saw your resumé and elevated it straight to the Board." He laughed. "It's highly unusual, I know, but they didn't even feel the need for a formal interview." He lowered his voice as if to avoid being overheard. "They held an emergency meeting and voted on it."

Caroline was breathless. "Already? When?"

"Late yesterday."

She thought back on her conversations with Reed. Was that what he'd tried to tell her? "Reed knows? And Fred?"

Bill chuckled. "Of course. They abstained from voting though. It's not really my business so I'm sorry if I'm being too personal, but I understand there could be a conflict of interest for them."

Caroline pushed the food around her plate. "Reed and I are seeing each other." There. She'd said it aloud to someone with the power to impact their professional lives.

"Okay, well." He cleared his throat again. "The only thing I need to know is whether you'd like to accept the position or not."

Caroline tipped her head back and stared at the ceiling. "Under the terms I established as your consultant?"

"Yes. But with one key addition. Fred asked me to convey that they understand you may have a contract to break with your current employer. They've added a stipulation that they will negotiate a buyout of your contract."

"Um." She took that in. "Wow."

Bill chuckled again. "Yeah. To be honest, I've never been asked to do that for a prospective employee before. Do you, ah, expect legal expenses to get out of your contract?"

"No. They won't be happy, especially since I probably just landed them a huge new client. But I'm not going to a competitor, so they don't have a leg to fight on." She took a breath. "So, yes! I would love to accept the position." She heard his sigh of relief.

"Wonderful! We can work out the details after the holidays. Will we see you at the party tonight?"

Caroline frowned at her food. "If my flight makes it in on time."

"Oh my. Well, good luck. If I don't see you, have a great holiday."

"You, too, Bill. And thank you for calling."

303

Caroline hung up and sat back. She would be working for Decatur. And she'd told the head of Human Resources about her relationship with Reed. If only she was home to celebrate with Reed!

She opened an app on her phone to check the status of her flight and then dug into her lukewarm food. Her flight would leave an hour later than scheduled, but at least she wasn't snowed in. She calculated the time. She'd be fashionably late, but she wouldn't miss the party altogether. Slightly more relaxed now, she was able to focus on lunch and think about Christmas. She still needed to wrap gifts. She imagined waking up with Reed on Christmas morning, watching the sun peek over the Manhattan skyline and exchanging gifts. Presumably they'd also visit her family and his to share the day with them as well. Thinking there would be more time to discuss it they hadn't taken the time to make plans before her trip. It was something she planned to change if they were still together a year from now. One thing she knew for sure was that her job at Decatur would give her a more reasonable work/life balance.

Finished with her lunch, she left a tip on the table and paid the tab. She had just enough time to get to the gate before the flight would start boarding. Once the plane took off for the last leg of the trip, Caroline turned her attention to making a list of the things she needed to do when she landed in New York. Remembering that she still needed to give Reed her arrival time, she sent him a text.

She was so anxious to get back that the flight seemed to drag. Wanting to stay busy, she pulled out her laptop and began fleshing out plans for taking

Hearts in Training

over the new department. By the time the plane landed she felt organized and ready to get to work. It took a few moments to remember she still needed to resign from Johnson & Jenkins and make things official with Decatur Industries.

Caroline texted Mason when she got to the luggage carousal and then waited with the crowd of passengers who were probably also hoping their bags didn't miss their planes.

Fifteen minutes later, she was wheeling her luggage to the exit Mason had indicated and was so elated to see a familiar face that she nearly hugged him.

"Glad you made it home safe, Caroline. Sounds like you've had a long day," he commented as he tucked her bags into the trunk.

Caroline settled into the back seat and relaxed against the warm, smooth leather. "Long, for sure. But thank you for being here. Are you missing the party?"

Mason smiled at her in the rearview mirror as he pulled into the web of traffic surrounding the airport. "I'll go when you go. I'm going to take you home to get ready and then take you on to the party."

She knew he was paid well for his services, but she appreciated his sacrifice all the same. "Thank you so much, Mason. Being able to go means the world to me. I promise to hurry so that you don't miss much."

Mason gave her a grin. "Take your time, Caroline. The good stuff won't happen before you

305

get there, so I won't miss a thing."

Caroline gave that a half-second's thought and then pulled out her list and reviewed it again. Shower, hair, makeup, dress. She wasn't likely to miss a step, but having a list gave her the feeling everything was under control. She had measurable steps. Mason drove like a contestant in a figure-eight race and managed to get her to the building in under twenty minutes. She wondered if that was a record for him.

She sprinted through the underground parking garage and into the elevator willing it to go faster somehow. Inside Reed's apartment she dropped her bags and took a moment to breathe.

Clicking heels preceded Angela's voice. "There you are! I've got the shower running and I've laid out your clothes. Which bag has your makeup?"

Caroline blinked at Angela and pointed to her carry-on.

"Good. Go hop in the shower and I'll get ready for hair and makeup. Don't get your hair wet!"

"Angela! I could hug you," Caroline sang as she hurried to Reed's enormous bathroom.

"We don't have time for that," Angela teased from the bedroom.

Caroline took a fast shower, just long enough to scrub the travel from her skin, toweled off, and rubbed on some scented moisturizer. On the counter, Angela had left undergarments for her. They were the same color red as the dress and sexier than anything she'd ever owned. She put them on and marveled at the perfect fit, and then pulled her robe from a hook near the door. She opened the door and found Angela ready for her.

"Why are you here?" Caroline asked as Angela started pulling her hair into place.

Angela shrugged, focused on Caroline's hair. "I heard you would be late and thought you might want help getting ready. It's a big night for our family and I wanted you to look and feel your best."

Caroline knew Reed thought of Angela as the more selfish sister, but there was nothing selfish in what she was doing right now. "You're a god-send, Ang. Seriously. A god-send."

Angela blushed a little and then stood back to critique her work. She'd pulled back the sides with glittering pins and left the rest to fall full and wavy down her back.

Caroline finished applying her makeup while Angela left and returned with the dress. Caroline reached out a hand to pet the red satin. "This is gorgeous."

Angela smiled, looking truly pleased. "You're going to look gorgeous in it."

A minute later Caroline had to agree. The dress fit perfectly and flattered her figure. She slipped on a pair of red satin sandals and pulled a few items out of her purse to deposit into a silver beaded clutch that Angela held out to her. She twirled on the spot and looked at Angela. "Ready!"

Angela grinned and linked her arm through Caroline's. "Let's go steal the show, Cinderella."

Chapter 23

Twenty minutes later, Mason pulled up to the curb of the hotel where the ball was being held and left the car with a valet. Both women giggled at his ridiculous display of pride when he stood between them and ushered them both into the ballroom.

They checked their coats and stood at the top of a short, grand staircase. Caroline oriented herself with the layout of buffet tables, bar, and dancefloor, and then scanned the crowd for Reed or her parents. Mason escorted Angela down the stairs and Caroline followed behind still searching for Reed.

When she reached the bottom of the stairs the crowd parted, and Reed stood there looking both handsome and imposing in his black tuxedo. Caroline's knees nearly gave out in relief and pleasure. She wanted to run to him and throw herself into his arms. Instead, she stepped up to him calmly and looked into his eyes. He was nervous, she could see it. Quietly, she asked him, "Have you seen a handsome CEO around here in need of rescue?"

A sparkle entered his eyes and she couldn't resist leaning up to kiss his cheek. Putting a hand to her back, he ushered her toward the crowd.

"Thank God you're here," he teased. "People keep telling me to have a Merry Christmas and I'm running out of things to say to that."

Caroline laughed and took pity on him, knowing that it was likely true. Leaning into his side, she patted his chest. "No worries, dear. I've got this."

Reed grinned down at her. "I know you do, babe."

Caroline looked around and noted several people giving them speculative glances. Elizabeth was among them, her phone peeping discreetly above her folded arms. Caroline looked back at Reed, curious for his reaction, but he didn't appear to have noticed. He was back to looking nervous.

"Reed, is there somewhere we can go to talk for a few minutes?"

His eyes flashed to hers, seemed to read something there and calmed down. "I have to address everyone soon."

That explained his nervousness. "It's good news, I promise. But I wanted to tell you before you hear it from someone else."

His hands settled around her waist and he pulled her in close, looking down into her eyes. "Share your good news."

She beamed up at him, eager to see his reaction. "I accepted a job offer today. It came out of nowhere and it was too good an offer to pass up." She watched his expression become speculative.

"Whose offer did you accept?" he asked quietly.

Struggling to keep a straight face, she answered him. "Believe it or not, it's this little family run place.

Decatur Industries. You might have heard of them."

Reed just stared at her for a split second and then lifted her off her feet and twirled with her. "Really?"

He set her down and she shrugged. "They made me an offer I couldn't resist."

Reed grinned. "Oh yeah? What was that?"

"My dream job." She lowered her voice. "With my dream man." She raised to her tiptoes as Reed leaned down to kiss her.

"Ah-hem."

They parted to see Fred and Gail standing beside them. Fred had a microphone in one hand and a champagne glass in the other. "Should we say a few words, son?" Fred winked at Caroline when Reed appeared to turn gray.

Caroline reached for his hand and pulled him along behind his parents toward the low stage where a band was set up.

"You're not going to get sick or pass out on me, are you?" Caroline intended to make him smile, but the closer they got to the stage, the worse he looked.

"I just might," he told her through gritted teeth.

"Which? Should I dodge or catch you?" They were nearing the stage and she could see Savannah, Daniel, and Angela waiting nearby to join them.

"Both," Reed confirmed.

Caroline squeezed his hand and then tried to let go so that he could join his family, but Reed held tight.

Hearts in Training

"Stay with me."

She nodded. "I'll be right here with you the whole time."

He gave her a funny look. "That would be helpful."

She frowned. She knew he hated being the center of attention, but she'd seen him control a room, and she'd seen him make speeches. She'd never seen him this nervous.

The Decatur family entered the stage and Caroline, feeling a little like an interloper, stayed by Reed's side as she'd promised. Looking out at the crowd she spotted a couple of reporters and a professional photographer, as well as her mom and Tony standing right up front. She managed a smile for them and then got caught in Elizabeth's disapproving look. She tried to remove her hand from Reed's, but he held tight, rubbing a thumb across her knuckles. She squeezed him back and reminded herself that he wanted her there. She straightened her shoulders and listened as Fred spoke a few words of praise to the hundreds of employees in attendance. Fred was charismatic and sure of the crowd's responses, just exactly how she knew Reed would be one day.

Fred wound down his speech and took a moment to look at his family gathered to the right of him, seeming to include Caroline in his proud gaze. For just a few seconds, his gaze lingered on her before turning back to the crowd.

"If you can hold your merriment for just a few more minutes, I have one more announcement." He paused to wait for the crowd to quiet down. "I'd like to introduce you to the newest member of our Executive team, accepting the open position of Executive Director of Training, and we hope the soon-to-be-newest member of the Decatur family, Caroline Trumbull."

Somewhere in her periphery she heard the crowd clapping and cheering, but her entire being focused on Fred's words. Did he mean the Decatur family as in Decatur employees, or as in the *family*-family? Before she could dwell on that, Reed moved to stand before her.

His expression was both nervous and heartbreakingly earnest, his voice low to express words meant only for her. She tried to maintain eye contact through gathering tears.

"Caroline, you are my perfect partner in every way. I knew it the first time you let yourself into my office and gave me attitude. Every day we spend together I become more certain that a lifetime wouldn't be long enough to spend with you." He smiled at her tears. "But, since a lifetime is all that I have, I'm offering it to you." He lowered himself down to one knee and she heard the crowd gasp. "I love you, and I'm asking you to marry me."

While Caroline reminded herself to breathe, Reed pulled out the most incredible diamond she'd ever seen. She pulled him to his feet and kissed him hard.

"Is that a yes?" He laughingly whispered against her neck when they broke apart.

She nodded hard and whispered, "Yes. Oh, my

God. Yes!"

She'd completely forgotten they had an audience until she heard Fred's voice boom into the microphone. "She said yes!"

The deafening cheers were punctuated by congratulatory pounding on Reed's back and hugs by his family. Then her mother and Tony were there claiming their own hugs and offering congratulations.

Caroline spent the next couple of hours tethered to Reed's side, greeting employees and reliving his proposal. She had a feeling people would be talking about it for years to come.

Reed never let go of her, either holding her hand or putting his arm around her. She floated around in a happy, tired daze, aware of the diamond sparkling on her hand, but even more aware of Reed's light-hearted mood. His earlier nervousness hadn't been for addressing his employees, it had been for her answer! Suddenly, she wanted to hug him, and kiss him, and make love to him all at once. She squeezed his hand, unsatisfied with the insignificant touch of fingers and palms when she craved so much more. Reed looked down into her eyes and seemed to understand. Excusing himself from the conversation, he led her into a corner alcove and pulled her into his arms.

"I need you," she whispered.

He groaned and crushed his lips on hers, kissing her with the depth of his emotions. "Can we leave now?" he whispered against her lips.

She rested her forehead against his collar bone. "Let's give it another hour. There are still a lot of people waiting to congratulate you."

"Us." He smiled.

"Us."

THEY LASTED half an hour. Reed made the excuse that Caroline had travelled all day, but several people gave them knowing looks. They said goodnight to Fred and Gail, earning a pleased hug from each of them. Gail reminded them about gathering on Christmas day.

Caroline apologized to Savannah that she hadn't spent any time catching up with her.

"No worries." Savannah reassured her. "We still have Christmas day." Savannah leaned in close to hug Caroline and whispered, "Everything will be ready."

Caroline hugged her tight. "You're the best almost sister-in-law ever!"

Savannah laughed and pointed at Angela. "Don't tell her that."

Caroline pulled Angela in for a hug next and whispered the same thing, earning a laugh from both sisters. One more hug from her parents and they collected their coats and retrieved Reed's car from the valet.

Twenty minutes later, they were home.

Caroline was exhausted in the aftermath of such

a long and emotional day. In the elevator Reed seemed content to just hold her, so she rested back against his chest and let him support her weight. The doors slid open and he pressed a kiss to the side of her neck before propelling her forward into the penthouse. The lights were low, the air was warm and still. She closed her eyes and breathed in the slight scent of the Christmas tree. Then she toed off her heels and padded barefoot into the bedroom. She heard Reed lock the outer door and then he was there, standing before her, watching her with the most poignant expression.

"For days I've been trying to find the right way to tell you how much I love you." He smiled for a second. "Then you had to go and say it first." He rested his hands on her hips and brought her forward two steps. "But I do, Carrie," he whispered. "I love you so much."

Beneath his hands, Caroline melted. She slid her arms under his suit jacket and tipped her chin up to see his face. "I know you do. You show it in all the ways you take care of me. And I'm glad you proposed because one thing I learned in L.A. is that I can't sleep when you're not beside me."

Reed kissed her softly and then lifted his head. "You've got to be exhausted."

"Dead on my feet," she confirmed. As much as she didn't want the day to end, she knew she wouldn't last much longer.

Reed turned her around and unzipped her dress, sliding the straps down her arms, baring her back to him. He pressed a kiss to her shoulder and slid the dress down to pool at her feet. "Wow," he whispered, his fingers smoothing along her exposed skin and sliding around the front to cup her breasts before dipping lower to explore hotter places.

Caroline pressed back against him and closed her eyes to concentrate on the sensation of his fingers exploring her. She felt the crinkle of Reed's shirt against her back and realized that she was far closer to losing control than he was.

She turned around and stepped out of his reach to undress him. She took her time, unbuttoning each button until she exposed his hard, lean chest. She unfastened his pants next, letting them fall at his feet to be kicked aside, along with his boxers and socks. Fully naked, Reed backed her up to the mattress and settled beside her to continue his exploration.

She reached up and put a hand to the side of his face, loving the feel of his skin. His eyes locked on hers as he rolled over her to take her mouth in a slow kiss. She tangled her legs with his, rubbing her toes against the hair on his calves, her more sensitive parts aching for release.

Quickly donning a condom, Reed was back in seconds, poised to enter her when he stopped. Sensing his hesitation, she opened her eyes and found him staring down at her, his expression solemn.

"You're mine, Carrie. Soon you'll have my name, hopefully someday my children. But you've had my heart since the first time I saw you."

She felt hot tears track down her cheeks. Shifting a little to take him inside her, she smiled up at him.

Hearts in Training

"My Reed. Always mine."

They came together in a flash of emotion and passion. Neither having the will or patience to drag things out any longer. Afterward, Caroline tugged the covers up over her and rolled to her side. Reed got up to dispose of the condom and was back in seconds to pull her into his arms.

He kissed the top of her head and settled in comfortably. "Sleep, baby. It's been a long day."

"Mm. The best day," she murmured.

Chapter 24

Christmas Eve with Heather and Tony went better than Caroline expected. Apart from now having three people call her Carrie, Caroline enjoyed watching Reed interact with her family. He truly seemed to embrace who they were.

Heather cooked Lasagne Bolognese for dinner, a Christmas tradition in Tony's family.

"Dinner was amazing, Ma."

Heather bustled around clearing the table. "Thank you, dear."

"Can I help clean up?"

Her mother shooed them out of the apartment's tiny kitchen. "It all goes in the dishwasher. Tony will help me catch it up later." Wiping her hands on a dish towel, she directed everyone into the living room to sit before the tree. Caroline took a seat on the couch and Reed sat beside her with an arm around her shoulders, pulling her in close.

"We have a couple of gifts for you," Heather announced. Beside her, Tony beamed. Heather picked up a couple of packages from beneath the colorfully lit tree and placed them in Caroline's lap.

318

Hearts in Training

Caroline opened the top package, a small silver jeweler's box. She pulled the lid off and gasped, tears instantly flooding her eyes and making everything swim before her. "Ma," she whispered, her heart squeezing painfully. She reverently lifted the necklace out and examined it. Her father's wedding ring had been turned into a pendant, a smaller ring with a sapphire stone twisted and welded inside. Her mother's engagement ring.

"It's beautiful, Ma. I can't believe you did this." She fingered the necklace. "Are you sure you're ready to part with them?"

Her mother was also teary-eyed, but resolute. "Of course. Your father would be so proud of you." She shared a look with Reed. "Of both of you." She gave a watery laugh. "So, consider this your something old, something new, and something blue!"

"You could always borrow your dress," Tony added. They all laughed. "Open mine next, Carrie-girl."

For once, the nickname made her smile, experiencing it as the endearment it was intended to be.

She held up a long envelope and Tony nodded. She opened it carefully and pulled out a cashier's check for $13,752.26. She looked at Tony in wonder and a little concern. Across from her, Tony had tears rolling down his wrinkled face.

"It's every penny, Carrie-girl. Every penny. The teller at the bank asked if I wanted to round it to make an even amount and I said, 'No Ma'am, I want to pay back every penny'."

Caroline couldn't hold back a sob. "Are you sure you can spare this?"

Tony straightened his shoulders and wiped his face. "Of course, we can. We already had most of it anyway. Now I've got a good job I was able to get a small bank loan for the rest."

"Tony, no! Don't take on debt just to pay me back."

"It's done, Carrie. You can't give it back and it's rightfully yours." Tony smiled at Heather. "We're doing great, ain't we, Heather?"

Heather shared his smile and then directed it at Caroline. "We really are Carrie."

"That's the best gift you could have given me."

Beside her, Reed removed his arm from her shoulders and leaned forward. "I have a bit of a gift as well, though it doesn't come from me personally. Your supervisor is so impressed with your performance and dedication that he'd like to offer you a promotion. It comes with a bit of a raise." Reed reached out to shake Tony's hand. "Congratulations."

Tony shook his head in amazement. "We owe you so much."

Reed held his hands up, denying this. "I'm just trying to be a good son-in-law."

Caroline's heart was ready to burst. She squeezed his knee and smiled into his eyes when he looked at her. "I love you so much", she whispered. Self-conscious that her mother and Tony were watching she took a breath and laughed, changing the subject.

"We have gifts for you too, but after all this they're going be a bit of a let-down." She kneeled under the tree and handed out the packages they'd brought for Heather and Tony.

They tore into the paper with an enthusiasm that was admirable in people their age and exclaimed over their gifts. Caroline watched with satisfaction. These were not people who would fake their reactions or pretend to be anyone they were not. They were genuinely happy, and for the first time since she could remember she felt pride for who they were.

Chapter 25

Christmas morning dawned crystalline and cold over the Manhattan skyline. Caroline rolled to her back and stretched. Reed was already up, and she could smell the coffee tempting her from her warm, comfy bed. Excited for what the day would bring, Caroline headed into the bathroom and then to the kitchen to claim her share of the life-giving liquid.

Reed greeted her with a kiss and a mug. "Merry Christmas, sweetheart."

"Mm. Merry Christmas yourself." She murmured against his lips and then took a scalding sip and sighed. "I can't tell which of those I needed more."

He cocked one eyebrow. "Need a reminder?"

"Yes, I think so," she teased.

Ten minutes later they took their mugs to the living room and sat on the floor to look at the tree and enjoy a little quiet time together before they would head to Fred and Gail's house for Christmas brunch with the rest of the family.

They exchanged gifts with a great deal of joy, laughing over the *His* and *Hers* coffee mugs, and Reed particularly enjoying the lingerie Caroline received from Santa. Caroline groaned over the desk plaque that said *Mrs. Boss-Man*. And when she

Hearts in Training

refused to put it on her desk, he offered her another one that said *Caroline Decatur*.

Reed held the first sign in his hand. "I'll have Maintenance install this outside your office."

Caroline tried to snatch it back. "I don't think so. People would never let me live it down!"

But Reed just smiled. "No one's going to mess with you, babe."

Caroline wasn't so sure, but she also knew she could handle whatever gossip was headed her way. Reed loved her and the company believed in her. That was all she needed. Crawling into his lap, she put a hand on the side of his unshaven face. "How about if you be the boss at work and I'll be the boss at home?"

Reed looked into her eyes and she felt it all the way down into her soul. "I can live with that." He pulled her tight against him and rolled her onto the floor. They made love beneath the soft, white lights of the tree and then lay in a contented stupor for a while.

"Reed! We need to get moving or we're going to be late."

Reed rolled to his side and surveyed her with lazy eyes. "We could skip it."

"We can't skip it! It's Christmas with your family."

Reed yawned and rolled to his feet to help her up. "Is this like the 'what to wear for pizza' conversation?"

Caroline looked up at him, confused. "What?"

He shook his head. "Never mind. What's the rush?"

"Your gift is there." And they had a schedule to keep if they wanted to be at their destination before dark.

Reed stopped and frowned. "We just exchanged gifts."

Caroline tried not to laugh at his expression. She nodded. "Yes. But I haven't given you your big gift yet."

Now he looked wary. She stepped up to him and put her arms around his waist.

"You got me a big gift? And it's at my parents' house?"

She cracked a smile. "Sort of."

"How big is this gift?"

She held up her left hand to show him the ring he'd given her. "Well, you gave me this *big* gift, so I thought it was only right that I do something just as extravagant."

Reed's eyes widened in alarm now. "Tell me you didn't spend that much money!"

That threw her. "How much was this ring?"

He narrowed his eyes. "People have purchased their first house for less. Please don't ever lose it."

Caroline smiled and patted his chest watching her diamond sparkle in the tree lights. "I don't plan

Hearts in Training

on taking it off. Ever." She peeked at it again. "No, your gift didn't cost me much. What I meant is the gesture is extravagant. Especially for you."

"Oh geez." He flinched. "Am I going to be publicly embarrassed?"

Caroline giggled. "I hope not. But with your dad, you never know."

Reed dropped his forehead to hers and let out a single laugh. "Alright. Let's get it over with."

TWO HOURS LATER Caroline was helping Gail, Angela, and Savannah finish the food and set the table. To Caroline this was pure heaven. She could hardly keep the joy out of her expression at being part of a big family. Finally, she had sisters, and with Daniel, a brother.

To her increasing embarrassment, Reed kept sneaking kisses while she worked, but his family seemed to take it in stride. Watching Fred and Gail, she supposed public displays of affection were normal for the Decaturs. She looked at Reed examining the gifts under the tree and smiled. Their first Christmas. They had so much to learn about each other, and now a lifetime in which to do it.

Brunch was festive and relaxed. Fred offered grace and they dug into the food.

"Gail, this food is fantastic!" Caroline was stuffed but couldn't resist reaching for another mini quiche. Fred and Savannah both laughed at Caroline's compliment. "Why is that funny?"

325

Gail gave Fred a look to behave himself. "Because" she answered, "I rarely cook. I just don't take the time. I enjoy it, but since it seems to be only at holidays and special occasions, they like to make a pretense of looking for take-out and catering boxes." Fred and Savannah laughed again evidently unashamed.

Feeling bound to take Gail's side, Caroline winked at her. "Well, having seen the pots and pans you two will have to help with later, I think it's pretty clear where all this excellent food came from."

At that, Gail and Angela laughed loudly. "Amen," Gail told her.

Beside her, Reed was impatient. "Are we done yet?"

Gail smiled. "Of course. Sounds like you're ready for some gifts." She gave a mock shake of her head. "Just like when you were children. You'd stuff your faces and race to see who got to the tree fastest."

The image filled Caroline with joy. She imagined the next generation of Decaturs, stuffing their little faces and racing to the tree while their parents sighed, and their grandparents laughed. Seeing Reed once again eyeing the gifts, Caroline's stomach clenched a little. What if he hated his gift? What if he thought she'd interfered? She took a spot on the loveseat and watched Reed as he joined her. No matter, the plans were all in motion so there was no turning back now.

The gifts were handed out one at a time so that each person could exclaim over it and give thanks. It warmed Caroline's heart to see that they were pleased with the gifts she'd chosen for everyone.

Hearts in Training

When it was Reed's turn, Savannah handed him a flat little box with a tag that read, *To Reed, From Santa.*

He looked at Caroline and then opened the box and tipped out a key and a printed card.

"Get out of work free card," he read, a smile dawning on his face. "You are hereby cleared of all work responsibilities until Monday, January third at seven A.M." He looked at the key and then at Savannah and back to Caroline. Caroline's heart swelled into a lump in her throat. "Eight days' vacation in your favorite place. A quiet, cozy cottage in Wolf Creek, New Hampshire. Merry Christmas."

Reed looked incredulous. "How did you pull this off?"

"Jamie. Your parents. Savannah. Angela." She looked around at the happy faces of her soon-to-be family. "It was definitely a team effort clearing your schedule." She laughed. "And Jamie deserves a raise."

Reed nodded, but she could see the excitement in his eyes. "Can I bring a guest?"

Caroline shrugged. Seeing the glint in his eyes she played along. "As long as you don't choose some floozy."

He laughed and pulled her in for a kiss. "Floozy seems a bit harsh. A trip like this was made for me and my perfect partner."

Caroline smiled against his lips, for once not caring if anyone was watching. "Oh boy," she whispered. "Good luck finding her."

327

He kissed her and held her tight. "I already have."

"So have I," she answered.

The End

Annie Kribs is a native of rural Michigan and full-time working mom who writes contemporary romance during her occasional respites from chauffeuring teenagers, working, cleaning, homework helping and watching superhero movies.

Other works by Annie J. Kribs

The Do-Over

<u>Wolf Creek Series</u>

Healing Hearts
Resurrected Hearts
Hearts on the Run

Connect with Annie at www.anniekribs.com, on Facebook at Annie J. Kribs, Twitter @ajkribsauthor, or Instagram @anniekribsauthor.

Made in the USA
Monee, IL
14 April 2022